Black-Eyed Peas on New Year's Day

An Anthology of Hope

Books by Shannon Page

Edited Books

Witches, Bitches & Stitches (anthology)
The Usual Path to Publication (collection)
Book View Cafe 2020 Holiday Anthology
Black-Eyed Peas on New Year's Day: An Anthology of Hope

Novels

Eel River
Our Lady of the Islands (with Jay Lake), The Butchered God, book 1
The Butchered God, book 2 (forthcoming)

The Nightcraft Quartet:
The Queen and The Tower
A Sword in The Sun
The Lovers Three (forthcoming)
The Empress and The Moon (forthcoming)

The Chameleon Chronicles
   (with Karen G. Berry, writing as Laura Gayle)
Orcas Intrigue
Orcas Intruder
Orcas Investigation
Orcas Illusion (forthcoming)

Collections

Eastlick and Other Stories
I Was a Trophy Wife and Other Essays

Black-Eyed Peas on New Year's Day

An Anthology of Hope

Edited by
Shannon Page

Black-Eyed Peas on New Year's Day: An Anthology of Hope

Cover art by Susan Dutton
Cover design by Mark J. Ferrari
Interior design by Shannon Page

ISBN: 978-1-63632-006-9

www.bookviewcafe.com
Book View Café Publishing Cooperative

"It's all wrong. By rights we shouldn't even be here. But we are. It's like in the great stories, Mr. Frodo. The ones that really mattered. Full of darkness and danger they were. And sometimes you didn't want to know the end. Because how could the end be happy? How could the world go back to the way it was when so much bad had happened? But in the end, it's only a passing thing, this shadow. Even darkness must pass. A new day will come. And when the sun shines it will shine out the clearer. Those were the stories that stayed with you. That meant something, even if you were too small to understand why. But I think, Mr. Frodo, I do understand. I know now. Folk in those stories had lots of chances of turning back, only they didn't. They kept going, because they were holding on to something... That there is some good in this world, and it's worth fighting for."

—Samwise Gamgee
The Two Towers (film version)
from the book by J. R. R. Tolkien

Contents

Introduction

In the waning days of October, 2020, as Election Day approached and I found myself doomscrolling through my social media feed and online newspapers yet again, worrying and fretting and desperately searching for even *one little scrap* of good news, I suddenly thought, *What we need is hope.*

And right on the heels of that thought came another: *Hey, I know: what if I got a bunch of people to write me stories of hope?* Thus, an anthology was born.

Writers are magical creatures. We can create whole new worlds—places to escape into, yes; but also, I would argue, places that we can manifest into the world we actually live in. Organ transplants, automatic doors, self-driving cars, video calls—heck, cell phones themselves—each first came out of the brain of a writer. What if we could also bring more hope into our world?

I wrote up a call for submissions and asked folks to spread it far and wide, and I harvested *so many* marvelous stories. Stories of magic and love, of tricks and twists, of astonishing technology and low-tech kindnesses…even a few entirely true stories.

I received far too many for a single book, so here are the best of them. I *hope* you will enjoy reading them as much as I have enjoyed collecting and assembling them!

Shannon Page
Orcas Island, WA
February 2021

At the Night Bazaar

Sherri Woosley

This, this magical twilight hour before the Night Bazaar opens is Orphan's favorite. Perhaps her favorite should be the hour before dawn when she wheels around scooping up the lost, forgotten, and discarded items that she collects to sell from her own tent, but no. Too much envy as she watches others leave through the golden portal, returning to their home worlds. To their loved ones. But Orphan has to wait. Someone—a parent, a family member, someone who has even a clue about who she is—could come to the Bazaar. So, instead, her favorite time is now, when hope is strongest. The sun's rays refract off the many tents that spread in a makeshift city; the smells promise everything from funnel cakes to stuffed grape leaves, incense to ointments made on a faraway moon.

Snow falls. Something on the ground bunches under the white flakes, creating a small mound. Orphan unclips the grabber that hangs off her wheelchair and presses the lever to extend the plastic pincers, tightening on the mound and lifting it from the snow. Sodden tickets from a carnival game. She cradles the pile of tickets in her hands and closes her eyes, breathing in the smell of pulp released by the disintegrating paper. First, she recognizes the desire to win, then the fierce drive of competition, and finally an overall sense of good fortune from the previous owner. Orphan exhales and opens her eyes. The tickets, like everything that Orphan claims, have a faint glow. Now anyone can feel what she feels. Orphan doesn't know if this ability to marry intangible to tangible is natural, maybe there is an entire world of people like her, but she suspects it is a by-product of living in the Bazaar. That she has developed an affinity for lost things because she is lost, maybe forgotten. Regardless, she adds the tickets to her bag. Perhaps this will be a lucky night.

From the far-off center of the Bazaar, the clock tower's bells chime. Golden light appears in the shape of a large door. The Night Bazaar is open. Like the randomness of the Bazaar's internal pathways, there is no schedule of portal connections, but Orphan clenches her hands into fists and hopes.

From her position in the main aisle, she watches the portal. It looks so easy when two women in bomber jackets and goggles step through the golden light, appearing from nothing. They are followed by a group of young mages in matching uniforms and the glowing badge that identifies each as an apprentice. More travelers pass before Talla, a handsome young woman with soulful eyes and a blue headscarf, appears. The blue complements her brown skin and dark eyes. Orphan waves in greeting, a smile breaking across her face.

Talla strides forward, an unfamiliar rucksack on her back, until she stops in front of Orphan. White flakes of snow sparkle on her headscarf and shoulders, on the soft cloth of her loose pants and tunic. Talla smells like the desert, or what Orphan imagines the desert to be like with wild wind and two scorching suns, shaggy animals with humps. Orphan has seen pictures at the art tent of Talla's world and space ships and something called Victorian England, but she hasn't experienced any of the possibilities outside of her imagination. She knows the Bazaar; it is home. But, maybe, a home shouldn't be lonely.

"Salutations." Talla bows and gives Orphan that half-smile she knows so well. "I'm glad to see you, but I can't talk. I have to find someone."

"Oh, but come with me first," Orphan blurts out. "Chef's macarons are right over here, best in the Bazaar." Frantic that Talla will leave on her own errand after so many nights of waiting by the portal, Orphan grabs for her hand. "Please."

Concern draws Talla's brows together.

Orphan drops her hand and wheels along the packed dirt path. The crowd is easy to navigate because most aren't stopping to look yet. They want to get deeper into the labyrinth that is the Bazaar where paths change like gears in a machine and the only constant is the clock tower rising from the middle.

A sweet smell wafts on the breeze and then she is in front of the large pastry case of Chef Bisous's stall. They are short, only as tall as Orphan in her chair, but their white hat reaches toward the darkening sky. "No, no, my friend. My macarons are not unwanted. Each is handmade." They point to colorful rows of macarons. "Tonight we have gingerbread marscapone, mint chocolate chip, and raspberry with a cream filling made with a special ingredient from Callisto. Quite costly. No freebies for you, Orphan."

Talla appears through the crowd and stands at Orphan's shoulder. Giddy, Orphan's eyes shine as she performs for her audience.

"I'm offended," she says to Chef, although she isn't. This is how the Bazaar works; bartering, slide scale of valuation, remembering what is foreign or precious to various cultures. Every night is different depending on when or where the portal opens. "Surely you have cookies that aren't perfect. Not the right shape? Maybe a little burn on the bottom?"

Talla taps Orphan's shoulder. "Listen, I have to go. It's important."

"This'll be quick," Orphan promises. "Hold on."

"My macarons are not cookies." Chef sniffs. "However, I might have one for trade."

"Now you're talking." Orphan speaks louder than she intended, wants to hurry before Talla leaves. She pulls the large bag that hangs off the side of her wheelchair onto her lap. "I have tickets to a carnival game tossed to the ground when there weren't enough for a prize, a scarf with a pulled thread, and a dress bought for something called 'homecoming dance' that was too long." Orphan reaches into the bag and hesitates over her treasures until the dress seems to hum. She holds up the dress. The tulle skirt has polka dots and the torso is silky.

"I'm sorry," Talla says, but then she starts coughing.

Chef leans over the case and makes grabby hands, but Orphan holds it away. "At least three macarons. One of each flavor."

"Too much for something no one else wants."

"You want it." Orphan adjusts in her chair, manually rotating her right hip to be more comfortable.

"Too long."

"Take it to Alliz. He owes me a favor." They are some of the many for whom the Bazaar is home: Chef and Alliz the costume maker and Apothecary. "It will look beautiful on you."

"It will." Chef pouts. "Fine." They snap open a pastry bag and slide the macarons inside. Orphan accepts the bag and takes a deep sniff. The smell makes her stomach growl with hunger. She offers the dress.

Chef holds the dress to their body and gives a thrilled little scream.

Orphan turns to Talla, triumphant, but her face falls as she sees the woman straighten from coughing, hand to her stomach and mouth twisted in pain.

"What's wrong?" Orphan's heart skips. She doesn't remember who left her at the Bazaar or when she discovered her special talent for selling junk, but she remembers meeting Talla. Her easy laugh as she set up a stall to sell the colorful rugs from her home world. Her acceptance of the wheelchair Orphan needed to navigate the crowded Bazaar. Orphan's first friend.

"I'm not contagious."

Orphan frowns and repeats, "What's wrong."

"A terrible illness is affecting my country. We traced it to a bacteria in our main water source, but not until after many people and animals had been affected. So many that my home world has run out of the cure." Her hand moves from her stomach to her chest as she struggles to inhale. "Young and old suffer with fever. We need an ingredient to make more medicine before anyone else dies."

"You're one of the sick," says Orphan. Her mind tries to process.

"I've been to the Bazaar. I have the best chance of finding someone who'll sell moganite."

Shame fills Orphan and she berates herself. So anxious to show off for some stupid macarons.

"I'll lead you to Apothecary's tent," Orphan says. "What do you have to trade?"

❉ ❉ ❉

APOTHECARY'S TENT IS ALONG the opposite arm of the Bazaar, past the tower clock, on an uneven cobblestone path that makes Orphan feel nauseous as she jounces along. Or, that could be her worry for Talla making her feel sick. They pass a used bookstore stall with a beat-up leather recliner, clearly wanted, and an unenclosed space with two tables in an L-shape covered with chakra jewelry for various spinal configurations. A gramophone sits on the corner playing records, a saxophone solo floating out of its bell.

There! One more and they arrive at a serious-looking brown tent with flaps down for privacy. Talla holds the flap to the side and Orphan rolls inside. Immediately she is struck by the smell of spices, sharp and bitter with a hint of too-sweet. Across the back wall stretches a shelf that takes up the width and height of the space divided into three sections. A spidery script labels each of the colorful jars that line two sections of the shelf. The other section contains mortar and pestle, scales, and other things that Orphan doesn't recognize.

"What do we have here?" Apothecary lowers her glasses as she listens to Talla's stumbled explanation. Hurrying through the Bazaar stole her breath. Apothecary looks into Talla's rucksack and takes out a blue stone the size of Jumper bugs, hefting it in her hand. "That's a nice collection of Ici gems, but you'll have to come back. Selling you that quantity of moganite would use all of my stores. Mine is from Deneb. Earth lunar hasn't been to the Bazaar in weeks and Titan's isn't as potent."

Orphan cocks her head. Deneb is a mining colony. Crowds were still coming through the portal, but she hadn't noticed any in the boots or union garb that miners typically wore.

Talla shakes her head, frantic. "I can't wait for the next time. It's been two months since the portal came. My friends and family are dying. Our doctors need me to return with the moganite tonight, before the portal closes."

Orphan places her hand on Talla's arm, but keeps looking at Apothecary. "You have enough moganite for the doctors to make the medicine. And the Ici gems are enough to cover the cost."

"Yes," Apothecary says to Orphan. She is another inhabitant of the Bazaar so they know each other by reputation, but have never interacted. "Look, I won't be able to make medicine for anyone else if I sell it all. I'll sell you half of what I have. That's the best I can do. No one can guarantee what comes to the Bazaar and I don't know when I'll get new stock from Deneb."

Talla opens her mouth to argue, but Orphan squeezes her arm. "I understand. I want to give you a gift." She opens the bag. Her hand hovers over the paper tickets to a carnival game, the macarons, and the scarf. Then, sure, she pulls the scarf from her bag and offers it.

"It has a pulled thread," Apothecary says with suspicion, refusing to take the cloth. "I'm not trading anything, Orphan. I've heard about your tricks."

"Not a trick," Orphan insists. "This is a gift. Take it."

Apothecary reaches and her fingers close on the cloth. She examines the maroon scarf, turns it over, flicks the pulled thread, runs a finger over the stitching on the logo of a gryphon with mechanical claws from a school on the other side of the portal. She closes her eyes and lets out a brief combination of sigh and sob. She wraps the maroon scarf around her neck, hands shaking.

Talla starts to ask Orphan a question, but Orphan puts her finger to her lips to signal silence.

When Apothecary opens her eyes, tears shimmer. "I'll sell it to you. All of it."

❉ ❉ ❉

THE PECULIAR DING-A-LING OF a dented brass bell reaches Orphan through the noise of the Bazaar. It is her bell, hung outside her tent, and one of her first finds. The bell was made to be heard and so Orphan hears it, anywhere in the Bazaar. A client has arrived at her tent.

"Follow me. It's faster this way," she says as they leave, veering left when Talla would have gone right. "We don't need to backtrack through the center. The portal is a straight walk from my tent. You'll be home soon."

"Why did the apothecary change her mind?" Talla presses a hand to her chest as they hurry.

"Forgotten friendship."

Talla laughs, startled. "That's not what I would have expected. How did a scarf make her think of friendship?"

"Whoever was wearing it last may have been with friends or a special friend may have given it. I don't know the history of lost things." The paved road is both smooth and downhill; Orphan is glad for the change from the uneven bricks. "It's like I hear the echo. Then I help the item find its forever home."

"And you think everything has a forever home?" Talla is dragging behind so Orphan slows.

"Think of me as a matchmaker of sorts."

"Is the Bazaar your forever home?"

They turn the last corner and Orphan lets out a whispered curse. She both wants to and doesn't want to answer Talla, but now there's a complication.

Two cats, one a grey tabby in spectacles and top hat and the other a striking calico wearing a tuxedo jacket, stand on their hind legs outside of her tent. Each is tucking away an elaborate silk parasol that must have been used to protect someone from the snowflakes. Orphan suspects her guest's identity and wonders if she and Talla can slip away without being seen.

"At last," says Tabby, dashing Orphan's hope.

"You're here," says Calico.

They speak in unison. "We present…Lady Tybalt." The tabby uses a paw to draw back the tent's flap.

"We've heard much of your wares and decided to see for ourselves." A white cat, Himalayan Persian with the distinctive thin "M" mark on her forehead, fluffs her elaborate ball gown and strikes a pose in the tent's opening. Orphan recognizes Alliz the costume maker's artistry. "Perhaps we will buy a little gift for ourselves. No doubt this upcoming holiday season we will receive treasures and delicacies and gowns of questionable fashion, all costing more than you could comprehend. But, we are looking for something special." The ornate collar at her neck boasts nine jewels, one for each Life she still has.

"I'm…honored." Orphan struggles to switch gears from the problem on Talla's world. Everyone at the Night Bazaar knows Lady Tybalt, consort to the tyrant cat king. Theirs is a home world of court intrigue and strife that sometimes bleeds into the Bazaar. The bleeding is literal; cat's claws are sharp. "Forgive me for not standing. I don't have an extra Life to spend on healing."

If she notices the hint of sarcasm, Lady Tybalt ignores it. Instead, she smooths her whiskers with a white paw and steps deeper into the tent with a tilt of her head that suggests she will reveal more only when they are alone.

Orphan looks at Talla and lowers her voice. "Sorry I can't go with you. Keep following this smooth path and when it curves around, you'll be on the main road to the portal. It's not far."

"Thank you so much." Talla grips her sack of moganite. "You've saved my country."

Embarrassed, Orphan shrugs, but Talla doesn't stop. "You saved me."

"We're friends. That's what we do, right?" But Orphan already feels Talla's absence.

"Come through the portal with me."

This is not the first time Talla has issued the invitation. Still, Orphan laughs it off. "My wheels won't travel over your sand."

"We have flying carpets, you know. We're not uncivilized."

Lady Tybalt interrupts. "We are waiting, little queen of garbage…"

"Oh." Orphan's cheeks burn, but she answers Talla by reciting the line that has become habit. "Someone might come looking for me. Maybe next time."

Talla shakes her head. "One day there won't be a next time." She walks away without looking back.

Orphan stifles the urge to cry.

With three leaps the tabby cat has left his post by the tent and passed by Talla, only to whip around and point the parasol at her chest. "You can't leave," he says. "Go back to the tent."

Rolling forward to intercede, Orphan is stopped by the other guard cat's head shake of warning.

Talla pushes the parasol to the side with the flat of her hand and says, "What do you mean?"

"We didn't give you permission to leave," Lady Tybalt says, swaying back and forth so that her dress makes a swishing sound.

"No one leaves until Lady Tybalt leaves," Tabby says. "Her presence is a secret and will remain so. It's a matter of court security." He tucks the parasol under one arm and extends the claws of his other paw. The tips are curved and sharp. The warning is clear.

Uncertain, Talla looks to her friend. Orphan has heard of bloody cat-fights in the Bazaar and doesn't doubt that these guards would fight. She doesn't want Talla hurt. "I won't be long with Lady Tybalt," she says.

Talla's shoulders slump, whether in defeat or exhaustion it is difficult to tell. "I need to rest anyway."

"Excuse me," Orphan prompts the guards, needing space to wheel through the front of her own tent.

They resume their posts, facing outward, at attention. Talla heads for a dark corner of the tent and sinks down into a bean bag chair, closing her eyes. Once she's situated, Orphan gestures in a circular motion as she begins her spiel. "Welcome. I sell anything you can imagine."

Lady Tybalt surveys the piles of forgotten toys, games with missing pieces, and broken furniture with an expression of disdain. "We've heard that you have…joy."

"That's expensive." Orphan scratches at a bandage that covers the stump below her left knee. It is long healed, the scar faded, but she keeps it covered so no one will stare.

Lady Tybalt huffs and the grey tabby leans into the tent from his guard position. "Pay her."

He flicks a coin stamped with the cat king's face to Orphan. She examines it before tucking it in a pocket. "Go get a bowl of curry."

"Payment?" The cat narrows his eyes.

"It's for Lady Tybalt; she'll pay. Better get two for her. The servings are small." Knowing that Lady Tybalt is watching the exchange, she adds, "The mango chutney adds the right flavor and the ginger is merely a suggestion. Make sure you go to the striped tent, second aisle over."

Tabby ignores Orphan to speak to the king's consort. "Ma'am?"

"We are hungry," Lady Tybalt says, her tongue darting out. "We hadn't realized it."

When Tabby's gone, Orphan rummages through a woven basket of toys until she feels a tingle. She leans forward and snags the toy, wresting it from the pile to produce a View-Master, the red plastic faded to pink.

"Look through there." Orphan turns the toy. "And slide the film circles in here. Keep trying discs until you find the right one."

Lady Tybalt smirks in elegant disbelief as she stabs the dusty film circles with a claw and holds them up to the light. Her eyes narrow. She inserts a disc. Her claw clicks the lever, again and again.

Orphan watches Talla sleep. Her chest rises in inconstant rhythm as she struggles to breathe. She needs the medicine too. Orphan feels time ticking, the big arms of the clock tower moving.

Just as the tabby cat enters, balancing two steaming bowls, Lady Tybalt lifts her skirt with her free paw and twirls around the junk tent, uncaring that others might be watching. He sets the tray down and looks up to see Lady Tybalt. After a moment of shock, he drops his eyes and retreats from the tent, backing up into a girl trying to enter.

"I've brought somethin' to trade," the girl says. She is between kitten and cat, so thin that her ribs show along her sides and one of her ears is tattered as if it had been bitten. Her collar shows she has only two Lives left. Orphan guesses the kittencat is from Lady Tybalt's home world, but possibly a mixed bloodline. That's how Orphan is too. She looks human-oid, but has nothing to show which home world her parents might have been from. "We found it after the last Bazaar. Mama said it was good." She opens her paw to reveal a plastic chess piece.

"Hmm. A white knight. What do you want for it?"

"Mama said to bring back food. Or money." The kittencat swallows. "For food."

What good is having nine Lives if you still die for being poor? Orphan unclenches her jaw and calls out in a too-sweet voice to Lady Tybalt, "Do you want your dinner?"

Lady Tybalt drops the View-Master and takes a step toward the bowls. She sniffs the air and then ignores the food; instead, she presses the toy back to her eyes.

"I said, do you want your curry?" Orphan already knows the answer. Her hands are on the bowl and she is able to claim it.

Lady Tybalt yowls in pleasure. She is lost to everything but herself.

Pocketing the white knight, Orphan extends the bowl to the kittencat. "Take this."

Eyes wide, the kittencat shakes her head. "I can't. That's too much."

"Well, it would be too much if you'd found a pawn, but this guy is my favorite. He can move in unexpected ways." Orphan reaches into her bag and pulls out the pastries from Chef. "So, I guess I owe you these, too." She winks.

Whiskers trembling, the kittencat accepts the bowl and pastry bag and hurries away.

The tuxedoed calico peers in. "That was Lady Tybalt's food!"

Orphan stares down the cat. "When it became junk, it became mine."

Calico pulls back her lip to expose a long tooth. "You knew that would happen. You tricked her into paying and then made her forget about it."

Orphan pushes against her seat so she can readjust. "It's not my fault if she no longer wants it."

The fur on her body stands on end so the cat looks larger, but Calico withdraws to her post.

Orphan exhales and then takes a deep breath in. The remaining bowl of food smells delicious, spicy and a little sour, and her stomach rumbles with hunger. Ignoring the sensation, Orphan wakes Talla. "Eat."

She moans in appreciation. "From the striped tent?"

"Of course. I only serve my guests the best."

Talla stops with the spoon halfway to her mouth. "Where's yours?"

"I've already eaten," she lies.

Talla only finishes half of the bowl before she sets it aside. Her brown skin has sweat across the hairline. Orphan feels her forehead. The skin is so much warmer than it should be. Is that crackling sound from her lungs?

"Not much longer," Orphan promises. "The disc is almost done."

Lady Tybalt brings the View-Master down, panting. Foam from her wild exertion dots the corner of her mouth. "I want another disc."

"No." Orphan shakes her head. "Joy without work is addictive. It's strong as a drug. I've seen it before. It's too easy and then—"

"I need another disc." Lady Tybalt ends with a wild yowl.

The tent curtain twitches open as the tabby cat peers in.

"Pay her," Lady Tybalt hisses. "Give her the whole bag."

The cat sweeps his top hat off. "Lady—"

"Do it," she snarls, the foam dripping.

The moneybag rattles against the rickety tray with the half-empty curry bowl.

Lady Tybalt examines each disc, tossing each away until one catches her attention. She covers her face with the View-Master and dances again.

Talla groans, her dark, soulful eyes open. "Promise me you'll take the moganite to my world."

Orphan's heart cracks open. "I won't. You're going to be fine. You'll take the first dose."

"I knew I had the infection bad, but I thought I had more time." Talla pulls her headpiece to the side so that dark hair spills out. Her eyes roll back in her head; her body slumps to the side like a puppet with cut strings. "I had to see you again."

"It's finished." Lady Tybalt looses a howl of rage. "I've seen everything on this one too."

"Get out," Orphan says, voice thick with unshed tears. "Talla needs joy more than you."

"I want to dance." Lady Tybalt's white fur is grimy with sweat, dust, and the dirt created by her swirling. "I have the king's ear. You must do what I say or he'll bring the whole army to rip you apart."

Orphan wants to scream with the agony of her friend dying, wants to understand why someone else from Talla's world hadn't come to get the moganite, why Talla hadn't told her she had to get to the portal immediately.

I had to see you again. Could it really be that simple?

Orphan looks around her tent at all the treasures she's collected while waiting at the Night Bazaar. The familiar glowing string of lights from some world's holiday that wrap the top of her tent. The calligraphy set with a pen that leaks. The robot hedgehog. These things have been her version of a family.

"You want another disc?" Orphan says. Negotiation is her specialty, but she is lightheaded at her own audacity. "It'll cost one of your Lives."

"Never!" The attendants rush inside. "The king would never—"

"He'll scratch your eyes out," says Tabby.

"He'll burn your tent to the ground," says Calico.

"He'll string his violin with your guts," they say together.

"Stop," Lady Tybalt demands. "Leave us."

The attendants drop to all four paws and dash away, surely to return with the king's soldiers.

"A human cannot use a cat's Life." Lady Tybalt's pink tongue darts out. "It's worthless to you."

"It's my gift. I can take your junk and make it a treasure." Orphan has never tried this before, doesn't know if the Bazaar will allow it, but she will make it be true through force of will. She has never wanted anything as badly as she wants this.

Lady Tybalt shrugs as if a Life means nothing.

Ping.

A jewel drops from her collar.

Orphan picks up the jewel and presses it to Talla's left temple.

Lady Tybalt drops to all fours and springs onto Talla's chest. Her ears flatten and she breathes into Talla's face. Her whiskers twitch and she breathes into Talla's face again. This time a smoky bubble forms from her mouth and then retreats down Lady Tybalt's throat. She kneads Talla's chest with her claws as if finding purchase and breathes a third time. A smoky form emerges from her mouth and hovers in the air over Talla.

Lady Tybalt leaps away, bored.

Orphan reaches out a trembling hand to guide the Life closer. Her body tingles with something like electricity, but that leaves a smoky taste on her tongue. She imagines walking through the air, no, spinning through the air like liquid lightning melting upwards. Heat spreads through her limbs and she cannot hold this Life any longer. It wants to expand inside of her, fill her, but Orphan is not empty.

View-Master discs fly as Lady Tybalt scavenges. She inserts a new disc and dances, her movements wild and uncoordinated.

Orphan shakes Talla. Talla inhales, chokes, and sits upright. Sparks flicker over Talla's body; her hair floats out from her head.

"What?" Talla's fingers scrape and pull against her skin. "What's happening?"

The sounds of a commotion come from the main aisle of the Bazaar. It is easy to imagine martial cats racing through the portal toward her tent. *Scratch your eyes out. Burn your tent. String his violin with your guts.*

"Almost daybreak. You need to get to the portal before it closes."

Talla rewraps her headscarf. "Ready."

Orphan wheels out the front of her tent and reaches deep into her bag, hand tightening on the carnival tickets when they tingle, full of potential to win.

The tower clock sounds, a wave of vibration spreading through the Night Bazaar.

Orphan holds the tickets up into the air, feeling the wind try to pluck them from her grip.

Cats in leather armor turn the corner, led by a Captain in a helmet racing straight toward her tent.

Orphan releases. The tickets scatter like dandelion seeds.

A nearby person snatches one up. Immediately a growing crowd scrambles for the tickets, desperate for a chance to win. The cat soldiers slow down, bogged by the bodies between them and the junk tent.

"She's right here," Talla calls, bringing Lady Tybalt out of the tent and into the false dawn. The cat's fur is matted and dirty, the View-Master still clutched in her paw. "It would embarrass the king if anyone saw her like this, right?"

The Captain slides to a halt, his gaze going from Lady Tybalt to Orphan. Talla releases Lady Tybalt and the cat wanders back into the tent, out of sight.

The Captain snaps at the air in anger. "We'll be waiting for you. Every time that portal opens. We'll wait." Then he follows Lady Tybalt, motioning to his soldiers to join him.

"Race you to the portal," Orphan calls to Talla as she wheels down a side aisle and then cuts over to the main path. Orphan waves at Chef, doesn't answer their confused, "Where are you going?"

Others are hurrying too; they don't want to be trapped on this side.

At the last moment, Orphan rubs her palms against her wheels like brakes. She stares at the golden light. Her heart beats so fast. She loves the Night Bazaar. She loves the mystery, the smells of foreign food, the way every night is different. This is home.

Talla rushes up clutching the life-saving moganite, her dark eyes holding Orphan's. She is only one foot from the portal. "I have to go," she says.

"You promised to show me the Library of Sinking Sands."

Talla gapes and Orphan almost laughs. She feels it inside, a frightened effervescence threatening to spill out.

"What changed?"

Orphan's cheeks burn, but she manages, "Someone came for me."

Words gush from Talla. "We can look for your parents, for your family, if you want. It'll be my turn to help you. Or, I can take you to the Library first, or we have this amazing—"

"Plenty of time to decide once we're through."

Talla nods. She takes a step back and disappears into the golden light. There's a flicker of blue sky and then nothing but the empty portal.

Orphan closes her eyes and pictures that flicker of blue sky. She imagines traveling through the portal to all the worlds she's seen in the books in the tent by the tower clock. She imagines not being alone. No more waiting. She wheels into the welcoming light, her whole body tingling like she is found.

SHERRI COOK WOOSLEY EARNED a M.A. in English Literature from University of Maryland, where she taught Academic Writing and Introduction to World Mythology. Her debut novel, Walking Through Fire, was long-listed for both the Booknest Debut Novel award and Baltimore's Best 2019 and 2020 in the novel category. Her short fiction is most recently published in DreamForge Magazine, Pantheon Magazine, and Abyss & Apex Magazine.

Website: www.tasteofsherri.com
Twitter: @SherriWoosley

The Last Date

Sarina Dorie

For nineteen years, I'd been waiting for some kind of magic to happen to me, like kissing a man and feeling lightning shoot through my body, or looking at a stranger across a crowded room and knowing I'd found my soulmate. I would probably have settled for finding a four-leaf clover and then meeting someone special immediately afterward. But no such luck.

By the third date with Jonathan, I had a sinking suspicion he wasn't the one. I just didn't know how to tell him in a way that wouldn't make things awkward when we were in Writing 121. Every time he smiled at me in that goofy way, or leaned his shoulder next to mine while we walked like he wanted to hold my hand, it just made it so much harder to break things off with him. For the last two hours I had endured awkward conversation over dinner, trying not to fault him for his poor posture, knocking over my water in his slightly cute but bumbling manner, or using a fork and knife to attack his sushi into submission. He certainly was amusing and didn't mind laughing at himself. I just didn't feel any magic when I looked at him.

As we left the stuffy Japanese restaurant and Jonathan walked me to my car, I welcomed the chill of cold air on my face.

He kicked at a pinecone on the sidewalk next to my Camry, his shoulders slouching even further. "Well, it's been a pleasure, Emma. Maybe we can go hiking next week."

Considering this was December in Oregon, we were lucky it wasn't raining on us at the moment. It was unlikely hiking was a good plan.

He leaned closer. I stepped back, avoiding his gaze as though I had no idea he wanted to kiss me.

I needed to get this over with. "I think we should just be friends," I said in a rush of breath. I stuck my hand in my pocket for my keys, ready to make a quick dash for it if he got weird. I didn't want a scene like with that last guy I'd dated, who had a tantrum because I wouldn't kiss him good night. Really, he had acted worse than my six-year-old brother. Pretty pathetic considering he was only months from graduating from college.

Jonathan stared off into the distance, his eyes dazed. I waited for him to say something, but he was silent, hunched over with his poor posture, looking both ridiculous and dejected at the same time. Rude dates, I could handle. Irate, I had a plan for. Catatonic, I didn't have a clue. I couldn't stand the stillness any longer.

"I, um, you're really nice and everything. I just don't feel like we're right for each other." My stomach flip-flopped when he didn't respond. "We can still hang out and do our writing homework together, but—"

He pointed toward the street lamp. I turned, seeing a leaf suspended in the air underneath, slowly spinning in place. My jaw dropped in wonder, watching the brown leaf levitate a few inches off the ground. Then I realized it must have been caught on a strand of spider web.

Jonathan grinned. "I never thought I'd actually see this! It's caught in a vortex and suspended in time and space."

I laughed, uncertain whether he was joking or not. "It's just stuck in a spider web. But it does look pretty like that. It looks…magical." My chest tightened with longing at that word.

"It isn't magic; it's a scientific phenomenon defying physics. You've heard of the Oregon Vortex, haven't you? That one is more or less permanent, but not very strong. Sometimes a fragment of space tears and we have temporary ones before the universe rights itself and gravity returns to normal."

"Right," I said.

He sounded like he actually believed what he was saying. This was definitely our last date. I didn't feel as bad breaking things off with him now that I'd discovered he was a nut. I fingered my car key in my pocket. I should have used this as my opportunity to walk around to the driver's side. Instead, I remained glued to the spot, watching the beauty of that leaf dangling and spinning in mid-air, ochre and sienna stains catching the light from above.

"You don't believe me, do you?" he asked. The hurt in his tone drew my eyes away from the dancing leaf.

He pulled out a wadded-up tissue from his pocket and pitched it toward the leaf. The tissue arced and stopped halfway to the ground, a foot above the leaf.

"That doesn't prove anything," I said. "It's light, just like the leaf, so it's caught in the spider web too."

His smile turned mischievous, his posture straightening. "If I can prove to you that it's a vortex, not a spider web, will you go on another date with me?"

"Sure," I said. Since I knew this was a spider web, I could prove it pretty fast by swiping my hand over the tissue to break the web.

I stepped forward and stretched out my hand, but Jonathan held his arm out to stop me.

"Wait. It isn't always safe to only put *part* of yourself in." Jonathan grabbed onto the belt of my coat and tugged me back. Then with a running step, he leapt into the air and pitched himself forward. He hung there suspended. Slowly he twirled in place. He grinned.

"Oh, my god!" I stared at his feet, dangling in the space above the leaf. This had to be a trick he somehow rigged because he wanted me to go out with him again. At the same time, I didn't want this to be a trick. I wanted this magic to be real.

"Care to join me?" he asked.

I stepped back, ran and jumped like he had. I knocked my shins against his, hopping up and down, well, more bobbing up and down, from the pain of it. It took me a second to realize there was no ground. I felt light, like being in water. Jonathan grabbed my elbow and we spun in unison. My long brown hair drifted into my face, buoyantly splaying in various directions, defying gravity in the lamp-lit street. If only someone was around to take a picture and capture this moment.

He winked at me. "You aren't going to deny this is a vortex any longer and claim we're stuck on a giant spider web, are you?"

I tilted back my head and laughed, feeling light enough to somersault in the air. Jonathan laughed with me, holding onto my sleeves to anchor me to him. I leaned against him, thinking nothing of our closeness until he lowered his face closer to mine. He hesitated, staring into my eyes.

There was something about the moment and the wonder of the vortex that made me feel giddy and drunk. I closed my eyes and kissed him, my chest tingling with warmth. It felt like magic, like they say it's supposed to in books or movies with triumphant musical scores overlaying a romantic scene. Only for me, the music was the percussion of my heart, adrenalin giving me the kind of high I'd never felt before.

When he pulled away, he had that adorably dopey grin on his face. I was breathless.

My feet encountered an uneven, though solid surface, gravity sinking down on me once again. I found myself standing on Jonathan's tennis shoes. My knees wobbled and buckled beneath me. I grabbed onto him to steady myself. Jonathan tried to move his feet out of the way and simultaneously keep me upright. Our legs managed to get twisted and we fell to the ground, grass breaking his fall and him breaking mine.

"No need to throw yourself at me. I can wait until a fourth or fifth date for that," he said.

I laughed.

Whether it was the magic of the vortex or the magic of that kiss, I decided I was willing to go on at least one more date.

❊ ❊ ❊ ❊ ❊

SARINA DORIE HAS SOLD over 170 short stories to markets like *Analog, Daily Science Fiction, Magazine of Fantasy and Science Fiction, Orson Scott Card's Intergalactic Medicine Show*, and *Abyss and Apex*. Her stories and published novels have won humor contests and Romance Writer of America awards. She has over fifty novels published, including her bestselling series, *Womby's School for Wayward Witches*.

A few of her favorite things include: gluten-free brownies (not necessarily glutton-free), Star Trek, steampunk aesthetics, fairies, Severus Snape, Captain Jack Sparrow and Mr. Darcy.

By day, Sarina is a public school art teacher, artist, belly dance performer and instructor, copy editor, fashion designer, event organizer and probably a few other things. By night, she writes. As you might imagine, this leaves little time for sleep.

You can find info about her short stories and novels on her website: www.sarinadorie.com

The best way to stay in contact with Sarina Dorie, hear about what she is writing, know when she has a new release, or books offered for free on Amazon is by signing up for her newsletter.

https://sarinadorie.com/newsletter-sign-up

The Family Business

Melissa Mead

Mother Gothel brought me to the tower before I was old enough to talk. I don't really remember anything before then. I must've been about five when she started the business. I was standing by the window while Nurse combed my hair. It only came to my ankles then. I laugh to remember how much I fussed and complained over brushing a mere yard or so of hair.

Mother Gothel flew by on her broomstick just as Nurse started the first braid. The glint of gold must've caught her eye. With one blink she was inside. Her empty broom lay across the hooks just below the windowsill.

I stopped squirming. Mother Gothel's visits were uncomfortable enough even when I behaved. She always peered and prodded, asked if I was eating my vegetables, and frowned the whole time. Today, though, she seemed pleased. A smile revealed her snaggled teeth and traced unaccustomed paths on her wrinkled face. She stroked my head with a gnarled hand.

"So, it's finally begun! Soft, too. Good, good. I'll bring you a present tomorrow, my pretty child."

"A kitten to play with?"

"What? No! Filthy things; they'd have you in tangles."

I swallowed my disappointment. It would've been nice to have company other than Nurse, who slept most of the time and snored like a congested elephant. "More books, then?"

Mother Gothel cast a questioning eye on Nurse, who confirmed, "She can read, Mistress."

Mother Gothel didn't look pleased, but she muttered, "Can't have her agitated and fussing. Very well. But I'll bring something else, too. Much better. Much more important."

❊ ❊ ❊

I BARELY SLEPT THAT night for wondering what the present might be. When your whole world consists of two rooms and a long spiral stair with no door at the bottom, the smallest change is a miracle of novelty. Still, I'd hoped for something more exciting than the small glass bottle she brought with her the next day.

Mother Gothel let me smell the liquid inside. It was dark green and smelled like a blend of the climbing roses that grew on the tower and the rampion that Nurse insisted that I eat with every meal, and it made my scalp prickle.

Mother Gothel made Nurse draw a bath and wash my hair, although I protested that we'd just done that yesterday. Then she poured the green liquid onto my hair and began shampooing it in.

At first I tried to pull away from the old enchantress's bony fingers, but her touch was surprisingly gentle. She hummed and muttered to herself as she massaged the stuff into my scalp, chanting words that I couldn't understand. The tingling grew stronger, almost prickly, but the heavy flowery scent made me too drowsy to care. She rinsed my hair, and Nurse toweled it dry and put me to bed.

❊ ❊ ❊

THAT'S WHEN THE BUSINESS began in earnest. My hair started growing at least two inches a day. I learned mathematics by calculating how long it would take my hair to reach each story of the tower when I hung it out the window to dry. At first I reveled in the attention. Nurse wasn't the huggy sort, and Mother Gothel had never shown me much affection. Now the old sorceress sat by the fire with me for hours, tenderly brushing and combing my ever-growing mane. Once a year, at the beginning of summer, she cut it off right at the base of my skull. Nurse said she had it spun and woven into cloth to make hair shirts for pilgrims.

I felt tremendously proud to be part of something so important. By the time I turned twelve, though, it wasn't fun anymore. My life revolved around the care and nurturing of my inhuman hair. By year's end it reached nearly to the base of my tower—about sixty feet. Mother Gothel laid a compacting enchantment on it that kept it from filling the room so I could move near the end of a cycle, but living under that enormous coiled beehive of a coiffure was no easy task for a child. Maintaining it in the smooth and glossy condition that Mother Gothel demanded was even more arduous.

Mondays and Thursdays were washing days. This quickly became too complicated a matter for a simple bathing tub. Mother Gothel and a barely-sensed army of invisible servants would escort me down a flight of stairs into a room that the sorceress kept locked at all other times. Inside, in the middle of the marble floor, was an enormous pool of warm water. It looked bottomless. I'm sure it went at least to the bottom of the tower. A low couch sat at the very edge of the pool. Mother Gothel made me lie on this so my neck wouldn't snap when she loosed sixty feet of hair from its confining enchantment. Even so, my head always bent backward when those weighty coils first slithered free.

Then the invisible servants would take over, washing my hair in the swirling water and dousing sections of it with Mother Gothel's latest shampoo. She was always concocting something to make my hair longer, stronger, brighter, lighter, finer, softer. If I looked behind me out of the corner of my eye I could see skeins of it floating in the air like the tentacles of an enormous golden octopus, held up by the invisible hands. It didn't seem to belong to me, this vast hirsute entity with the unseen staff scrubbing and rinsing it. Sometimes I read or sang while this was going on. Sometimes I fell asleep, only to be awakened by the touch of Mother Gothel's hand caressing my scalp, followed by the vast gurgling rush as the water drained away until next time.

With greatest care, the invisible hands wrung most of the water from my sodden tresses, one hank at a time. Then Mother Gothel helped me into my neck brace, a wooden bowl that clamped onto my shoulders and balanced on the top of my head, and piled all that heavy, wet, magically compacted hair into it. She kept a grip on my arm as, step by careful step, I made my way back up to my room. In fine weather I'd sit before the tower window with my head propped on a cushion while Mother Gothel released the enchantment again and my hair spilled out the window like a golden waterfall to dry in the sun. Cold or rainy days were less pleasant. Nurse and the invisible servants would move everything against the walls, except the chair in the middle where I sat, build up all the fires, and spread out sections of my hair like the rays of a soggy sun. Sometimes I'd wake in the chair to find the Tuesday/Friday ritual of brushing and combing the still-damp mass already begun. (Fortunately, combing out tangles doesn't hurt when the tangles are more than ten feet away.)

On Wednesdays and Saturdays Nurse and I had a half-day free once the invisible hands had plaited my hair, coiled the braids into the familiar magicked pyramid and pinned them down. Needless to say, I looked forward to Sundays, and rest.

Even more, I looked forward to the first day of summer. I considered it my birthday, since I had no idea when my real birthday was. Mother Gothel always saw to it that summer began on a Wednesday or Saturday. (I just figured that ordering the seasons about was one of the powers that came with witchcraft.) When the invisible hands had finished braiding my hair on that day they didn't bind it up as they usually did. Instead, Mother Gothel would approach with a pair of gigantic, wicked-looking shears. The blades would press against the back of my head, and the weight of a year's worth of hair would fall away, leaving me feeling buoyant and bouncy. The golden braid would undulate out of the room like a sixty-foot sea serpent as the hands carried it away to be spun and woven. Mother Gothel would follow, chortling and rubbing her hands together and not even glancing back at me.

The first day I'd run up and down the tower stairs, rejoicing in my abrupt lightness. (And scaring poor Nurse, who wasn't used to my being so freely mobile.) I'd spend the next few weeks dancing, spinning in circles and trying not to notice the golden fan behind me reaching further each day. By the end of the month I'd be tripping on my tresses again, and Nurse would braid and coil my hair before Mother Gothel noticed.

When I wasn't being shampooed or shorn, or coaxed to eat more of that wretched rampion, I read. Mother Gothel had learned from my childhood tantrums that boredom, with attendant pacing and hair-pulling, endangered my precious asset, and she'd reluctantly taught me two spells. One allowed me to tighten or loosen the binding on my hair, thus adjusting the weight to relieve my stiff neck. The other allowed me to read two books at a time from an enchanted library. When I finished the allotted pair, they vanished and two more appeared next to my breakfast rampion. At first they were dry educational texts. With time, I learned to stretch the spell. When I turned sixteen and Nurse vanished without a word, leaving me alone except for Mother Gothel's visits, I extracted books that I knew the old witch wouldn't have permitted. Fairy tales. Histories. Travel catalogues. Anything that gave me a glimpse of the world outside my tower. I learned that there were millions of people in the world, and cities like great stone anthills. I learned about horses, and the freedom of galloping over miles and miles of open earth with no walls to block the way. I learned that it wasn't generally considered socially acceptable to lock one's supposed daughter in a sixty-foot-high doorless tower in the middle of nowhere. It was cruel, too. I'd finally realized the truth of that.

Once I tried to escape. One late spring afternoon (a carefully-timed Wednesday), I loosened one long braid of my hair and wrapped it around one of the hooks where Mother Gothel parked her broom. With a bit of broken glass, hopefully sharp enough to cut hair, hidden in my dress pocket, I edged out onto the windowsill and tried to figure out a way to climb down my own braid.

Mother Gothel swept down on me, shouting at me to stop. When I didn't obey she magicked me back inside.

She didn't touch me. She was a witch. She didn't have to. She simply removed every last magical binding from my hair, and left me immobilized in the middle of a static-laden flaxen cloud. Even moving a few steps meant dragging yards of the stuff after me—across the carpet, which turned the static into little lightning daggers. Finally I just piled some hair into a soft heap and slept on it. I dreamed of horses, flying, and scissors.

❈ ❈ ❈

ANOTHER YEAR PASSED. My annual haircut restored my spirits for a while, but now I was feeling the full weight of my hairy burden again. I was sitting at the window with my chin propped on the sill, studying the grass and wondering what it would feel like to walk on it barefoot, when something moved on the plain below.

I sat up with a jolt. I'd never seen anything larger than a rabbit out there, and this thing was walking on two legs! The sight was so alien to me that it took a while for me to realize that I was looking at another human being. My heart began to pound. I started hyperventilating. I watched the person come closer and tried to think of all the things I'd read that one said during a conversation. Hello. How are you. Lovely weather we're having isn't it. Pleased to meet you. What's your name. Oh yes. Names were important.

Then I realized that I didn't know if I had one. I didn't think "Pretty Child" counted.

❊ ❊ ❊

BY NOW THE OTHER person had reached the base of the tower and was looking up at it in curiosity. My mind had gone blank. I peered out the window at the stranger. It looked like a man. I tried to think of what a man might be doing out here.

"Prince," said my stunned, monosyllabic brain. "On a Quest."

"Thanks," I answered myself, and the prince must've heard, or caught some movement, because he called out, "Hello?"

My brain panicked. I blurted out, "Happy Saturday!"

He laughed, but it wasn't a bitter laugh like Mother Gothel's. It didn't mock my foolishness. It made me feel like we were sharing a joke. I'd never shared anything before, unless you counted my hair. "It is a fine day, isn't it?" he shouted back. "A good day for a long walk, which I've had. Would you mind if I came in?"

Now I was holding the windowsill to keep upright, and very glad that it was a Saturday afternoon and both Mother Gothel and the invisible hands had left. I knew Mother Gothel would never allow such a thing. "There's no door," I said, dismayed.

"No door?" He sounded horrified. He vanished out of sight, and I was afraid he'd left, but he was just walking around the tower, checking for entrances. Of course, he found none.

"Is your name Rapunzel?" he hollered up to me.

"I don't know!" I hollered back. "Should it be?"

The man burst into hysterical laughter that sounded almost like crying, and started to walk away.

"Wait! Wait, your Highness!" I used the enchantment to unreel the first few ells of my braid and flung it over the windowsill. "Don't go! Climb up this!" I unwound the whole braid and lowered it as quickly as I could. After a few moments I felt an uncertain tug, then a harder yank.

"Ow! Wait; let me fix something." I lifted up an armload of hair and wrapped it around the nearest hook before letting it fall again. "Now climb."

It seemed to take forever before I saw a set of white knuckles gripping the windowsill. I thought it was just because of my own impatience, but as my visitor heaved himself over the sill and landed, gasping, on the floor, I saw another reason. My prince was old. Probably not as old as Mother Gothel, but his hair was gray and his face weathered and lined. Nothing like the princes in books. But the scent of leaves and grass, of outdoors, clung to his clothes.

He groaned and picked himself up from the floor, and looked from me to the "rope" he had just climbed.

"That was your hair?" he cried.

I nodded. The binding spell was already working, twirling and weaving my braid into its usual compact pile. I thought that was why he looked so horrified, as though the giant braid were a venomous snake.

"I climbed your hair?"

Mother Gothel would probably have a similar reaction, only worse, I thought, as my brain chose that moment to start working again. Those boots had surely broken many strands, even whole locks. But I didn't care. In fact, I felt more exhilarated than I ever had. "Yes."

"I didn't know…I'm so sorry…did I hurt you?"

"Not once I wrapped it around the hook," I said, feeling overwhelmed. This strange prince didn't even know me, but he felt bad that he might've hurt me. Mother Gothel would've been doing a damage assessment. I remembered several scenes from my books, and decided that if this prince got to the point of kissing me I wouldn't mind, even if he was old, maybe even forty or more. I tried to think of what I was supposed to do next. "Um, would you like something to drink, or eat? I have lots of rampion left." I offered him a bowlful of the interminable greens. He stared at it.

"Rapunzel," he muttered, shaking his head. "It figures."

This was getting frustrating. "Excuse me," I said. "I know my social skills are woefully underdeveloped from lack of practice, but I'm reasonably intelligent and doing my best to be polite, and you just aren't making any sense."

He chuckled, shrugged his shoulders until they popped, and sighed. "Where I come from, we call those greens rapunzel."

"Well, Nurse used to say 'You are what you eat,' and goodness knows

Mother Gothel makes me eat enough of the stuff, so it might as well be my name. It sounds rather pretty. Would you mind if I use it for my name, at least until I find out if I've got another one?"

"But don't you know?" He looked distressed. I was afraid I'd committed a horrible faux pas.

"No, not really. I'm sorry. I haven't had much use for a name before. No one else to talk to, you see. Um… What's yours?"

"Harry," he said, with a bemused glance at my towering coiffure.

"You aren't making fun of me, are you, your Highness?" I said, more sharply than I suspect was polite.

"I swear I'm not. It's Harry, not Hairy. Short for Harold. Why do you keep calling me 'your Highness,' child?"

"Aren't you my prince? The one who rides out of the sunset on his noble steed to steal me away? Or maybe rides into the sunset. Anyway, we ride away from here. That's the important part. Then there's something about kissing and Happily Ever After, but right now I'd settle for the getting out of here part."

"How did you get in here in the first place?" he said, rather plaintively for someone older than me. "And do you mind if I sit down? My knees are killing me." He looked around in vain for a seat.

"Mother Gothel just levitates, but you can sit in my chair. Don't worry; my legs are very strong from climbing the stairs every day. Standing won't bother me."

He sat.

"Mother Gothel brought me here. If you're not a prince, what are you doing here? We're so far from anywhere that when Mother Gothel sends a message to another witch she has to use a phoenix, because any other bird would die before it got back."

The man ran his hands through his graying hair. Once I fell asleep with my head on the windowsill while my hair was drying, and I got sunstroke. He looked sunstruck now.

"I've been walking the earth for eighteen years," he said. "And I'm as far from a prince as you can get. But I think I'm your father. Let me explain."

I listened to his bizarre tale of cravings and garden theft. The more I heard, the madder I got.

"You traded me for a SALAD?" I shouted.

"I traded you for my wife!" he shouted back, and stopped. "Wait. That doesn't sound much better, does it? Especially since the year after that she ran off with a cabbage farmer from Farport. The point is, I regretted it right away, and I set out to find you."

"Before or after the cabbage farmer?" I knew that was ungracious, but I'd been expecting a prince who'd take me away from the tower, not the man who'd put me in it. He could've at least traded me for something interesting, like papayas or vanilla beans.

"After." He looked at the floor. "But that's still seventeen years of walking. Please, give me a chance to prove myself. Let me rescue you."

I had to admit, it seemed stupid to turn him down, even if he wasn't a prince. I accepted. I should have asked him more questions. Like what he planned to do after we left the tower. Like why Harold had spent seventeen years looking for a daughter he'd barely even seen, and how he'd even had any idea which way to go. How he'd known, all those years ago, that the witch's hidden, walled garden even held the rampion that my mother had so craved.

But I didn't. I was so excited at the prospect of living in a world unbounded by round stone walls that I unwound my hair and wrapped it around the hook again, and didn't even think to be surprised when my father produced a pair of freshly-sharpened shears for me to cut it off with.

The instant the blades sheared through my hair, a wind shrieked through the tower. The stones rumbled. I clutched the windowsill, and when the shaking stopped I looked up to see Mother Gothel hovering on her broomstick just outside the window, glaring at me.

"What have you done?" she bellowed. In a blink she was inside the room, shaking her knotted fist at me. Then she noticed my would-be rescuer huddled on the floor, and kicked him in the side.

"You! What do you think you're doing? We had a deal! You got what you wanted. Now get out!"

"Greedy old hag. Those shirts are everywhere! You can afford to share the profits."

She kicked him again, and he groaned, but shouted, "You owe me!"

"I owe you a trip out the window, face-first into the rose thorns!" Mother Gothel countered.

"You both owe me an explanation!" I shouted, and they stopped and stared at me. Mother Gothel even looked a bit frightened. "You said my hair went to make shirts for the pilgrims. You said it was a good deed."

Harold chuckled and stood up, keeping a wary eye on Mother Gothel. "Good for her purse. Talk about your pot of gold! Cloth-of-Gold made from your hair is worth more than the real thing. Pilgrims couldn't afford shirts made from it. My mother-in-law here has made enough coin to fill several towers, and you're living on stewed rampion."

"Don't listen to him, my pretty child," said Mother Gothel, but her voice wavered. I'd snatched up the shears again, and she couldn't seem to look away from them.

"Why not, Mother?" said Harold. "Because your granddaughter might find out that she's entitled to a fortune that you won't let her touch because you think of her as your pet sheep?"

When he said "fortune," his brown eyes took on a greedy golden glint.

"That's what you wanted, too," I said, feeling something twist and break deep inside me. "The fortune. Or at least part of it. That's why you were looking for me."

"But I really am your father," he protested, and Mother Gothel didn't contradict him. "She tried to do the same thing to her daughter—your mother—but the rampion didn't make her hair grow. It just gave her cravings. But you, you're..." He stopped. "You're my only daughter!"

"And Mother Gothel's my grandmother," I said. They nodded in eager unison, and I turned cold. "All that means is that this is a family business," I said. "It's an ugly, selfish business, and I want no part of it."

I stiffened, waiting for Mother Gothel to strike me with some horrible enchantment, but she just stared at those scissors.

"And you can't do anything about it, can you?" I said as realization sunk in. "Because I cut my hair off myself, and it won't grow back unless I let you use that shampoo on it again." I grinned. Feeling giddy, I swung my legs over the windowsill and began to climb down my last enchanted braid.

"You'll never manage on your own!" Mother Gothel cried.

"You won't find a prince out there, you know!" her son-in-law added.

I ignored them. When I reached the bottom of the tower I stripped off my shoes and stockings and walked away, barefoot, through the grass. I didn't expect to find a prince.

But if I were lucky, I might meet a nice cabbage farmer.

❊ ❊ ❊ ❊ ❊

MELISSA MEAD LIVES IN Upstate NY. You can find her work in several places, including *Daily Science Fiction*, *Intergalactic Medicine Show*, and *Cast Of Wonders*. Her Web page is here: https://carpelibris.wordpress.com/

Thank God for the Road

Nancy Jane Moore

We'd planned to make Flagstaff by nightfall, but an hour outside Gallup one of the solar panels on the bus roof started to flap around. Emily and Jo climbed up to check, and discovered several more loose panels.

It was too hot to sit inside while they fixed it, so the rest of us put up sun shades and rested by the road. Not a cloud in the sky, nothing but cactus in any direction, so hot and dry that every time you took a deep breath, moisture dried up all the way down into your lungs.

I sat with Irene, who was teaching me another story.

Irene's our oldest member—over sixty now. But crowds grow real quiet when Irene tells a story.

I'm the youngest by a good ten years: I turn twenty next month. And I'm a guitar picker, not a storyteller. But Irene wants me to learn to tell. It didn't take me long after I joined All Star Traveling Revue to figure out no one ever says no to Irene.

"It rained for days and days," I said, sing-song.

"You have to put more feeling into it," Irene said. "You have to make people know what it feels like when the roof is leaking, and every time you run outside you get soaked to the bone, and you can't imagine ever being dry again."

"I'd like to feel like that."

"No, you wouldn't." But Irene knew what I meant. I've never seen that kind of rain. The places I know get a little drizzle, and everybody's grateful. There are parts of the country where they get too much rain instead of too little, but we never go there. They don't get enough sun to power the bus.

"You've got to make the audience feel wet when you tell that story. You've got to make them shiver, even if it's 97 degrees and hasn't rained in seventeen months."

So I thought back to a time in Austin when they'd had a little rain and we went swimming in Barton Springs. The water was icy cold. It's the only time I remember being wet all over. "They didn't think they'd ever be dry again." I shivered.

"That's more like it."

We got back on the road in early afternoon. "We could stop in the Painted Desert," someone said.

"Yeah," I said. I've never been there.

"Not enough people there to do a show," Jo said. She was driving. "We'll go as long as there's sun. That way we'll make Flag tomorrow."

Sun powers the bus's generator directly. We've got batteries that run a stove, a computer, a few amps, but we haven't got one big enough to run the bus. We don't drive after dark.

I sat up in the front, staring out at the expanse of concrete. The road is crumbling, helped along by cactus and other plants too tough for even drought to kill or cement to stop. An obstacle course. No one ever stays in one lane.

It's desolate here, but not the desperate desolation you get driving east from Denver across the Great Plains. It's not as flat, and things here are the way they were meant to be. The plains weren't supposed to turn into desert, but this place has been bone dry for a thousand years.

The first vehicle we'd seen all day came along about an hour before sunset. Jo was struggling to see in the setting sun. I cupped my hand over my eyes and moved to get a better angle. "Looks like a car."

We stopped. Common courtesy. Though we all checked to make sure we had weapons handy. We're friendly, but we're not fools.

The car held two grown women with three little kids in the back seat. Boxes and suitcases were tied onto everything but the solar panels. The women got out; the kids stayed in the car.

Jo and Irene got off the bus. I tagged along behind. "Where you heading?" Jo asked.

"Central Texas. We hear there's work. Heard anything?"

"We haven't been there since spring," Jo said. It was November. "But they had rain. Might be work."

"You musicians?"

"Musicians, actors, storytellers."

"There a living in that?"

"So long as we travel. Every place needs entertainment."

Irene was making friends with the kids, telling a funny story. I heard giggling.

Jo said, "What do you hear from out west?"

"Things got pretty bad after that last earthquake in L.A. Lots of refugees heading everywhere else in California. Jobs dried up."

"Along with everything else," the second woman put in. "Things seem better in Arizona. They said in Flag there was snow in the Grand Canyon."

I've never seen snow. "Oh, Jo, can we go see it?"

"Maybe." Snow is water.

"We almost stayed in Flag. The water wasn't too pricey and there was work. But we got family in Texas."

Jo nodded. "Be careful in New Mexico. They haven't had much rain."

Irene yelled up to the bus windows. Someone threw down a bag. She took out a couple of rag dolls and a little box and gave them to the kids. They squealed, delighted.

Jo frowned—we sell those toys—but no one tells Irene no.

The car went on east. We drove thirty miles and pitched camp near some Anasazi ruins.

"Funny to think," Emily said over dinner, "that highway used to carry thousands of cars at a time. Now we travel all day and only see one other vehicle."

"Thousands of people? That's crazy. There's not that many cars anywhere."

"Look how big it is. Had to be a lot of cars once."

"Emily's right," Irene said. "Used to be everybody had a car, everybody drove this highway."

Irene remembers.

"But oil got pricey and water got pricier, and none of the car makers adapted 'til too late. That's why the only vehicles left are mish-mashes like ours.

"Here's the funny thing, though. People have been traveling this pathway for a long time, probably back before the Navajo and the Hopi lived around here. It's the natural path. But this big highway didn't get built until the 1960s. And it's been falling apart pretty much my whole life—I doubt it's had any repair in fifty years. This huge highway was a good road for ninety years, maybe less."

I was surprised. You look at a big road, and you think it must have been there for all time.

"My daddy used to tell a story. Seems when his grampa was a little kid, five years old, his parents moved from Texas to California."

"Was that the Dust Bowl?"

"No, earlier than that, when times were flush. 1923, '24. They drove on this very road, except it wasn't even paved back then, much less wide and divided.

"They met another car on the road. The folks in it had been in California and were headed back to Texas. Just like us, they stopped and chatted. Nobody else coming; it didn't matter that they blocked the road. Just like now.

"They were driving one of the first cars ordinary folks could buy, a Model T Ford. The future looked bright. With cars, people could go anywhere, live everywhere. Nothing was too far away anymore.

"So people built these all these highways and the cities grew to super size. But when the rain stopped falling, the cities died. In another hundred years, this highway will be gone. Though there'll probably be some kind of road. Your kids"—she pointed at me—"might even be driving down it.

"Our grandparents and their grandparents built a major civilization around the automobile. And it lasted a hundred and twenty-five years."

We all got quiet. Even I know a hundred and twenty-five years isn't long, not for civilizations.

Finally I said, "So what do we do about it?"

Irene smiled—a big smile, the largest I'd seen in some time. "Why, we start over, child. We try again. It's going to be harder, because we haven't got the resources to be careless this time. You have to pay real attention to build something that'll last longer than a hundred and twenty-five years.

"That's why we're out here, telling stories and singing songs, letting everyone know that there is more to life than just surviving. That's our job." She paused. "Getting the rebuilding started, that's your job."

She hooked me, then and there. Youth always knows it can do something better than those who came before. Besides, you don't say no to Irene.

❄ ❄ ❄

Now, FIFTY YEARS LATER, I'm not so arrogant. I know I failed more than I succeeded.

But the road's still here—just two lanes of concrete now. We jackhammered out the rest, let the land take it back.

A group in New Mexico sent some old spaceships up to bring spent comets down for water. It's expensive—makes gold look cheap—but it made the Southwest livable again. Nobody wastes it, not this time around. We at least learned that much.

The Southwest is still desert and it's still hot, but people are making lives here again instead of just passing through or withering away. The road is too busy for people to stop and chat in the middle of it, but not so busy that people don't pull off to the side and visit.

You can't have civilization without a road, but you can't let the road take over all of civilization. That's what we aimed for when we rebuilt it.

I think Irene would approve.

❄ ❄ ❄ ❄ ❄

NANCY JANE MOORE is the author of two novels, *For the Good of the Realm* (June 2021) and *The Weave*, both published by Aqueduct Press, as well as the collection *Conscientious Inconsistencies*, the novella *Changeling*, and numerous short stories. In addition to writing, she holds a fourth degree black belt in Aikido and teaches and writes about empowerment self defense. She blogs on most Fridays on the Treehouse Writers blog (https://treehousewriters.com/wp53/) and can be found regularly on Twitter at @WriterNancyJane. A native Texan who spent many years in Washington, D.C., she now lives in Oakland, California, with her sweetheart, two cats, and an ever-growing murder of crows.

Some background to the story:

Despite being set in the near future, this story contains one bit of real-life history. My father and his parents traveled from West Texas to California in 1923 on a road that was not yet the famed Route 66 or the current Interstate 40, and they did indeed stop and chat with folks coming back east somewhere in the middle of Arizona. The story has one more personal connection. My sweetheart read it when it was first published and, due to his love for road trips, was inspired to write me a fan letter. I responded, we met in person at WisCon, and that is why I now live in California.

Changing of the Guard

Mindy Klasky

I entwined my tendrils in Iliana's hair, using her senses to show me the soldier who tossed and turned beneath my branches. My sylph sat back on her heels and folded her wings across her back, content to watch now that she had finished cleaning his head-wound. "*He is waking up,*" Iliana thought. My tendrils stretched as she leaned closer to the sleeping human, peering at him through her night-large eyes.

"*He'll be thirsty,*" I replied. "*Fill the cup.*"

She took her stoneware vessel and held it to my bark, collecting the life-sap I leaked for her. My sylph touched her tongue to the liquid, curious as all her kind are. She detected the smoky essence immediately, the manly elements the wounded soldier would need to restore his memories, to remind him why he had wandered into the forest.

I knew, of course. I'd seen soldiers stagger beneath the canopy before, dazed and confused by their bloody human battles. I'd seen the humans flee their wars, coming into the forest because they were injured. Or afraid. Or both.

My tendrils quivered with Iliana's heightened interest. My sylph was far gone in her fascination with humans. "*What have you put in this?*" she asked.

"*The things he needs. His body is different from yours.*"

"*I can see that.*" She added a smile to the thought and reached across to help the soldier into a sitting position. His eyes snapped open, and she stared at his curious round pupils, huge in the dim light of the forest night.

"Wh—" He did not bother finishing the word; instead, he reached for his weapon. I had already told Iliana to hide the krakik. I had seen the damage that burning weapon could do. I was willing to help her play nursemaid, but I was not willing to be hurt. At least not by a silly weapon carried by a belligerent human male.

Of course, when I told her to hide the dead iron weapon, I created another opportunity for her to feed her compulsion about humans. I showed her yet another path out of the forest and into their world. I hoped she wasn't ready to take it. Yet.

Iliana's voice was as musical as wind-struck bells when she spoke to the human. "I have taken your weapon. You will not need it here in the forest."

"In the forest?" He scrambled to his feet faster than he should have, and through Iliana, I sensed the blood drain from his face. He glanced about in fear and revulsion, and I knew he did not remember stumbling beneath the trees. He could not recall his decision to come to the forest, fleeing the noise and filth of battle by the human stockade.

Curious skin these humans had. They wore all their emotions on their faces. Their blood beat just beneath the surface, betraying half their thoughts to anything with a tendril and a sylph's senses. The soldier's anger and fear warped his voice. "How did I get here?"

"You walked. Or stumbled, more precisely." Iliana frowned, struggling to speak the right words aloud. It was hard to find the proper ones, nearly impossible, because she was only accustomed to thinking her thoughts directly to me.

The soldier opened and closed his right hand, as if he still held his ugly krakik. "You lured me here! I've heard tales! I know about you sylphs!"

"Lured?" Iliana shifted her perch on my roots, automatically opening her wings for balance. The brave soldier caught the moonlight off her iridescent scales, and his face blanched even more. His lips were as pale as Iliana's moon-spun hair, and he flinched as she demanded, "What do you know about sylphs?"

"We've heard all about you in town! We know you enchant men and take their seed. You breed babes and then dash them against the roots of trees, feeding your forest with human blood."

"That is not true!" she cried, and her hands spread protectively across my bark. Her thoughts to me were shocked: "*Do you hear how he accuses us?*"

"*They* all *accuse you, not just this one. The humans are afraid of you. Of me. Of the forest.*"

I meant the words to be soothing, but Iliana's agitation spread to the rest of our flock. Through my roots, I sensed the willows beginning to whip their withes down by the lake, and the sturdier trees moaned where the wind passed through their branches.

Iliana heard the unrest, the imbalance she had created. She folded her wings with precision, taking deep breaths to calm herself before turning back to the human. "You were injured," she said, "and I cleaned your wounds." Iliana used her sensible voice, the one she saved for birds and squirrels and other creatures with small brains. "Drink this, and you will feel better."

She offered him the cup, and he started to dash it away, but something stayed his hand. He dipped a broad finger into the nectar and sniffed it suspiciously. After a long pause, he tasted the wetness on his own flesh. Apparently, he detected nothing odd about the drink because he swallowed the rest of it greedily.

"*He is thirsty. Should we give him more?*" Iliana sounded anxious and excited, like a bird preparing to fall from its nest for the first time.

"*He's not strong enough for more. Not yet. Patience, my child.*"

"*I am not a child!*"

It was an old argument between us, worn smooth as the bark on a river-washed snag. "*Pay attention! He's waiting for you to answer him.*"

She blinked hard as she turned back to the human, shaking her head so her long white hair flowed down her back and cascaded over her wings. Her excitement trembled across my tendrils. She found it hard to meet the human's dark eyes, impossible to keep her thoughts from his hard lips, which were rapidly regaining their ruddy color. Her attention was snared by the muscles that tightened beneath his hairy arms, and she stammered a little as she shifted back to speaking aloud. "I— I am sorry. Did you ask me something?"

The human shook his head, as if he wished to clear away the sight of her moon-white hair, her wings, and her cat's eyes. "I was only saying I should have taken my chances with the battle." He jutted his chin back toward the stockade. "At least there, I'd be my own man."

"Ah, then," Iliana nodded sagely, settling back onto my roots. "Now I understand your earlier anger. I would have shown you more respect if I had known you were the king."

"I never claimed—" he spluttered. "I did not say I am the king!"

"But you said you would be your own man," Iliana countered sweetly. "Even *I* know only the human king is his own man. The king owns all the other humans. The other humans must serve the king."

I was pleased that Iliana remembered the things I had taught her about the humans, about their life in the stockade. After all, I'd had a long lifetime in the forest to learn how the humans worked. I'd studied the occasional parties of men and women who passed beneath my branches. I wished, though, that Iliana had chosen a different time to show off her wisdom, to present her soldier with her truths.

"Are you calling me a slave?" the man bellowed, and once again, he clenched his hand around his missing krakik.

Iliana's wings opened for flight, and I knew it took all of her will power not to retreat to my lower branches. The sight of her glistening membranes stilled the soldier again, changing his breathing and the scents he broadcast into the forest night. Iliana responded by fluttering her wings so they caught the moonlight just...so.

The soldier calmed as if he were hypnotized.

"I am calling you a human man," she finally answered, and her musical voice lanced the last of his tension. "I know nothing more about you, or about the ways of your people." I could hear the longing in her tone. Even the human man, with ears as dull as earth, must understand. She whispered, "I would give my wings to see your town behind the stockade."

"Don't say that!" he responded immediately, and then flushed at the vehemence behind his words.

"Why not? I am a sylph. I can say whatever I like, so long as it is the truth."

"I've heard of your sylph truth." Bitterness wafted off him like the scent of rotting acorns. "You lead good men astray. Your forest takes the best of the king's soldiers. They wander from their posts on the stockade walls and they get lost in your forest, never to return."

She stared at him solemnly, the moonlight glinting from the vertical slit in her eyes. "We take only those who wish to be taken."

"Tell that to the widows left in the stockade."

"All right," she said agreeably and moved to his side. Her head reached only to the middle of his chest, but the tips of her wings hovered by his lips. She reached out and settled his hand on her narrow shoulder, ready to help him back to the world of men.

"What are you doing?" He pulled back as if she had set his fingers in a snarl of maggots.

"I am helping you to go home. We can speak to the widows then."

"You're not coming anywhere near the stockade! I didn't mean..."

"Ah," she sighed. "You lied to me."

"I didn't lie!" he growled. "This is madness! All of it!" He staggered back, shaking his hand as if to shed the memory of Iliana's touch. "Madness!" He turned heel and stumbled down the path, back toward the stockade. Back toward his human war.

"*Wait!*"

"*He can't hear you.*"

"*I know,*" Iliana thought miserably, and my heartwood ached.

In those two words, I realized how close she was to leaving, how much she had been seduced by the mystery of the human life beyond the forest. We'd been years traveling to this fork, and now I thought my bark would crack. After pulling strength from my heartwood, I made myself think, "*Go after him, child. Make sure he gets to the stockade.*"

"*I cannot do that. I cannot leave you.*"

I let a breeze capture the broad sides of my leaves, lifting them from her hair, her wings and her eyes, as if an early morning fog were dispersing over the forest. She hesitated for only a moment, sniffing the air to make sure that no stray flame burned, that no metal axe lurked nearby. Then, she skipped down the forest path, tracking her human into the night.

❊ ❊ ❊

SHE TOLD ME ALL about it when she returned, so excited by her time inside the dead wood stockade that she forgot I could sense her adventures in the perfume of her breath, in the restless weight of her body as she sprawled across my roots. I lowered tendrils into her hair, entwining myself in her, telling myself I was acting to comfort her, to ease her sylph soul. My heartwood pulsed with a bitter wash of jealousy. She had loved her night with the humans.

Of course, the soldier never realized that she followed him. She had slipped past the human guards at the stockade gate, folding her wings about her body so they thought she was only a beam of moonlight.

Once inside the stout wooden walls, she could not decide where to look first. There were so many sights. Torchlight flickered from one structure, where loud song rang out and the smell of fermented grains tickled her nose. More fire leaped by the gate, as the guards warmed their hands over open flames. The sooty smell threatened to overwhelm her, and she needed to remind herself that no trees lived within reach of the fire. All was safe.

She soon lost her soldier, but she followed the other wondrous folk who roamed the night-time streets. There was an old blind man, cranking the handle of a dead wooden box that shrieked with music. There was a haggard woman, carrying a basket of the first autumn apples, gleaned from a stingy orchard just outside the stockade walls. There were three children, boys, jostling each other to peer into the chinks of a building wall, smothering their giggles as they watched some amusing sight.

My Iliana was enchanted by all of the humans. There was so much to do and see in the village, so many experiences, so many sensations.... Now, secure in the forest that had been her life, she exhaled a deep breath, letting the scents and flavors of the human world roll across her tongue.

Although she did not ask me, I added a sleeping draught to her nectar when she finished her tale. I did not dose her with one of the heavy elixirs that the humans distilled from my distant cousins, the poppies. Rather, I brewed a sweet syrup that soothed her mind and reminded her that she was safe in my embrace, protected for as long as she would stay. I wove my tendrils deeper into her hair, even twining them around the tips of her wings.

She slept for several hours, and when she woke, her wanderlust had lessened. She fetched me water from the lake, and she spent the day tending my roots where they broke through the rich soil. She scaled away a persistent patch of lichen, and the breeze hummed in my leaves as I watched over her with satisfaction.

A week passed, and I enjoyed better care from Iliana than she had provided in years. Still, I could not help but notice that she gathered bitterroot by the shores of the lake. I smelled it on her hands when she came back one night, and when she slipped away the following evening,

I was not surprised to sense woodsmoke in the distance. It takes a large fire to boil enough water to render bitterroot.

Her pale sylph skin was flushed when she returned in the stretched light before dawn. The blush made her look almost human, even more than the bitterroot dye in her hair. Midnight tresses curled down her back and between her wings. Some of my tendrils curled away from the heavy scent, but I forced myself to enfold her in a viny embrace. She sobbed as dawn broke over the forest, but I could not say if her tears were for the forest she longed to leave or the village she longed to enter.

✾ ✾ ✾

MANY NIGHTS LATER, THE human soldier returned. His scent was blown on the darkling breeze, sharp against the forest smells, far stronger than the distant rank breath of the stockade. Iliana could have sensed him if she'd chosen to, but she was busy tending to me, working hard beneath the moonlight to scrub a fungus from one of my roots.

She startled when he cleared his throat, whirling on him with anger in her cat's eyes. She did not like to be interrupted. She did not like to be surprised.

Through my tendrils, I sensed her heartbeat quicken as she recognized him. Her wings fluttered prettily above her head, and a curious lethargy spread through her long-boned limbs. "It is only you," she sighed, affecting human disinterest as she ran one hand through her dark hair.

He strode across the clearing, krakik at the ready. "You witched me!" he hissed.

"I am a sylph, not a witch," she answered quite reasonably. Perhaps she was not afraid of the krakik because she had never seen the burning it could do. He jabbed the weapon beneath her ribs and clutched at her black hair. His cruel hands drove her to her knees, forcing her flesh against my roots.

I could not resist. I twined a pair of tendrils into his hair.

"*What are you doing?*" she asked, and there was worry in her voice, concern for the soldier. She did not know if I would hurt him. Even then, she did not imagine that he would hurt her. Hurt me.

"*I'm listening to him. I'm feeling him. Be careful, Iliana. His anger is mixed with fear.*"

"Sylph, witch, what do I care!" His human voice seemed even harsher, coming on the heels of our silent conversation. "You stole my soul with your charms! You've walked my dreams."

"Oh, so now you think me a dream-catcher?" Her words were light, even though her cheek stung where he pinned her against my bark.

"*Iliana, don't push him.*"

She ignored me, her eyes so wide in the forest night that it was hard to tell that her pupils were vertical slits. "What exactly do you think I am, human? Where do you think I get my powers?"

"You suck them from good men in the stockade. You drain us to feed the forest. You leave us unmanned with our wives, and then you make us doubt ourselves in battle. All so you can please your trees!"

Before she could react, before I could even warn her what he was thinking, he pointed the krakik's muzzle toward my roots. The shock of the burning shivered through my entire trunk.

One root was seared all the way through, the smooth wood curling up on itself, crumbling to charcoal beneath his bitter flame. I thrashed my branches in agony, recoiling my tendrils from his hair, from his smelly human body, from the stink of his anger. The surrounding forest writhed in reaction to my pain, branches whipping as if a storm blew across the lake.

For Iliana's sake alone, I pushed down the impulse to crush the human. I smothered the urge to drop a branch on his ridiculously thin skull.

Iliana tried to protect me, throwing herself at the human and knocking away the krakik. She shrieked as she attacked, and as she beat him, she scattered iridescent scales from her wings. "You...you *human*!" she shrieked, pelting him with clods of earth. "Get out of my forest! Leave us alone!" Her hair blew in her eyes, and she shrieked wordlessly as she tore its dark curtain to the side.

That eerie howl froze him, and his hands fell to his sides, powerless as one of her missiles hit him in the middle of his chest. "You've changed," he finally said.

Iliana glared at him as if he were a patch of leaf-blight.

"Your hair—" he said.

My sylph launched herself at the human, buffeting him with her wings. She turned her fingers into claws and her teeth into tiny daggers. He stood up to her attack for a full minute before he fled to the forest's edge.

❊ ❊ ❊

THE NEXT WEEK PASSED quietly. Iliana brought me water from the lake, more than I needed, pouring it over my roots as if she could wash away the harm the human had caused. I took what nutrients I could from the sorrowful bath, and I completed the process of healing myself, channeling my vessels away from the root severed by the krakik's burning tongue. Iliana curled beneath me like a child, letting me weave a bower above her head. Despite all the attention she paid to me, she refused to speak, refused to answer the questions I set inside her mind.

"Why are you mourning, little one? I am fine. See?" I waved my branches as vigorously as a sapling in its first winter storm. *"The human has done no lasting harm."*

She said nothing, only shifting to preen her wings in the moonlight. She ate nothing, drank nothing, forgot even to watch the moon rise. When she was not sleeping, she stared out at the forest's edge, at the stockade that was beyond her sight. My tendrils told me she hated herself for staying, and she hated herself for still longing to go.

I knew what I needed to do, and I knew she would never ask me to do it. When she brought my water that afternoon, I drank deeply, drawing more into my heartwood than I ever had before. My pith swelled, pushing against the tight constriction of my bark until I thought I would burst from the pressure. Iliana was too preoccupied to notice.

Creating the tincture took all of my skill. I knew it would kill her if I added too much of one agent. It would drive her mad if I used too little of another. I mixed the potion carefully, and twice when I thought I was done, I let the stuff seep back into my core, uncertain that I had the right to make this decision for her.

Finally, though, I was satisfied with my creation. I was certain it would act as I desired. As Iliana needed.

I let a new-grown tendril weave through my sylph's hair, caressing her face for the last time. *"Awake, little one."* She obeyed reflexively, attuned to my commands as all her people had been since the first tree grew from the grasslands. *"Pick up your cup."*

The liquid I had crafted just filled the vessel, exactly as I had planned. It came from my heartwood. The taste would be bitter. I gathered my thoughts around her mind, numbing her tongue to the stuff and speaking as if she were a newly sprouted seed. *"That's it, little one. Drink, and you'll be better. Tip the cup. Drink the drink. All will be well. All will be well."*

My tendrils told me when the last of the drink burned down to her belly. She set down the cup in a daze, and then she turned toward my trunk, tracing my deep whorls with her thin, thin fingers. The draught began its work immediately. Her eyes widened, the pupils expanding as if she stood in broad daylight, alone, unsheltered, beyond the forest fringe.

"What was that?" she asked with wonder. Wonder and ignorance, and I knew that I had lost her.

"It was a cure, my child."

She ignored my endearment, forgetting already that she hated the title. Instead, she stretched her arms above her head, as if she were awakening from a long winter's nap. I sensed the blood beating closer to the surface of her skin, raising a new heat in her face. *"A cure? But nothing ails me."*

"Nothing now." I managed to shape the thought without letting my windy sorrow tremble the words. Although her feet stayed still, I could feel her move away from me. I could feel her mind withdraw from my touch.

"What was in it?" she asked, and her words were music beneath the forest canopy. Even the birds stopped to listen.

"Things you may not know," I thought, but it was too late. She could no longer hear me.

Iliana's first human steps were like a newborn fawn's. She moved, cautious and graceful beneath my branches. I could not make myself pull back the last of my tendrils; I could not relinquish her entirely. She seemed taller as she stood at the edge of my reach, and her voice was deeper when she studied the forest.

"You did this to me, didn't you? You changed me, to make me human?"

I ruffled my branches in admission, but she could not truly understand me. I think a look of sorrow crossed her face, but I've never been able to read the hot flesh of humans, not without my sylph's eyes and ears.

"You want me to go to the stockade."

I wanted nothing of the kind. I wanted her to stay and tend to me. I wanted her to bring me water from the lake. I wanted her to clean the lichen from my bark and to pick away burrowing insects so the birds would not harm me. I wanted to feel her sylph hair beneath my tendrils.

I wanted her to be happy.

"You want me to go to the stockade," she repeated, and her voice was full of wonder. I sensed the moisture in her human eyes as she gazed at me in awe. "Thank you." Her whisper barely shook the air, barely reached my quivering tendrils. "I'll never forget you."

Impulsively, like a human child, she leaped back to my trunk and threw her arms around me. I could not keep my tendrils from closing around her one last time. I hoped she had not yet mastered the humans' ability to lie.

Before I was ready, she drew away, rubbing at her arm where a rough patch of my bark had scored her pink flesh. That was my parting gift to her, although she did not realize it at the time. She was so concerned with the slight seep of blood from those tiny, clean scratches that she did not notice the last grasp of my tendrils. She did not feel her useless wings plucked loose, falling to the loam between my roots.

She did not look back as she made her way to the forest's edge—and the stockade.

❄ ❄ ❄

THE SUN HAD SET when I heard the human crash through the forest. My first thought was to reach out for Iliana's mind, to summon her awake, so she could lead the intruder away, guiding him with her laughter and fluttering wings to a place that was safe for all the forest.

Of course, there was no Iliana. There was no place safe for all the forest.

The wind sprang up, and I realized this was not just any human approaching. This was *him*. Iliana's soldier. Reflexively, my roots drew back, trying to burrow deeper in the protective earth.

He passed me by at first, stumbling along the path with a scarce-shielded oil lantern. The stench of burning coated the air, making my leaves heavy and stiff. He muttered as he walked. I could not keep from stretching my tendrils after him, hoping for a few words about my dear Iliana, but he was already too far away for me to touch.

Just when I thought he was gone, I sensed the oil again, and he came lumbering back along the path. Something must have caught his eye this time. He squatted in the earth before me.

"Ahhhh." The single syllable escaped him, a cross between a sigh and a moan. He knelt in the loam and crossed his arms over his chest. I dared to drop a single tendril into his matted hair, and I began to understand.

"Iliana…" He turned her name into a mourning cry. He fingered the ragged base of one of her wings, the jagged edge where it had kissed her flesh. When he raised his hands in the moonlight, they were coated with silver dust.

Like any human, he drew the wrong conclusion. For a frantic minute, he dug about my roots, circling my trunk to search for Iliana's earthly remains. He might as well have shouted that he was looking for bones. As he dug, he muttered to himself, and I learned what had driven him to the forest.

He had been standing watch on the stockade walls, guarding his precious town and his glorious king against the barbarian invaders. In the moonlight, he thought he saw Iliana. He thought that she was wandering the village streets. He had left his post, deserting his brothers as he chased a sylph.

His commanding officer had berated him, no longer able to tolerate the soldier's strange behavior. He had become untrustworthy, ever since he had been spirited away in the middle of the last battle. Even as the soldier cried out that he sought Iliana, he was stripped of his command and told he could no longer serve his king.

The soldier had returned to his home, only to find that his human wife had barred the door against him. She cried through the dead wood, telling him he was possessed. He was mad. He would not see his son again.

And even as the soldier raged against his wife, he looked down the dark and twisting street and he thought he spied Iliana. He thought he saw her, with her hair dyed black and her wings stripped away, walking through the night without the fear a human woman would possess.

He'd called for her. He'd chased her. He'd run through the streets, ignoring the men who had been his brothers in arms. The soldiers jeered at him from their posts along the stockade walls.

And yet, he could not reach Iliana. She shimmered just ahead of him, and then she disappeared, like moonlight, down a dark alley.

And so, he had left his pitiful town behind its dead wood stockade. He had journeyed into the forest, in the deepest, darkest night. He had traced his way back to the place he had first found in the dream-state of his injury, of his lost blood.

But Iliana was gone.

Now, as sunlight broke over the forest, the soldier sank into the loam, collapsing against my trunk. He clutched his head between his fingers. "I saw you in the streets! You came to bring me to your forest! You chose me to be yours. You chose me, when they were all convinced I was a dreamer and a traitor and a fool…"

His anguish was too much to contain. He raged to his feet and slammed his fist against my bark. He had traded his life as a soldier, as a husband, as a father, and yet he found no sign of Iliana. He was left with nothing except my sylph's shimmering wings, already thinning away under the moonlight.

If he had come in another week, there would have been no sign at all of my Iliana.

But I was wrong.

In the darkest shadows beneath my branches, he found another sign. He tripped over Iliana's stone cup. Slowly, like a child, he raised it to the moonlight. He consecrated it to some new service, cradling it between his palms. He would have drunk deep, but it was empty.

He must have remembered Iliana's actions when he was injured. It took him only a moment to find the niche on my trunk. He settled the cup against my bark.

For just a moment, I thought to summon all my knowledge of poison and pain and hurt. I could destroy this puny human with little effort.

That, though, was not the way of the forest. I would not murder this one—not when he presented no direct threat. He lived a bloody, smoky life because that was what he was bred to do. He knew no better.

But perhaps he could be taught.

I leaked sap into the cup. Only when clear liquid neared the brim did I add a few drops of a special substance, a compound brewed close to my leaf-tips, close to the moonlight.

He drank like a human, greedy and quick. Those last few drops that I added made him tired. But I was pleased to see that he remembered to shutter his lantern before he staggered across my roots. He still gripped one of Iliana's wings in his fist as he curled up against my trunk.

It would do him no good to awaken with sorrow. I wormed a tendril between his fingers, worked my way around the shimmering wing. Moonlight and the breeze had taken their toll. It took little effort to urge the fragile scales to drift into the night air.

Now that I could employ more tendrils without worrying about frightening the human, I set about completing the healing I had begun with those few drops at the top of the cup. I brushed his face. I wove into his hair.

In the moonlight, the soldier had lost his ruddy bravado. His skin looked silver beneath the night sky. Human age had painted his dark hair gray.

He was unaccustomed to my touch, and the whisper of my tendrils stirred him from his dreams. He muttered in his sleep, reaching reflexively toward the krakik at his waist. I rustled the tendrils nearest his ears, trying to match vibrations to the words I thought. *"Easy, little one. Sleep easy. Sleep deep. You do not need your fire-stick and your fear. Sleep in the peace of the forest."*

His face contorted, and his mouth worked. His eyes flashed back and forth beneath their lids. I softened my voice, resorting to a blanket of thoughts rather than words. *"Peace. Comfort. Security. Peace."*

The soldier twisted in his sleep, his hand still groping for the krakik. My tendrils fluttered in concern, and I longed for Iliana's smooth hands, for her agile fingers that could have cast away the weapon. My burned root ached, throbbing where the soldier's head rested against its charred surface.

I renewed my efforts. *"Peace. Cool. Quiet. Water."*

Without warning, he bolted upright, as if I had jammed a root against his spine. His eyes were wild as he gazed around the forest, and his breath came in sharp, short pants. His fingers closed over the krakik, and I pulled in my sap, trying to conserve my heart-blood in my soft core. The other trees sensed my agitation, and their limbs frothed the air above our heads.

I pulled back all of my tendrils, making myself blind and deaf as I cursed my wooden hope. I had been a fool to let the human drink from the stone cup.

The sound was so slight, I almost missed it in the frenzy of thrashing branches. It took my deepest heartwood to recognize the noise, to realize that I had heard the hard slap of metal against water. Daring to uncurl a tendril, I reached toward the lake. I stretched toward my flock that stood in rings about the water.

Concentric circles lapped the shore, licking the lake's edge like a vixen cleaning a newborn kit. I lowered my tendrils, grasping about the loam at my roots. The human was there, quivering and alert. The stone cup had fallen upside down, leaking a single drop of sweet sap onto the forest floor.

That was all. Nothing else. No krakik.

I lowered my tendrils slowly, not wanting to frighten the human. "*Peace*," I projected. "*Gratitude. Hope.*"

At first, I did not think he understood. He looked down the forest path, as if he even now longed to break for the stockade. I sensed a moisture about him, and my longest tendril discovered salty tracks of water creeping from his eyes down his cheeks.

I had done all I could. The man was not for the forest. I began to draw back my tendrils, to smooth out my roots so he could easily walk back to his people. Perhaps they would forgive him over time. Perhaps they would come to believe that he had, in fact, seen my Iliana.

As the last of my tendrils fell from the human's face, his throat worked. He grabbed the viny length with shaking hands and raised it to his mouth. For just a moment, I feared his sharp, white teeth, but then he brushed me with his lips.

"Life." The whisper was so faint inside his mind, that I could have imagined it. "Life," he repeated, and then added in a flurry the thought of *tree*, and *water*, and *moon*, and a hopeless, sorrowful shimmer that might have been *Iliana*.

I wove my tendrils into his hair and called more sap to my surface.

USA Today bestselling author Mindy Klasky learned to read when her parents shoved a book in her hands and told her she could travel anywhere through stories. As a writer, Mindy has traveled through various genres, including traditional fantasy, romantic comedy, and hot contemporary romance. In her spare time, Mindy knits, quilts, and tries to tame her to-be-read shelf. Learn more about Mindy at www.mindyklasky.com.

In Case of Emergency

Karen G. Berry

The little black pot had a tail, which curled neatly around its base. Laurinda added herself to it a pinch at a time; stubbornness, regret, generosity, no more than a speck of caution, a generous helping of shamelessness. It wasn't quite enough. She threw in weekends with unsuitable men, her too-loud laugh, obscenely low necklines and a ladle full of impropriety. "I have no guilty pleasures," she intoned over the mixture.

Laurinda watched the churn and swirl of the various ingredients as the pot heated and shivered. Its tail swished away to reveal three tiny black feet, on which it began to prowl the table. It moved unevenly, with a dip and a thump, a tap and a sway. "Oh dear, little pot, don't spill," scolded Laurinda. "You've got so much of me in there."

The pot's tail shot out and began to act as a rudder to keep things even. The stewing continued, with occasional whistles and tiny eruptions of steam. "That's much better, darling. You do such nice work," Laurinda said calmly, watching the progress of her elixir.

After three circuits of the tabletop, the pot settled, as did its contents. It emitted what sounded like a small belch. "All done, precious?" Laurinda leaned over and studied the contents, inky black and shot through with fiery pinpricks. "That looks volatile. I hope I never have to use it."

The pot twitched its tail.

Laurinda ladled the mixture into a small bottle. After corking it tight, she held the bottle as it cooled, turning it this way and that to watch the morning light catch glints of emerald, lapis, and ruby. "It's cool now," she said to the pot, which seemed to be waiting at attention. "I think it's safe."

She affixed a paper label upon which she wrote, *BREAK ONLY IN CASE OF EMERGENCY.*

With a sigh, she tucked the bottle on a shelf, hiding it behind a photo of herself at the nude beach in Hawaii. "Just look at me," she murmured to the pot, which had settled again, rewrapping its tail around its feet, as invisible as any sugar pot there on the table.

"I was a knockout, wasn't I?" She smiled, shook her head slightly.

A knock rattled her front door.

"One second, darling!" She adjusted her hat, smoothed her lipstick, and grabbed the handle of a small suitcase. She lingered with her hand on the doorknob, taking one last look at the home of her single years. The door rattled again with the urgency of a bridegroom.

"I'll be back soon, and just think, I'll be married." Laurinda winked at the little black pot, and turned to the door. "Coming, darling!"

With a smile, she was gone.

❀ ❀ ❀ ❀ ❀

KAREN G. BERRY LIVES, works and writes (for a living) in the suburbs of Portland, Oregon. She is the co-author of three mystery novels about a woman who disappears when life gets too stressful, which seems like a good idea right now. Karen is also the sole author of seven more novels and one nonfiction book, *Shopping at the Used Man Store*, which inspires spit-takes and hopelessness in nearly everyone who reads it. She does not consider herself a poet, but her poetry has appeared in numerous journals and anthologies and even won some prizes. If you are burningly curious, more information about her life, books, and dogs can be found at https://karengberry.mywriting.network/

Circus

Paul McMahon

The posters went up all around the neighborhood during the night, stuck to telephone poles across the street from our solid wall of run-down brownstones. Behind the telephone poles stood another solid wall of brownstones, except these were a little more run-down. Posters hung from the posts beside each staircase, and clung crookedly to the windows of the few vacant buildings as if they were blown there by a great gust of wind. Everyone came out to look. They each featured a group photo of the performers and clowns in front of a striped tent, and I couldn't look away from the sheer size of the woman smiling dead center among them while two people balanced on a wire far above her head.

Julie Delphny snapped her gum beside me, making me jump.

"You ain't gonna go to that," she said.

I knew it, but I didn't like that she did. "Why not?"

"Shows like that's for rich kids."

She looked at me and her pale blue eyes had the effect on me they always did. They tangled my thoughts.

"Oh," I said.

She nodded once and then skipped away to find someone made of tougher stuff to play with.

I caught myself staring at one or another of those posters all afternoon. I felt a little guilty, staring at that big lady so often, but since I wasn't going to see the circus for real, I figured there was no harm in it.

❀ ❀ ❀

THAT NIGHT, MY DAD came home with circus tickets for the whole family. A stranger named Thackery gave them to him for pointing him toward city hall. People always did things like that. Dad befriended everyone he met, just as easy as you please.

It took some time for him to convince Mom the tickets were on the up and up. When she finally conceded that they were legit, he tried to convince her to come with us. She wanted nothing to do with it. Fortunately, though, Dad had me to help. After Mom went to her room and closed the door, I waited a full five minutes and then went in.

"Julie Delphny told me we're not rich enough to go to the circus."

Mom climbed off the bed and led the way.

❀ ❀ ❀

MY LITTLE BROTHER BJ made it through the high wire act but started fussing when the clowns came out. Mom held him and kept him quiet while they goofed around. She remained in a good enough mood afterward that she agreed to wait while Dad and I checked out the sideshows. Mom made me promise to look after Dad so he wouldn't do anything crazy.

I did well until I saw the big lady from the poster. You couldn't tell from the poor mimeographed picture, but she had the same soul-shattering pale blue eyes as Julie Delphny. I squeaked through the throngs of people and made it to the wooden sawhorse barricade to get close to her.

"You have beautiful eyes," I said when she looked at me.

"Bless you, sweetheart."

I blushed because I hadn't intended to speak out loud. Someone else spoke and she turned away, so I stayed and watched her for a while.

When I remembered I was supposed to be watching Dad, enough time had passed that I knew I was in trouble.

I worked my way out of the crowd and saw him immediately, standing apart from everyone and talking with the Ringmaster, of all people. I marched over and took his hand and heard him saying: "Anytime," and "Whenever," and "As long as you need."

❀ ❀ ❀

THE FIRST ONES THAT arrived were the organ grinder and his monkeys. Capuchins, they were. Well trained at mimicry and pick-pocketing. Of course, they didn't do much thieving as part of the circus, but it seemed to be their favorite talent. In their first ten minutes they brought me three plastic toy wallets, three vinyl girl's pocketbooks and an expensive-looking necklace.

"It's only for a couple of days," Dad assured Mom later that night. The organ grinder, Joe, fell asleep on the couch, while the monkeys, One and Three (Two had died a few months earlier), climbed into the crib to sleep with BJ, adopting his cooings, droolings and farts as their own.

❈ ❈ ❈

THE NEXT DAY, THE high-wire act showed up, a married couple, Wenceslas and Bella. Their green sparkling outfits attracted the attention of the entire neighborhood. Mom glared at me while Dad hugged Bella and shook Wenceslas's hand. Inside, Dad, Joe, and Wenceslas broke down the kitchen table to make floor space. It seemed like a ridiculous amount of trouble to go through; we had the kitchen and a big living room on the first floor, plus three smallish bedrooms on the second. This was plenty of space, but Dad insisted. It didn't dawn on me until Mom's bedroom door slammed that Dad expected a lot more people to show up.

That night, through their door, I heard Mom tell Dad that she wouldn't speak to him again until our apartment was returned to normal.

But she did.

❈ ❈ ❈

THE NEXT MORNING I sat on the front steps, feeling like a celebrity. All the neighborhood kids played in the street, Tag, Hide and Seek, Treasure Hunt, and each of them stole sidelong glances at me. When One and Three came outside and mimicked my posture beside me, some of the kids began staring outright.

Julie Delphny sat in front of her own building, two apartments down and across the street, concentrating on something in her lap. She was the only one who never once glanced at me.

All activity ceased when the big brown van turned onto our street. It crept along, gliding slowly between the walls of brownstones, allowing kids to scamper out of the way. They watched, slack-jawed and wide-eyed, as it passed. Julie Delphny glanced at it, but her expression didn't change.

The van stopped in front of me and the whole street held its breath.

With a rumble, the door slid open. The hand that curled around the edge had too many fingers; the face behind it peered at me with bulging eyes.

The sideshow had arrived.

I stood to the side and welcomed each person as they passed, enjoying the awe-struck expressions of the neighborhood kids until that giant leg appeared in the van door.

I gaped at her as she stepped onto the sidewalk and smiled up at the sky. Her eyes reflected its pale blue perfectly.

I had to come down off the stairs so she could ascend. When she smiled at me, it felt like a dream. By the time she entered our apartment, and I reclaimed my place on the stairs, Julie Delphny was gone.

❀ ❀ ❀

An hour later, I discovered that I'd lost my bed to the fat lady. Dad cornered me when Mom wasn't nearby to ask if I would sleep with BJ for a few nights. The fat lady, he explained, was too big for the couch and no one from the circus would risk her lying on the floor for fear of not being able to get her upright again.

I resisted because I'd just come from BJ's room, and Wenceslas and Bella were arguing in there. I angled and cajoled until Dad said I could sleep in my own room, but on the floor.

"What if she rolls off the bed?" Mom said behind him. Dad winced, then turned to her. He took her upper arms in his hands and placed a kiss on her forehead where her brow creased. "Tommy will be okay," he said. "This is good for him. Broadens his horizons."

I took the opportunity to slip into my room.

"You're the boy who told me I have pretty eyes," she said. She sat on the edge of my bed. My cheeks heated up and I dropped my gaze. My accidental slip of thought that day seemed like the worst mistake I'd ever made.

"You're embarrassed? Why should you be? No one ever told me that before, you know." I looked at her without really wanting to. Her smile was kind, almost loving.

"All anyone else notices is my size." She sighed. "But I guess I shouldn't complain. They do pay me for the privilege."

I wanted to tell her she wasn't that big, but even my eleven-year-old brain knew that was a lie. I didn't know what else to say, though, and since the pressure to say *some*thing was so great, I went with what I had.

"You're not *that* big."

She laughed, loud and long, her body juddering in her gray camisole. "Oh, child. You've got charm enough to forge a river, just like your father. I certainly hope I *am* that big, or all these people will have been throwing their money away!"

I felt my cheeks redden even more, but despite that, I said, "You have a wonderful laugh."

She smiled, hugely. "Thank you, child," and then she was the one reddening. "Truth is, I haven't had occasion to use it much."

❊ ❊ ❊

THE CLOWNS ARRIVED THE next afternoon. I was on the steps, watching for Julie Delphny. Dad and Joe the Organ Grinder chatted a few steps above me, talking money and economics and unions. I didn't understand it, nor did I want to.

A tiny white car turned onto our street and began weaving drunkenly toward our building.

"Here they are now," Joe said.

The car was half the size of a VW bug, and as it neared, I recognized its spattering of colorful polka dots. It angled into the curb in front of our stairs and stopped. One little door opened and out they came, orange and yellow and silver and red, big noses and floppy shoes. They single-filed up the stairs, beeping and honking and squeaking greetings as they passed.

Through the open kitchen window I heard Mom say, "No way," followed by the rapid murmur of Dad trying to calm her down.

Stookey, the head clown, rose from the car. He stood six feet tall without counting his tiny purple top hat. He bowed with a flourish, first to me, then to the neighborhood kids on the other side of the street. He waved his hand in the air and then pointed to the little car, directing everyone's attention. He slammed the car door and the vehicle collapsed into a two-dimensional cut-out, which he picked up and folded over until it could fit into the large bib pocket of his white overalls.

The neighborhood kids cheered.

Stookey turned toward our building, but before he could step onto the stairs, the door opened.

Out came BJ, snug in his tram, shoved along by Mom. Behind her came Dad, still trying to soothe her but getting nowhere. It remains the only time I've ever seen his charm fail.

"Allicia, it's temporary!"

"Fine. Call me when they're gone and we'll come back." Mom's cheek was smeared with white and red clown makeup. How many had kissed her before she'd had enough I'd never know.

"Come along, Tommy," she said to me. "We're staying with Grandma."

I looked at Dad, but he stared after Mom as she fought to control BJ's carriage on the stairs. One and Three clung to each side, trying to hold the wheels still. Joe whistled low and the capuchins leapt onto the railings and saluted at attention, except One stuck his tongue out and kept it there.

"Tommy," Mom said.

I sighed, ready to give up, but noticed Julie Delphny across the street, watching us, blowing a big pink bubble.

"I'm staying," I said.

"Don't argue with me, young man. It's not safe for you here."

I shook my head. "I'm perfectly safe here," I said as Mom reached the sidewalk. She glared at me with her full matronly gaze.

"Get down here, Tommy. Your grandma wants to see you."

I swallowed, panicked that Julie might hear her talking to me like a child. Dad's hands found my shoulders.

"If Tommy wants to stay, Tommy stays," he said.

"Who's going to look after him? You?"

"Yes, me," Dad said. "You act like you're leaving him to fend for himself."

She dropped her eyes to mine. "Somebody's got to take care of Dad," I whispered.

Mom looked like she had something else to say, but Stookey leaned over and planted a kiss on her unblemished cheek. She jerked away from him. Whatever she muttered under her breath made his purple tie spin with a goofy rattle. She headed down the street and didn't glance back.

Stookey came up the stairs, each of his feet making a *sproing!* as he lifted them. He slapped my palm as he passed. I looked for Julie Delphny, but she had gone inside. Again.

❋ ❋ ❋

THE FAT LADY'S NAME was Olga, which I learned because she used it whenever she wanted something. "Olga needs room, it's too hot," she'd say, or, "Olga wants more butter on her toast." One afternoon she came thundering down our hallway hollering: "Hurry out of the bathroom, Olga has to pee!" Two clowns scurried free, their shoes slapping the floor like beaver tails while they ran with the waists of their pants balled in their gloved hands. Olga shimmied through the door, slammed it, squealed, flung it open again, and threw One into the hallway. He hit the wall but landed on his feet, where he pointed his tongue at the closed door and then walked away like an astronaut traversing the surface of the moon. It wasn't until later I realized the capuchin was mimicking Olga's walk.

I didn't give Mom another thought until after dark, when the first inkling of hunger hit. The fridge was empty, only enough jelly to almost cover one slice of bread. I opened the cabinet for the peanut butter and leaped back when Sammy the Contortionist, growled: "Sleeping here."

I folded my slice of jelly bread and headed upstairs to bed.

THE NEXT MORNING, I woke when the first ray of sunlight fell across my eyes. I listened to Olga's breathing for a little while, then rose and stretched the kinks out of my back and legs. All the kids' cereals were gone, but I found some granola. No milk, though. Since all the bowls were piled in the sink, I poured the cereal into a coffee mug and ate it with my fingers.

Out on the top step, Joe stared into his open calliope while One and Three played tag along the handrails. The Double-Headed Boy and the World's Smallest Man played jacks on the sidewalk. Two clowns pedaled oversized tricycles up and down the street.

"Has anyone seen Bella?"

Wenceslas stood behind me, looking worried. His green sequins looked like dull scales in the shadows.

"Thought she was with you," Joe said.

"She was. Don't know where she got to."

"I'll go look upstairs," I said.

"Would you?" He stood aside, then followed me.

I avoided my room, whispering that Olga was sleeping, and led him to BJ's room.

We found Bella.

Her green sequined arms were wrapped around Stookey's back, while over the clown's shoulder her eyes opened wide and she gasped at the sight of us. Blotches of white and purple paint smeared her face, making her expression somewhat clown-like.

"Bella?" Wenceslas said behind me.

Stookey spun with the sound of a top. He threw his head back in a clownish bawl and spurted solid streams of water from his eyes.

"Wenceslas, wait!" Bella cried. She tried to run toward him and tripped over Stookey's shoe, pulling him down on top of her in a heap.

"Stop him, boy!" she yelled at me. Stookey clung to her, bawling, while she slapped at him, trying to get away. I ran downstairs, then stepped out into the sunlight.

"Where'd he go?" One and Three both pointed up. There was Wenceslas, walking along the power lines across the street, a block and a half away and not slowing.

"What's going on?" the organ grinder asked.

"Stookey and Bella," I said.

"Shit."

Wenceslas seemed to shrink as he got further away. After a moment, Bella came out, scrubbing her face with what looked like Stookey's polka dot sock. One and Three turned their backs to her. She scanned the neighborhood, then looked at me.

"Where is he?"

I looked up. Wenceslas had disappeared.

Bella took a deep breath. "Which way?"

I pointed down the street.

Bella bumped past me and climbed the nearest telephone pole as rapidly as I'd ever seen One or Three climb anything. She stuck her arms out and headed off along the topmost wire. I watched until she, too, shrank out of sight.

LATER THAT AFTERNOON, I had Dad collect money from the performers so I could buy groceries. With the change, I bought a box of chocolate-covered raisins and ate them on the bench outside the store. I searched the power lines for some clue that Wenceslas and Bella had reunited but saw nothing. I watched the people coming in and out to shop. None of them pointed at me or asked me what it was like to live with so many stars. Most of them didn't notice me at all. I envied the way Dad could make friends by offering strangers things they needed. I was too young to have anything anyone needed, and I wouldn't for a long time. I ate my last raisin and headed home.

I hugged the shopping bags to my chest, being careful not to trip, and made it without incident.

In my absence, someone, probably the Strongman, had carried the sofa out of the living room and placed it on the sidewalk. Olga sat there, her arms outstretched and her face turned up to the sky. My feet stopped moving.

Julie Delphny sat on the arm of the couch, talking with Olga.

I hurried into the apartment and put the groceries away, then looked for Dad to let him know I'd made it home safe. I headed for a low murmur of voices in the living room and discovered the clowns surrounding Stookey. As soon as one of them saw me, their voices turned to squeaks and whistles. Stookey frowned at me, tears fountaining while each of the others stepped forward and swiped an 'X' on his white overalls with a black marker. I left them to it and headed upstairs.

Joe the Organ Grinder chatted with the Strongman in the hall.

"Where's my dad?"

"Haven't seen him," Joe said. He looked at the Strongman, who said the only word I ever heard him speak.

"Sidonio."

I looked at Joe.

"The Ringmaster," he said. "Your dad went to meet him."

Back downstairs I saw through the kitchen window that Julie Delphny was still here.

I wanted to go out and ask Olga about Dad and Sidonio, about Wenceslas and Bella, about the clowns in my living room, but I stayed where I was, watching Olga and Julie Delphny talk and laugh as the shadows grew.

❀ ❀ ❀

IT WAS LONG AFTER the clown court broke up that I gathered the courage to step outside and sit on the top step. My gaze wandered to the power lines, but except for a few pigeons, they were clear. I pretended not to notice Julie and Olga, watching instead two boys across the street, tossing a baseball back and forth.

I kept my gaze from wandering left even though I longed to know whether Julie was looking at me. I hoped Dad would return, wanted the clowns to come out, wished One and Three would sit beside me.

Finally, Julie scooted off the arm of the sofa and took Olga's hand. After a moment's hesitation, she leaned down and kissed the fat lady on the cheek. Olga chuckled.

"Oh, child."

Julie walked by, close to the stairs, and paused. "Hi, Tommy."

I nodded and raised a hand. She seemed to be waiting for me to say something, but I couldn't think of anything and after a minute she walked away.

"You like that girl," Olga said.

"Julie?"

Olga blew a puff of air that made her lips pop. "Is there any other girl around here?"

I started to nod, but swallowed when I saw Olga's expression. "I guess not."

"You smiled when she said your name."

"I did?" I watched Julie walk up her stairs and close the door behind her. I got up and walked to the sofa, but I couldn't bring myself to sit on the arm.

"Why didn't you say something to her?"

I shrugged.

"Do you always get so quiet when she's around?"

"Yes."

"For heaven's sake, why, child?"

"I don't know if she likes me."

"How can she? She doesn't even know you."

"I'm out here every day. Of course she knows me."

"She knows what you look like, but that's all you've given her to know. She needs to know more than that if she's going to like you." I peered into Olga's pale blue eyes, thinking about Julie Delphny. "And you don't know *her*, either. No more than she knows you."

Olga looked at me for a long time. She pointed at the two boys playing catch across the street. "Watch them for a minute. Tell me what they do."

I did. Every time one of them caught the ball and flung it again in the same fluid motion, he glanced around. When the boy nearest me caught my eye, his posture straightened and his expression became serious as he anticipated his next catch.

"They're looking to see if someone's noticed them," I said.

"Correct. And that's no way to live your life," Olga said. "People get to know you when you notice them back."

I swallowed, hard. "What do I say to her?"

"Say what you said to me. Now help me up, Olga's got to pee."

❈ ❈ ❈

MOMENTS AFTER OLGA MADE her way into our apartment, I spied Dad coming down the street with Sidonio the Ringmaster.

By the time they reached our building, the stairs were overflowing with circus folk. I sat on the sofa on the sidewalk and immediately two clowns and The Double-Headed Boy sat around me. The Penguin Girl asked to sit on my lap, and as soon as she settled, One and Three climbed onto my shoulders. Faces peered out of all our windows.

When Sidonio started speaking, Dad sidled sideways to stand closer to him. I watched Dad gazing at all the people from the circus who'd been staying with us. He winked when his eyes found me, and when I smiled his own smile grew huge, as if he was thrilled that I'd noticed him. I had an instant of remembering the boys playing ball, but then the performers cheered and started clapping each other on the back. Up the street, the brown van that had brought the sideshow people crept toward us.

The next few minutes were chaos. The sideshow performers started climbing into the van, and I barely stopped the Strongman before he climbed in. He was happy to move the sofa back into our living room. A lot of the neighborhood kids gathered across the street, many of them with their parents, all of them laughing at the clowns as they patted each other down, trying to determine which of them had their little white car. Stookey had gone missing. As the van drove away, the driver honked and promised to return for them.

It came back half an hour later and while the clowns piled in, I raced inside and opened all the cupboards to check that Sammy the Contortionist hadn't stayed behind.

Joe the Organ Grinder was the last to leave. He shook Dad's hand on the front step. "We'll always be grateful for your hospitality," Joe said.

"Thanks," Dad said. "We enjoyed having you."

Joe cocked an eyebrow but said nothing.

One and Three hugged me before falling into step behind Joe as he walked back toward the circus. One walked like an astronaut traversing the moon, and Three kept throwing his head back with his wrist on his forehead, imitating Stookey.

In the kitchen, I found Dad struggling to put the table back together by himself.

"Quiet in here," he said.

I nodded.

"Walk to your grandma's, Tommy. Tell Mom it's okay to come home."

I picked up a table leg and began screwing it into its hole. "Why don't I help you finish this and we can go together."

He looked at me for a little while, then nodded.

❀ ❀ ❀

WE LEFT LESS THAN fifteen minutes later. Together, we walked down the stairs and started along the sidewalk.

"I wonder if your mom missed me...us."

"I'm sure," I said. "But you shouldn't ask."

"Really?"

"You should tell her you missed her. Tell her how special she is."

He didn't respond to that, but I could tell he was thinking about it.

Across the street, Julie Delphny's door opened and she stepped out.

"Hey, Dad?" I said.

"Yeah?"

"You need to get Mom on your own."

"Why?"

I didn't answer. I was already walking across the street. I stepped right up to Julie Delphny's stairs, looked up into her pale blue eyes.

"Hi, Julie," I said.

❀ ❀ ❀ ❀ ❀

PAUL MCMAHON LIVES IN the great outback of Massachusetts amidst an army of wildlife that wants to hunt him down and kill him. Sometimes it seems his kids are in line with the coyotes, foxes and fishers to take a turn. He writes to escape the stress of being prey. His work has appeared in the New England Horror Writers (NEHW) anthologies, *Wicked Tales, Wicked Witches,* and *Wicked Haunted,* and many others. His first novella, *Chilopodophobia,* is available from Grinning Skull Press, and he is currently finishing up a mosaic novel titled *Bower's Cloud,* about an invasion of lethal plants ending life on Earth.

Fire Cat

M. J. Holt

I felt the sharp claws latch tightly into the calf of my left leg through my jeans. I couldn't stop rushing down the fire escape. I felt the press of Mr. Smith at my back. Behind him, his son Abe carried Mrs. Omaki. Behind them were more people. In front of me, dozens of people were using the exterior fire escape that I had barely given any thought to when I rented my place.

A fireman helped me to the ground. I moved down the alley and into the street. The cat didn't let go of my leg. Blood ran down my leg into my shoe. I looked around and saw a man carrying a thin Christmas tree, while others carried pets, shopping bags, and wrapped presents. Hanukkah was done. Christmas loomed. Kwanzaa followed, then the new year. I had intended to be gone and alone by today.

The fire trucks had already stopped at our building when Mr. Smith pounded on my door yelling at me to run. The interior stairwell was filling with smoke. He had yelled and yelled as I slung my large purse over my head, and grabbed my coat and a hoodie. My huge purse holds all that I need from tampons to a certified birth certificate, not mine, and much more. My father had taught me about running.

Up the street away from the burning building, I sat against the wall of a newer building and draped my hoodie over the cat. She stayed very still. I petted her in short strokes like her mother would have licked her. I felt her relax, but her claws still gripped my leg. Finally, she retracted them. I lifted her to my chest and almost flung her over my shoulder.

She weighed nearly nothing. I wrapped her in my hoodie and slipped her into my purse, then put my coat on and walked down to the pharmacy at the end of the block. I bought gauze pads, ace bandages, antibiotic gel, cat and human food, and drink. The fire was odd, so I bought a burner phone and a couple of sim cards. I traded two hundred bucks for a gift card. That's how I get a credit card in this almost cashless society.

More fire trucks and a dozen ambulances filled the street. Police threatened the reporters who crowded toward the survivors. I heard the reporters say that people had died in the fire.

Across from the reporters, I found a cold yellow metal box, probably a generator to run lights later. I sat on it and cleaned the blood from my leg, slathered antibiotic gel on it, and pressed the gauze into the gel. I bound the ace bandages to my leg using the pressure I could get by wrapping them tightly to staunch the blood flow from the tiny wounds.

I watched the reporters jockey for position to take pictures and figure out how to spin the story. I used my phone to watch the media frenzy. On my screen was a blond woman with tons of sympathy for the now homeless people. I'd watched her vlog reports before and liked her best.

A tall man wearing a porkpie hat with an ace of spades in its band and garish clothes pushed his way through the reporters, earning every cuss word hurled at him. I instantly didn't like him. He elbowed a small blond woman in the sternum, knocking her onto me, and I hated him. I realized that she was the reporter I'd been watching. She tipped her camera to show the street as she caught her breath. I gave her a sip of water, then wrote her a note. "Turn off the sound and any voice recorder and I'll talk to you about the fire."

"You escaped it?"

I nodded.

I showed her that I was watching her cast, and she did as I asked.

I stopped her partway through her first question. "That's the wrong question. Everybody is scared and feels like shit. We're all homeless, like you said. The right questions are these. One, who told you the building was on fire? Two, when did you hear the fire engines? Three, when did you hear the fire alarm? Four, what floor do you live on and describe the fire. You're going to need to do dozens of these. It's not for livecast. Record, then splice it all together."

She gave me one of those looks.

I said, "Do four, and see what you've got. It should bury the asshole who elbowed you. People died. I don't know who, but families with kids, desperate old people cheated out of their pensions lived there. The place was loaded with people like that. It's the holidays. Christmas Eve."

"And then there is you."

The cat softly mewed. "Yeah. Give me your direct number. No on the air crap. No description. Zero about me. I'll let you know if I remember more. Do yourself proud."

I limped away to feed the cat in a quiet place where no one could identify me.

❄ ❄ ❄

A DOZEN BLOCKS AWAY in a less poor part of town, I found a halfway respectable motel. It was a three on a scale of zero to ten. Zero is living in the rough. One is a shelter. Two is a place like the one that just burned. Three is clean sheets and a bathroom window I can get out of. The motel had large plastic evergreen trees decorated in colored lights and large red and green balls that would look good in the dark. I took a corner ground floor unit, paid for the night in cash, and didn't mention the cat. Hard plastic ribbons and bows attached to the metal doors with magnets made each room look like a surreal present. Inside, it looked aged and worn with no decorations.

When I looked in my purse, I didn't see her, but then the bag that held the bandages, food, and the burner moved. I put my purse on the bed, laying it on its side, and turned on the TV. It took a while to get it off of the automatic porn and onto the mundane channels. The local channels were running soaps, but the national channels made the hotel fire their drama of the moment.

I jacked my phone into a power source and bluetoothed it to the TV. I saw the blonde walk through the mess made by the fire. Mostly poor-looking people gathered on the sidewalk. She would focus on some action and stay on it while talking about what she saw. I wondered if she was asking my questions. I had no reason to believe she would.

The cat emerged from my purse. Her eyes were too wide, which I took as a sign of her terror. Poor cat. Obviously a she-cat because of her muted calico coat, her long hair hung in matted clumps with small areas that looked groomed. She lay still for a few moments then started shaking again. I opened a can of cat food and emptied it onto a flier from a take-out restaurant. I pressed the edges of the can so that they were smooth and put water in it. She soon quit shaking and I went on to think about what incriminating things had I left behind.

❋ ❋ ❋

THE CAT AND I set out at four in the morning for my former residence. She rode in my purse in the paper bag from the pharmacy. Plywood covered the front of the building. A couple of boys sprayed graffiti on it. In the debris-strewn alley, the fire escape, worse for wear, looked sturdy enough to hold me. I let the cat out of my purse. She looked around. The cat had her stunned look down pat.

She tried to follow me up the rickety fire escape only to get her paw caught. I went back to her, freed her paw, and carried her until she wiggled. The building sat on a steep hill, and the first floor was street level on its other side. I let her jump into the first-floor hallway and climbed up to the next floor.

My unit smelled of wet char and smoke, but looked undamaged. Time-worn grime gave the white walls a pale-yellow hue. The two-inch-wide slats of the Venetian blinds, new when grandmothers had been girls, darkened the room. I used a small flashlight to search. I pulled my soft backpack from the closet shelf. Shoes went in the bottom with my clothes rolled tightly on top of them. After that, I searched for any thumb drives I might have dropped and didn't find any. I tossed the bed, and did one last check of all the drawers. Under the dresser I found a pad of notes, not mine, that I kept. I'd bought the pillow, so I rolled it and put it under the flap of the backpack like a bedroll. I tossed the bedding out the window.

From below, I heard, "Look at this."

A bedraggled woman with a kid held the bedding.

"Take it," I called to her.

"You got a mattress?"

"And a bedstead. Come up, carefully, and take it all."

"Toss it."

I pulled the window from the frame, pushed the mattress out, and tossed the bed parts on to it. It took a few minutes. I took the box springs to the fire escape door and pushed them over the side. The woman had two shopping carts and loaded the bulky pieces into them. Two pre-teen kids ran to her and they took pieces of the bed frame. I said, "Merry Christmas," then lost sight of them carrying away my DNA in the deep shadows of the early morning dark.

The fire escape swung and sang the song of broken parts as I descended. I sat on the ledge to the first floor to let it settle down. When its song ended, I heard mewing from the cat and responses from kittens. *Shit*, I thought, but I liked the cat. On the first floor, she crouched in front of an air grill. I used my jackknife to pop the cover off and the cat slipped into the space behind it. She came out with a kitten that she put on my shoe and went back. She brought out two more kittens. *Great*, I thought, *now I have a cat and three kittens*. Oddly, the thought cheered me.

Getting up, I bumped a small pile of refuse and saw a caution yellow vest and hoodie with a clip-on badge reading *Jess Tarkington*. The picture was androgynous, but so am I. I put on the hoodie and vest over my hoodie, and clipped the badge on after smudging it with soot.

The cat left the kittens with me and went to another grill. I carried the kittens to her and listened. Weak mewing came from behind it. I pulled it off, and out came another kitten with thin, shiny red electrical wire wrapped around its yellow furry body.

❊ ❊ ❊

As I UNWRAPPED THE wire from the kitten, a piece of hard plastic hit against the side of the small duct. I used my phone flashlight to look down the duct and saw more red wire wrapped with yellow and black wires. Why would there be an improvised explosive device in an air duct in this building? Then I asked myself, how did the kittens get into the ducts?

I moved to the door of the unit next to the duct. I kicked the locked door open and saw that the unit looked like a bare work room. Wire and a nearly empty box of gel fire starters that ignite with a match lay on a small table. If the apartment had caught fire, this all would be gone. The unit smelled of gas. I opened the window, sneezed, and reached into my pocket for a tissue, but it wasn't my hoodie pocket; Jess's pockets held black heavy-duty latex gloves.

I don't have fingerprints, so I don't worry about them, but I didn't know what chemical booby traps this place held. I put on a pair of gloves and searched the unit for how the kittens had gotten into the duct system.

A man-sized hole cut in the floor of the kitchen, on the street side, had cut the air duct in two. A trail of kitten paw prints led into the duct. My light revealed a stack of the fire starters on a wooden beam next to a huge post that had to be part of the building's superstructure. A broken, nearly burned-out piece of metal sat between two fire starters. A black plastic box that looked like the receiver of a remote garage door opener sat on the beam. The wires had not been cut to fit and the excess stretched away from the fire starters and ended with a female plastic connector. It looked like the other end of the piece I had found on the kitten. Thinking that this was clever, I stared at this, then looked up. Right in front of my face I saw a gas stove with one burner torn apart. I looked at the burner next to it, and realized that the broken part was the igniter for the burner. The gas smell was from the stove. The kitten had saved this end of the building from burning by getting tangled in the wire.

The cat and kittens were not in the hall, and I didn't find them in the open duct work. A little sad, I went to my purse and backpack. Rustling in my purse stopped me from picking it up. Inside, the cat, back in the paper bag, nursed her babies. I shifted the bag so they wouldn't get hurt when I picked it up.

"Hey, you," said a man from the end of the hall. I turned my head only enough to see a man dressed in a caution yellow hoodie and vest at a door.

I stayed hunched over and said, "You need to look in that room there. You gotta report it. Looks like somebody rigged a device to start a fire. The wire detached and something pulled it into the air duct, there in the hall, by your foot. I had packed up some other evidence when I found it. Nothing like that, though. Take a good look and tell me what you think."

He said, "The evidence truck is across the street."

"I'll put this in it and be right back. Look in the kitchen. There's bunch of fire starters on a beam under the kitchen floor. Looks like somebody MacGyvered a gas stove igniter to set it off. Maybe a rat disturbed it. I'll be back."

He went into the unit. I pulled the hood around my face and went down the quarter flight of stairs to a vestibule that exited onto a side street. I stripped off the vest and the hoodie with the clip-on badge, and dropped them inside the doorway. I pulled my own dark gray hood over my head to hide my face and walked in the opposite direction of the fire inspectors.

❈ ❈ ❈

THE SIX OF US rested on the bed. The kittens played and the cat went into needy overdrive. I groomed her with my comb while I watched the local all-news stations. The story of the fire seemed to cycle on about every fifteen minutes, when the story changed and they reported that first-hand reports were posted online by fire survivors. I went to my blond woman's vlog to see what she had. People, some boldly showing their faces, and others masked by darkness, told their stories. Every story echoed the others: fire engines, neighbors knocking, no fire alarm. I listened to them all. My blonde hocked her interviews to the media on a reuse link. She claimed that 50 percent of revenues went to a list of homeless shelters that had taken in the displaced people.

The newscast became background noise until I saw a flash of a picture of the desk clerk who rented the rooms. He griped, "I don't know anything. I was burned out, too. I got nothing, and they fired me that afternoon. No severance. Unemployment says they got no record I worked there."

A newscast showed a still photo of an old geezer, well-dressed and mighty in his geezerhood, and identified him as the owner of the building. The picture had been taken through his living room window. The photo was so sharp I could read the headlines on the newspaper he held. I found the photo online with others that showed an extravagant Christmas tree next to a bar cart.

I knew who he was before I moved into his building. I probably would have been gone if he had showed up sometime in the eight days I'd been there, but he hadn't. I had planned to kill him in a mugging.

I thought about the unit with the fire starters. He could have entered by that side door, gone into the unit, and fixed the place to burn the day of the fire or weeks before.

The kittens distracted me from thinking about work. I played with them and received tiny bites and scratches. The first three kittens who the mama cat found behind the grill were her girls—calicos. The little yellow one checked out as a boy.

While the kittens nursed, I called myself and tested the new app I'd written to disguise my voice. It worked. I made a business call to another burner phone.

"He's still alive," I heard.

"Yeah. Sorry about that. I can get him. Might take out a couple of cronies."

"I don't care."

"Fine. Bye."

I timed the call. Under fifteen seconds.

I LET THE CATS play in the storage locker that held my car. From the trunk I took a metal case used to transport vaccines. It held the tools of my trade: IEDs, chemicals, guns, knives, and more. Trained with our tax dollars, I took the long course in terminations. When people ask what I do, I say I'm in personnel. That's boring enough that they change the subject. I find it funny.

From the case I took two ampules. Mixed together, they formed a reliable organophosphate nerve agent. The second choice looked like it would be easier to deliver than my first, a mugging that I had chosen to limit the collateral damage.

I left the cats to play, changed into nice clothes, applied reflective glitter makeup to disguise myself for the cameras, and went out. I bought a gift-boxed bottle of whiskey like the one I saw in the photo. Back at the storage unit, I carefully opened the box wearing Jess the fire inspector's gloves. Using a tiny needle topped with an ampule-sized funnel, I drained one and then the other chemical into the bottle. I heated the wax over the bottle top, like I'd been taught, hiding the needle mark, and put it back in its box. The box came with a separate, ornate gift wrap box.

Earlier, I had searched for the name of a law firm that represented him. I wrote "To a Great Client" on the gift card and signed the firm's name.

I changed from nice clothes into cheap generic black jeans and hoodie. I wiped off the glistening of makeup and put it on in a different pattern, put in bright blue contact lenses, and tied back my hair. A short, cheap yellow Dacron wig and a big billed gimme hat covered my head. I looked fat-headed. I left my purse and the cats in my car, and walked to the building that housed the law firm on the card. I called a ride, and had him let me out in front of the wrong house and drive off. I jogged to the guy's house and rang his doorbell.

A woman answered, took the package, and gave me a five-dollar tip. Several minutes later as I walked down the long street a car came up behind me. I stepped onto the verge. The woman who had answered the door stopped and asked if I wanted a ride. I said that I did. She asked who the gift was from, and I gave the law firm's name. The back seat was crammed with suitcases and garbage bags.

"He killed those people. He wants to tear down that building. You don't kill people for a real estate deal. I'm gone."

She continued to vent, telling me that she was going out of state to her sister's for the holidays. She rambled on until we got to the lawyer's building and I got out quickly. I went inside, asked where my next delivery was and the guard didn't know because there never had been one, but he let me use the restroom. I rubbed the dazzle makeup haphazardly over my face to change the pattern.

Back at the storage locker I changed, swept the whole area, poured bleach over it, and let it dry. I drove out of town. All the garbage came with me and I disposed of it in small amounts as I drove home. I stopped only for take-out food, cat supplies, and naps at rest stops. I could see my driveway when I spotted the sign "VET OPEN for the Holidays." The yellow kitten's eyes had swollen shut on the trip home. The vet examined and treated the cat and kittens. Afterward, we shared the crackers, caviar, and the New Year's Eve dinner I had bought.

Second week of January, the blond reporter vlogged my recent target's funeral. She reported that the wife had returned to find him ill and he died the next day. Everyone accepted that the flu took him. A long line of homeless people and others had spit on my target's grave while his wife stood by serenely.

Months later, a message popped up from one of my offshore accounts. The deposit information showed that a client had paid me a bonus. It came from a burner phone number I recognized. I'd been paid the day after the holiday target's estate had settled. Oh how she had hated him.

The cats enjoy excellent health due to our vet who lives up the road. We go back and forth between our homes and she cares for the cats when I'm out of town. I've never had a friend before.

❄ ❄ ❄ ❄ ❄

M. J. HOLT ABANDONED the big city to live on a certified organic farm with her husband and many animals on a peninsula in Puget Sound where she writes full-time. Her stories have appeared in "Low Down Dirty Vote Volume II," "Alternate Theologies," "Short-Story.me", and her poetry may be found in the poetry anthologies "300K," and "Timeless Love", "Gutter Eloquence," and other periodicals. She earned degrees in history, English, education, and holds a Masters in English Literature. Her novel, *The Devil's Safe*, is coming out in early 2021. She is a member of SFWA and MWA.

Letters Submitted in Place of a Thesis to the Department of Chronology

Stewart C Baker

Miki Almeyde
Wildhorse Lake, Oregon
November 1st, 2036

Dr. Albete Arejo
Chair of Chronology
Universidad de Nuevo Orégon
Forthmont 14, 3164

Dear Dr. Arejo,

Do you remember, I wonder, the first class of yours I attended? I was young then, full of misplaced knowledge—I'd never set foot outside the timestream. Yet I believed I knew the answers to our past and our present.

Of course, for you it's only been two years. I forget that sometimes, here in the era when storms come down like vengeful plagues from an arcane, long-vanished theology.

Anyway. Do you remember the first thing you said that day?

"The basic principle of chronology is this: The past cannot be changed, the present changes always, and the future is unknowable."

It's the kind of crap they peddle in chronology for non-majors, the kind of useless aphorism that gets people thinking we're nothing more than high-tech voyeurs. Because if you can't change the past, if you can't know the future, what's the point? Why bother?

I laughed—*that*, I'm sure you recall—and you spent the rest of the class grilling me, tearing down everything I thought I knew until by the end I didn't even bother trying to answer. I just sat there with my head down, cheeks flushed, until the chime rang and I could scurry out the door and back to the privacy of my dorm. I've never felt so humiliated, and don't think I ever will again.

But the experience humbled me. I tossed out everything I thought I knew and re-examined every foundational chronological study with newfound skepticism. The only times I ever raised my voice in class after that were when I had questions. You probably thought I was trying to get back at you by playing dumb, but I genuinely wanted to learn.

And I have learned. *You* taught me, Dr. Arejo, despite yourself and your self-interested myopia about the basics of chronology. That's part of why I insisted on having you as my thesis supervisor, even though we never did get along.

I'm sorry. I've been blathering on like we're old friends, and yet you must have no idea why I've sent this to you. And I'm sure my choice of medium—this antiquated, inefficient printed letter—is just as baffling. (I'm sure you're wondering, as well, how I got back to the past and why I'm a full forty years after the date of my assignment. How it could be possible that I've evaded the automatic return built into every chrono-casted journey to the past? But I'd rather not get into that. You'll find out soon, anyway.)

As far as you're aware, I've been holed up in my library cubicle for the three months since I returned to the present, putting all I learned into a thesis so you could graduate me and get me out of your office, out of your department, out of your life.

Truth be told, I almost didn't send this letter. I'd decided to let my original message (which you should be receiving shortly in the form of a rambly netsend) stand alone, in all its youthful folly. But then this afternoon, just before we were ready to step out on our trip, Julie—

No. No, that won't mean anything to you. Not yet. I'll send you another letter, later on.

Yours from a greater distance than you can imagine,
Miki

❁ ❁ ❁

from: almeyde-m-2668954.uno.estu
to: arejo-a-8891370.uno.facu
sent: Forthmont 10, 3164
recd: Forthmont 14, 3164
subj: I can't do this anymore.

DR AREJO. HI.

First of all I just want to say that I'm sorry.

I'm sorry.

Ha ha. Sorry, a little nervous here.

The truth is, for the past three months, I've been getting kind of obsessed. Sounds normal for a student working on her thesis, right? But that's not what I mean.

I can't stop thinking about the people I left behind. I can't get over the fact that they'll live their whole lives never knowing who I really am, where I went when I vanished that last night.

Because yeah, they saw me vanish. Julie and Alessandra—the women I went back to watch. The two who, when they were older, played such a pivotal role in trying to prevent what we call the era of storms.

I know this must be a surprise. I've never said a word about it when we meet in your office to discuss what I learned in the past, and what I planned to put into my thesis. I just didn't know what to do, how to say it without you revoking all my departmental privileges and locking me away from our chronocasters and our fabricators. And *that* I couldn't bear to consider.

So I nodded my head when you spoke and spat out the crap you wanted to hear, like "if we must blame those long-dead peoples for what happened to our planet, we should in equal measure pity them," or "capitalist-consumerist lifestyles in the terminus years played an integral part in the final turn away from a radical utopian dream." Or—only occasionally, when I didn't think you were really listening anymore—I'd give little eulogies for rain.

Rain! God, I miss that.

Have you ever felt rain, Dr. A? Ever felt the nascent electricity of a big storm crackling over the hairs on your skin, smelled that wet-on-dust scent that's so lovely the ancient scientists who researched it named it after the blood of the Gods?

To be honest, I'd be surprised if you have. Even though you're well-respected in the department, an expert in your field, I don't think you've ever stepped to a time when we don't live in the climate-controlled arcologies built by our forebears from the ruins of the world. If you've stepped to any time at all.

I'm calling you a fake, Dr. A.

An armchair chronologist, a spectacled nerd who'd rather push numbers around in a proof than try to disprove that line you fed us the first day of class about the past never changing.

But that's not why I'm 'sending you. I want to explain the loud explosion which should be rumbling through the halls of the chronochamber just around now (Don't bother running down there—it's already over. There's nothing left but ash and molten metal. I've been very thorough).

I'm 'sending you as well to insert this wonderful little cognitive virus which, by the time you read this sentence, will already have wiped out everything you know about chronology and which will propagate from your cortex and out into the wider 'net until every article, every file, every unfinished half-thought on the nature of time and the practicalities of chronology is gone.

Ain't the post-material world just grand?

Ha ha. Another little joke.

Although I guess you won't find it very funny.

But that alone isn't enough. I don't want you to suffer. I want you to know *why*. I want you to know what I found on my assignment to the past that changed me so much. Why I feel I have to go back, to disprove that old clunker of yours about the past never changing.

So here's the few hundred words I managed to force out on my thesis before I decided, instead, to escape this time-obsessed, too-ordered world. To get back to Julie and Alessa, to explain it all to them and to *do* something, damn it.

I'm sure the prose isn't up to your standards. Really it's less of a thesis chapter and more of a confession. I'd apologize for that if I thought you'd even bother to read it.

❈ ❈ ❈

The Historical Context of the Years before the Era of Storms.
Chapter 1 - Rain, Snow, Sun, Wind
by Miki Almeyde

HERE AND NOW, IN our comfortable, engineered arcologies, it is easy to look back on those who lived in the twenty-first century as fools, as clueless barbarians bent on ruin and death.

Our texts all teach that they acted as they did out of selfish pride. But it must be understood that living without a clear view of the future changes everything. Even in our own age, do we not constantly look at time without thinking of the consequences?

Therefore, if we must blame those long-dead peoples for what happened to our planet, we should in equal measure pity them their short-sighted hopes, their misguided dreams.

And of course there was the weather. Oh, the weather! Rain, snow, sun, wind. What I liked the most were the storms, when low-hanging banks of dark gray cloud painted the sky with deep, rich signs of life to come.

Despite the arguments of scientists, how could anyone who had never seen beyond those gently rumbling, drawn-out summer storms suspect what was to come within a few decades?

This first chapter of my thesis, then, rather than setting up the historical contexts of the lives of Julie Hope and Alessandra Olvera—the leaders of the Climate Now! movement who vanished mysteriously in the 2030s—contains a brief account of my last night in the twenty-first century.

I had spent a year living as a student by then, and had long since befriended Julie and Alessa. At first, I viewed them as my subjects, as a pair who between them made up all the contradictions and confusions of the period.

Alessa was a would-be bohemian, a budding artist who cared deeply about equality and justice. Julie was a socialite who lived to be seen spending. (This was before her transformation later in life when she became a leading voice on climate change at the 2026 summit in Xi'an, that terrible summer when the world's forests ignited and the Antarctic shelves shed so much ice that the tides rose and rose and kept on rising.)

But as I spent longer in that misleading calm before the global storms, I could not hold myself at arm's length. The lifestyles and outlooks of the time changed me into someone who was not quite a twenty-first-century woman, but not a product of our post-material society, either.

Maybe this will make more sense if I just describe the night I left. The night I realized I loved them both, that I couldn't view them as subjects anymore.

I wanted to show them something they'd never forget. Something they could carry with them forever as a token of remembrance, although of course I didn't intend to tell them who I really was, where I came from.

❊ ❊ ❊

THE STORM THAT NIGHT was a prime specimen of the pre-desertification Pacific Northwest United States. I took a long walk for the feel of electricity on my skin, the scatters of rain and damp gusts of wind. When the sun finally set, I took the last of my cash over to a gas station, picked up a box of wine coolers, and headed over to Julie's and Alessa's dorm room, just down the hall from my own in the all-girl's floor.

Julie answered the door. That night, she was wearing one of those hideous half-dresses everyone seemed to think was attractive. Despite myself, my skin flushed with heat that had little to do with the warm humidity of that mid-August evening.

"Hey," I said.

"Hey," she responded. Making it mean much more.

"I brought booze."

"How daring. Come on in."

I did. The room was a mess, like always. Posters and photos littering the walls—so much dead paper, always and everywhere. Alessa was crabbed up on her usual chair with a sketch pad.

I gave them both a wine cooler and they drank it down—Julie eagerly, Alessa reluctantly, both of them looking at me as they did. I was about to vanish from these girls' life completely, and I had to say something, but what? I couldn't think straight. Even though I'd just drained my wine cooler, my tongue was bone-dry.

I fished a second one out of the pack, then raised it up and shouted out "To weather!"

Alessa rolled her eyes, but opened a second bottle too.

Julie laughed out loud. "To weather!" she repeated, following it up with a drink.

We had a few more, each one making the room seem brighter, warmer. These are all the little details that never come out in the historical accounts, no matter how many times you patch them into your cortex. Not even the most advanced technology is the same as being there in the flesh.

Being there like that affected my achronological present, even if it didn't alter the time stream—of course I don't have to remind you how impossible that is. And I have no doubt that it played a strong role in how my future will play out, but I'll write more on that later.

Anyway, we drank some more.

"Hey," Julie said, after that. "Let's... Let's go out in it. Since you like it s'much."

"It?" Alessa's forehead had that little crease she got when she was confused and didn't want you to know it.

"It," Julie said. "The, uh. The weather. I mean. What's? What's the worst that could happen in a storm?"

I burst out laughing and couldn't stop. They both looked at me funny when I refused to explain, but what could I do? I was hardly going to come out and say that within the next forty-three years, super-hurricanes would wipe out the Eastern Seaboard of the United States, an endless string of enormous tornadoes would pulverize the Midwest, and the West Coast would be choked or drowned or swallowed up in an endless stream of rising seas and fire and smoke and mudslide. I was hardly going to say, "And don't move to Europe or Asia or Africa or South America or Australia, either, because what happens there is *worse*..."

"To storms!" I said, instead, "and everything that happens in them." Then I fell over backwards, slightly missing my seat. Maybe they would think I was drunk.

Maybe I was.

After that, I thought they'd both forgotten about the suggestion of going out until Alessa suggested an abandoned house as a destination, and off we went. The walk helped a little with the alcohol. The prick-prick-prick of rain against my skin, that humid promise in the air. I left my jacket undone just for the feel of it all. Julie kept trying to hit on me, and I kept feigning ignorance—I loved getting her all worked up.

Alessa hung behind, and she didn't look too well. She'd always been a lightweight.

So it was as we arrived at the house. Julie dragged me inside almost as soon as we got there, then into a side room, slamming the door behind her a little too loud.

"You," she said, staggering toward me and trying to undo her jacket. "You have… You…"

She frowned, stopped, fumbled at her jacket some more until she finally got it off, then started on her dress. But she only got one arm free before she blinked a few times, shook her head, sat down on a moldy pile of blankets and fell asleep, leaning against the wall.

As I've already said, I'd gone over to their place that night intending to take them somewhere special, to try and open up their minds to the future they would find themselves in. To warn them in some obscure and careful way of the world their children would live in. But all I could manage was to stand there like an idiot, watching my plans fall apart with a mix of pressure and promise building in my temples like the tension in the air before a jagged slash of lightning and a peal of thunder tear it to nothing.

Maybe this is what that last generation felt like, I thought, when they realized what they'd done to the world. When they realized that too little, too late wasn't going to save them. I wandered off to look for Alessa, but she was passed out too, in a seat just inside the main door.

So I went out in the rain, luxuriating in the feel of it on my skin. How could anyone worry, with that cooling influence? I felt myself relaxing, decided I'd just go back to their dorm with the both of them and to hell with this century's backwards normative drives.

I staggered back inside and shook Alessa awake, then dragged her into the side room and shook Julie awake, too. And only then realized I'd forgotten about the return timer.

"Listen," I told them. "I have something important I have to do. But, uh, I have to disappear for a while. I swear I'll come back. I love you too much to lose you. Both of you you, I mean. Not just one of you you."

They stared at me like I'd grown a second head. In retrospect, I may not have been quite as sober as I hoped.

"I'm serious," I said. "And, um, don't try to follow me."

Then I bolted into the rain, not stopping until I almost fell into the river. I had to get further away, was all I was thinking. I didn't want them to find out about who I was like that—I wanted to tell them on my own terms.

I could hear them shouting back in the downpour behind me, getting closer. Concern in their voices, and fear, and love, and hope, and all sorts of other contradictory emotions. And I realized something: I felt just the same. That the "historical context" we talk about as an essential part of chronology was, frankly, a load of crap. People are people whenever they are, and that's the key to understanding them.

It always has been, and it always will.

But I had a more pressing problem than redefining chronology as we knew it. There wasn't a way across the river I could see, nor a way past Julie and Alessa and back in the other direction. So I did the only thing I could do under the circumstances: I jumped into the river, and hoped my timing was better than my judgment.

❋ ❋ ❋

DOESN'T MAKE A VERY good thesis, does it, Dr. A?

All the same, it sums up my feelings. The more I think about that night's events—about that mad rush into the storm, that crazy leap into the ice-cold churning river—the more I'm convinced that a lot of chronological study lacks clarity, lacks nuance.

It's true that they could have done more, the people of that time. It's perhaps even true that they should have. And certainly we shouldn't just forgive them for the mess they made. But it's wrong to leave them there, with the chronological resources at our disposal.

No, it's more than that. Chronology itself is wrong. We're just as cynical and apathetic and foolish as they are if we don't go back and set things right as best we can.

If you've bothered to read this far (or maybe if you've skimmed to the end), you'll discover that I'm nowhere to be found. You'll discover I've taken everything I can and destroyed what I can't. That the chronocaster is gone forever, a useless pile of slag and dust you won't remember how to rebuild.

I'm leaving, in other words, and I won't be coming back. You say it's impossible to change the past, but I'm going to try my damnedest.

Miki

❀ ❀ ❀

Miki Almeyde
Wildhorse Lake, Oregon
November 1st, 2036

Dr. Albete Arejo
Chair of Chronology
Universidad de Nuevo Orégon
Forthmont 18, 3164

DEAR DR. AREJO,

I hope this letter finds you well, and that you've come to peace with your situation. I know it's an uncomfortable one, and the truth is that if I hadn't been so angry I might not have put you in it to begin with.

You have to understand how I felt back then. I honestly thought I was going to prove you wrong—you and every other Chronology researcher who swore and swore and swore that the past was immutable, the future inherently unstable.

You were right, though, at least about the past. As the years went on, Julie and Alessa and I tried everything we could to turn back the course of climate change, but it was just too damn big for us, even when we finally, finally, finally got the producers and governments and consumers of the world on board.

Xi'an was an eye-opener for all of us. I'm not sure you still have the history texts to realize it, but that was the year it became absolutely certain that the world was doomed. The seas rose three meters in three short months, the forests of the Amazon ignited, and the temperatures kept getting hotter and hotter. At the climate conference, Julie got all the nations of the world to sign radical new protocols which pushed us from carbon-neutral to carbon-reducing, and a team from China introduced a new form of nanobiotic which would lower the melting point of water. That was how desperate we were. (Alessa was on a trip to Brazil, painting and sketching, trying to show people the world around what it was like there.)

But it was futile, of course. Too little, too late. Things kept getting worse, and eventually we realized there was no hope in staying where we were. No chance for humanity in the era of storms.

You'll remember in my previous letter that I mentioned Julie, that I mentioned a trip we were taking. The thing is, we've been researching chronology—not climate change reversal—ever since that conference. I've shared all the files and knowledge and equipment I stole forty-odd years in the past (and a thousand or so years in the future), which for you is only four days ago. Working together with scientists around the globe, we've figured out a way to step *forward*, into the future, not the past.

Tomorrow we were meant to step to 2840—a date I'm sure you'll recognize as the founding of Nuevo Orégon.

But yesterday, there was a storm. A big one, even for now. A good deal of our equipment was ruined, and we lost Julie. She died in the storm when our supposedly shatterproof bunker collapsed after being pummeled for hours by hail the size of cattle.

In these turbulent times, she lived long and well. And I'm thankful, don't get me wrong. I'm glad I came back. I'm glad we got to share our lives together—me and her and Alessa. But it just seems so unfair, so frustrating, when this time tomorrow we would all have been safe in the calm of the 29th century, after the storms have passed.

Of course all my friends and family have tried to console me. All these surrogate grandchildren, these unrelated loved ones I have. I don't think they'd quite understand if I told them that, tomorrow, when they step, I won't be going with them. That Alessa and I are going to stay here with the memory of Julie, and face out the end of the world, hand in hand.

But I wanted to let *you* know, I wanted in some obscure way to make peace with all of my past by letting you know that, even though you were sometimes a frustrating ass, Dr. A, in the end you were right.

You *can't* change the past.

But that's never really mattered, has it? Just because something is impossible doesn't mean you shouldn't try. Even though I didn't succeed in changing anything, I found happiness. I helped others find happiness. That's what it means to be human, Dr. A. Remember that, and it will make the future a much brighter, better place than all the chronology in the world.

Yours in passing,
Miki

✺ ✺ ✺ ✺ ✺

STEWART C BAKER IS an academic librarian and author of speculative fiction and poetry, along with the occasional piece of interactive fiction. His fiction has appeared in *Nature*, *Galaxy's Edge*, and *Flash Fiction Online*, among other places. From 2017-2020, Stewart was the editor-in-chief of *sub-Q Magazine*, an online magazine of interactive fiction. Stewart was born in England, has spent time in South Carolina, Japan, and California (in that order), and now lives in Oregon with his family—although if anyone asks, he'll usually say he's from the Internet, where you can find him at https://infomancy.net

The Eighth of December

Dave Smeds

West Berlin was draped in grey as the band's limousines rolled through the streets. An unbroken mantle of clouds threatened a downpour, but held onto its bounty like an avaricious politician, turning the last hour of daylight into outright gloom. Faded buildings paraded by. People huddled at bus stops, toying with umbrellas as if certain they would need them at any moment. No smiles.

Vic Standish consulted his watch. In less than twenty hours he would be boarding his Lear jet and be done with this city. Most of that time would be filled playing the gig or holed up in his hotel room, with only one necessary detour in between. He was ready to be gone. In the past two days the Bürgermeister's liaison had shown him and his mates the best the city had to offer, but its façade held too many cracks: The barbed wire and guard turrets were still there at Checkpoint Charlie. A policeman stood at nearly every major intersection. The smear of paint on a brick wall didn't quite conceal the swastika graffiti underneath.

Seated next to Vic, his drummer Lenny was reading a paper containing a bold headline about the deepening crisis in Yugoslavia. The Soviets had just delivered more armaments to the Serbs. The U.S. was contemplating increased air strikes to aid the besieged Islamic enclaves. The United Nations had given up its attempts to mediate.

Saturday, December 2, 1995. The Cold War was casting a frigid shadow. The citizens of West Germany wore haunted, worried faces of stone. Vic had no doubt it was the same a few miles away on the communist

side. Their mental photo albums were open—if they were old enough—
to pages showing tanks rumbling into Hungary in 1956, into Czechoslo-
vakia in 1968. Closer to home, they were remembering the Wall going
up, splitting the city, never to come down.

Vic knew something of what they must be feeling, though as an American, his corresponding memories were of the Cuban Missile Crisis, of
umpteen civil defense drills during his teenage years, and of his father
building a bomb shelter beneath their house. How had the world become
so hostile again? There had been a time, after Nixon went to China, after
the Vietnam War ended, after détente, after Jimmy Carter brought Israel
and Egypt to the table at Camp David, when people and nations had
steered toward a gentler course.

That was in another lifetime, Vic reflected. Back when he owned a different name. Back when he used to tour Europe with his old band. Back
when people listened to a different kind of rock'n'roll.

Everything had changed, and trying to recapture the past was futile.
In the here and now, he had to concentrate on what was possible. Maybe
the music wasn't the same, but at the very least, he could help take the
crowd's mind away from the concerns of the moment. Wasn't that his
job?

As the quartet of limousines approached the stage entrance of the coli-
seum, a cluster of several hundred fans cheered and waved banners. VIC-
TORY! GREATEST BAND EVER! said one sign, which brought a wry shake
of the head from Vic. Faithfulness was one thing, but exaggeration was
another. He remembered a concert in '69 when he and his sidemen had
had to sneak in through a maintenance tunnel to get backstage, and even
that didn't compare to what he'd witnessed at Beatles and Stones gigs.

Lenny was grinning, though. For him, the adulation was a brand-new
experience. The band's fourth album was emptying off the shelves as fast
as it could be restocked. The tour was cresting a wave of momentum that
would put them in the public consciousness for good. No more one-hit
wonders, no more promising journeymen, destined to vanish as soon
as someone new came along. Even if the band never cut another track,
Victory would not be forgotten.

Vic let a smile nudge the corners of his lips. Yes, it *did* feel good, didn't
it? Even to an old fart who had seen it all before. It set his blood to flowing, made him think of tight young groupie bodies—even though he

didn't indulge in the latter's charms anymore—and made his hand itch for the hard, phallic shape of a microphone in his grip.

"We're gonna blow 'em away," Lenny boasted.

"Yeah." Vic accepted it as an obligation. "Let's do it."

❃ ❃ ❃

THE AUDIENCE REAFFIRMED THAT English-language rock'n'roll acts could make it no matter where in the world they played. The crowd rose to their feet as Victory lit into its self-referential piece—a minor hit on the radio, not even released as a single—but one that always made a connection during the live show with its long, repeated chant: "Victory! Victory! Victory is here!" It was two-thirds of the way through the show. Vic was stomping back and forth across the stage, sweat streaming down his bared chest, shouting the lyrics, egging the Berlin residents to a higher and higher pinnacle of frenzy.

The pounding in his heart came from three separate stimuli. First was the euphoria of being center stage, holding the attention of so many at once. Second was the nostalgic high of being successful at a craft at age fifty that he had been master of since age twenty-one. Third, he was terrified.

He was afraid because he wasn't in command of the mood. It had gone beyond him, driven by the screaming guitars, the heavy metal arrangements, the visceral beat of the drums. The Germans were releasing their pent-up tension, letting it flow out in waves. Glorious and necessary as the catharsis was, Vic knew it had the potential to spark a riot. He fought back visions of trampled twelve-year-old kids, of eyes being jabbed out. His bouncers at the edge of the stage, huge men who had once played football or hockey at semi-pro levels, were earning every bit of their salaries now—throwing overexuberant fans bodily back into the upraised arms of the hundreds who had abandoned their seats and mobbed the front of the stage. Those arms waved back and forth, their owners' eyes gleaming with worship as Vic stalked back and forth. That awe would turn to rage if Vic did what he wanted to—which was to run for the nearest exit. God help him if his voice were to falter or if a fuse blew and killed the speakers. The people had come to purge their demons. The process was in full swing, as unstoppable as an orgasm in mid-ejaculation. If he denied them their release, they would rip him to pieces.

He had no choice but to keep going, keep pretending that he was the one orchestrating the moment. If the horde lost the focus he was providing, the best description of the result would be chaos.

The song reached its final, crashing note. Vic sobbed. He wanted desperately to switch to a ballad, quiet the savage exultation, put some moderation into the waving fists, the screaming women, the feedback loops from the amps. But he couldn't.

Victory didn't do ballads.

❁ ❁ ❁

THE BAND HAD BLOWN them away, all right. Vic sat in numb awe in his dressing room, dismissing the invitations of the other members of the band. They were heading off to celebrate with one final night of alcohol and Berlin women, and if they had any brains left, condoms as well. He was in no mood to extend the altered state of consciousness. He would let it dissipate while he had the strength to survive it.

Vic's body ached. He took a final swallow from a bottle of Evian. Two liters down his throat since the end of the encore and he was still dehydrated. A fifteen-minute shower in the ludicrously tiny stall in the back of the room had merely diluted the layer of brine that hugged him like a second skin. Fresh perspiration was still oozing from his pores, though where he was finding the fluid to produce it, he didn't know.

A knock sounded on the door. Hurriedly he picked up the wig he'd removed prior to the shower and refitted it with an expertise born of countless repetition. He'd need to adhere it better before he went out, but it would hold for the length of time needed to deal with a visitor.

He rose and unlocked the door. Fred Brownell, his manager, slipped inside. Vic restored the deadbolts.

Fred was beaming, his bowling-ball torso resplendent with a silk cravat and a suit that must have set him back a few thousand deutsche marks. He set his valise down on the makeup counter and opened it, showing a sheaf of box office receipts next to his laptop computer.

"You're back at the top again, kid. I knew you could do it. You just topped this place's Guns N' Roses attendance record."

Kid was a relative term. Fred was sixty-one years old, his skin as tough as old leather from too many years of lying on beaches and from too many drugs—though he had forsworn both when he turned forty-five.

"I'm back?" Vic asked, groaning from fatigue as he eased into a folding chair. "What are you comparing it to? We don't talk about those days, Fred."

"Oh, fuck the rules," Fred replied mildly. "One time won't hurt. There were a lot of good times back then. I would think you'd be glad to get back to home base."

"Home base? I never hung around any scene like *this*."

"Don't be such a glum asshole." Fred raised his arms, spun in a circle, as if to point out that neither of them was in his grave. "All I meant was, it's good to see you out of retirement."

"We've been recording and touring more than five years now, Fred. It's not a recent development."

"Victory never did anything like this before," the fat man insisted. "This tour is hitting that old level. You moved those people out there, kid. Even with fake hair and a fake voice, you worked magic. They were there for you."

Fred obviously hadn't seen what Vic had. From backstage, the manager had watched the energy rise, gotten a boner at the thought of all the profits, and pictured reality the way he wished to.

"Bullshit. They were there for themselves," Vic said. "Don't make it into something it's not. I'm just a guy with some songs. The rest of it is just an illusion. It is now and it was back then."

"People don't buy tickets just to hear songs," Fred said. "They could play their copies of your CDs if all they wanted was the tunes. They came for Vic Standish the man. Maybe it *isn't* the way they used to come for Brad Taylor. But it's close enough in my book."

"Whatever you say." It wasn't worth arguing the point. Fred was Vic's closest associate and he loved him like a brother, but the man couldn't be talked out of anything. That's what made him such a good negotiator of contracts. Let him believe what he wanted to.

After Fred left, Vic pulled off his wig, reverting once again from a long-haired dark brunet to a short-haired blond with a deeply receding hairline. He popped out his contact lenses, which altered his brown eyes to blue. His eyebrows were that shade of variegated brown that worked with either type of coloring, especially after he donned his thick-framed glasses.

"The old days," he muttered, checking himself out in the mirror. In the old days, his body had been lean and taut. Ribs would show when he removed his shirt. His cheekbones had stood out and his arms had been ropy with veins. He hadn't totally gone to pot since then, but the thyroid problem had taken its toll. He looked nothing like he had in his youth, and now with the wig and contacts gone and his body stuffed into an overcoat that exaggerated his bulk, he barely resembled the man who had been on the stage ninety minutes earlier.

He slid out the door unobserved. The security men were concentrating on the entrances, per orders, Vic having learned that the best way to give fans the slip was to be where the guards weren't. He avoided the limousine waiting out back. Instead he filtered through the fringes of the group by the exit, parting them like the stern German corporate executive he appeared to be, and grabbed a regular taxi. No one gave him a second glance.

Cautious habits died hard. Rather than stay with the same vehicle that had taken him aboard at the ICC, he got out at a major hotel and furtively slipped into a second taxi. This car delivered him to an older, two-story home depressingly close to the Wall. The building was well-maintained, but across the street was more agonistic graffiti overlaid upon vestiges of World War II bomb damage.

Despite the late hour, the lights were on. A stout housekeeper bedecked in apparel just as no-nonsense as her expression led Vic to a bedroom that looked and smelled like a patient's room at a hospital, complete with adjustable bed on rollers and an oxygen tent covering the upper body of the man on the mattress.

"Hi, Andrew," Vic said. The invalid opened his eyes, smiled, and waved the housekeeper away. She left with a Teutonic glare at Vic that implied in no uncertain terms that he should not exhaust her charge. Both men waited until the sound of her footsteps confirmed that she had descended the stairs, out of conversational hearing range.

"How's it goin', Brad?" Andy asked, rubbing at his eyes. He didn't seem to have been sleeping, though the dark purple semi-circles under his lower lashes hinted that he should have been. "Or should I say Vic?"

"It's Brad to you," Vic said, unfamiliar as it was to hear the name roll off his tongue.

"Hated to miss the concert," Andy said. "Kept trying to talk the doc into letting me go with my portable oxygen. I hope you brought down the house."

Vic shrugged. "You could say that. Those young bozos I perform with know how to rock. Sometimes I still wish I had you and the other guys behind me, though."

"Well, we all make our choices, don't we?" Andy gestured at his wasted body. "Guess I took some detours I would have avoided if I'd known what I was in for."

"I wouldn't say we had any options about what either of us did. Things happened. Things bigger than any of us. We couldn't have known what would come down."

"Oh, the world is a motherfucker, that's true. But that don't mean there's no component of responsibility." For the first time, the sick man seemed to locate a reservoir of strength. His tone carried weight as he asked, "Have you thought about my idea? You'll be in London on the eighth. It's the perfect place."

"I'll think about it. I've got…a bit more to lose than you."

"True," Andy replied. "But also more to gain." He coughed, and with it came a gurgle from deep in the lungs.

"Shit," Vic said. He handed his friend the glass of water from the bed-side. "That sounded bad."

"Oh, I'm not dying yet," the other man joked. "They say I'll probably make it through the winter. I've got a New Year's party planned. Can't let people down."

❋ ❋ ❋

BACK IN HIS HOTEL room, Vic brooded. He had managed to be chipper and good-humored through the last of his short visit with Andy, but now the unfiltered pain of seeing his friend in a terminal condition was keeping him awake. That, or he was still juiced with adrenaline from the show, even though by rights he should be deep into the rebound by now, catatonic until the alarm clock forced him to get up and head for the airport.

He turned on the television. An actress who looked like she'd never had a period disrupt her adult life cooed over the latest development in tampons. He reached for the remote, annoyed—didn't northern Europe have any commercial-free stations? Perhaps, like everywhere else, the local government simply wouldn't fund that sort of thing anymore.

A change of channels brought him an old American movie, with John Wayne speaking German in a high nasal voice that tended to go on long after his lips had stopped moving. He killed the volume and let the picture flicker at the corner of his visual field.

Hell. It wasn't as if he didn't know why he was restless. Andy had resurrected a ghost.

The clock on the nightstand had long since rotated its digit counters into the a.m. half of the night. December 3rd. Five days short of fifteen years since the turning point.

Vic unfolded the clipping that Andy had given him just before they had said goodnight. It was a rock critic's essay from *Rolling Stone*, written in 1975, analyzing who had been the greatest movers and shakers of the past decade.

Vic Standish was unknown, of course. Brad Taylor headed the list, up above Lennon and Dylan, Jagger and Hendrix. On the first page of the article, there was a picture of a lean, fair-haired, thirty-year-old man with a speck of hazel in the iris of his left eye, right where Vic Standish had an identical mark.

A spokesman, the critic called Taylor. The voice of a generation.

The essay's tone was so reverent it sounded like a eulogy. In some ways, it might as well have been one.

Vic recalled the writer's name from a later issue of the same magazine, the special edition that appeared a few weeks after the murder of John Lennon—the one with his naked body wrapped around Yoko Ono. When Vic had first seen the cover on a newsstand, Lennon's closed eyes and damp washcloth posture, along with Ono's somber gaze-into-space, had led him to conclude that it was a photograph of the corpse. He had nearly set fire to the whole stack before he learned that it had been taken by Annie Leibovitz hours before the murder, and that Lennon himself had suggested the pose.

That issue had also contained a mention that in East Berlin, the state radio station had broken its usual ban on Western rock music and aired ninety minutes of Beatles songs as a memorial. That little snippet of trivia had bubbled to Vic's mind when his plane had touched down for the current gig. More than one aspect of his life seemed to be closing full circle this weekend.

❊ ❊ ❊

MAY, 1981: FRED WAS sitting with him in a Los Angeles patio café, doing his best not to be stunned by what Brad had just announced. To his credit, Fred did not try to protest. He nodded mournfully and leafed through the pieces of paper Brad had just given him.

"This is how I see it," Brad said. "John Lennon and I shared way too many similarities. We're both rock'n'roll legends. Both us had fans literally tear clothing off our bodies to have a piece of us. He took a hiatus. So did I. We both lived in New York most of the last five years. Now there are these."

Fred's frown evolved into a scowl. The papers he'd been handed were death threats, written by at least three separate lunatics, only one of which the police had been able to track down.

"These are as bad as you said," Fred muttered. "It's really got you spooked, eh, kid?"

"Damn right it's got me spooked." Brad's hand shook as he reached for his coffee, just thinking about it. "I'm not going to become a target for another Mark David Chapman."

"So you're going to fake your own death." Fred didn't phrase it as a question; he spoke as if anchoring the concept firmly in his brain. He was a perceptive man. He had caught on that his client had made up his mind and nothing he could say was going to change it. The one thing he might fuss about was the financial loss, but the plan, as Brad had delineated it, would give Fred quite an income flow over the long haul.

"Yes."

Fred sighed and reached out to shake Brad's hand. "It's been a fun ride, kid. I think you're crazy, but you have my support. Where are you going to do it?"

"Grand Cayman."

❋ ❋ ❋

GRAND CAYMAN IS AN island where all sorts of things can be bought. In June, 1981, Brad Taylor's body was found, throat slit, in the kitchen of a bungalow on the beach several miles from George Town, a vacation residence he had owned and visited frequently for several years. At least, the public was led to believe the body was that of Taylor. It actually belonged to a derelict purchased from a morgue, but to pin it with a different identity required active lying by only two individuals outside

Vic's tight-knit circle—a police detective and a coroner, both well-paid for their falsehoods.

Reported missing were several important pieces of Brad Taylor memorabilia, including his favorite guitar. Naturally Vic—as he would henceforth be known—had taken these articles with him, but their absence was attributed to robbery by the same man who had done the killing.

The search began for the thief/murderer. Several of the island's usual suspects were rounded up and questioned in the "guilty until you pay us off" style of the local authorities. A description of a man who had supposedly been seen near the bungalow on the day in question was distilled out of that activity, but the artist's composite showed a lanky, dark man with dreadlocks, a description that applied to so many transients in the region that it was useless as a means of narrowing the list of suspects. Then a radio station in New York received what purported to be an anonymous letter from the guilty party. It rambled on in a fashion reminiscent of the Zodiac killer, saying that Brad Taylor had been murdered for his immorality and decadence. In the envelope was a lock of hair that matched that of Taylor, and an exact list of the missing items from the bungalow.

The media had a field day, but when the excitement ended, the authorities had no leads. The case went as cold as the ashes, supposedly those of Brad Taylor, that were scattered over New York Harbor in early July.

❀ ❀ ❀

DECEMBER, 1981: VIC, STILL lying low in the Caribbean, rendezvoused with Andy on Tobago.

"I wanted to tell all my old bandmates," Vic said as they shared dinner at The Beachcomber. Parrots sat on perches just outside the open windows of the restaurant. Palm trees waved in the slight breeze. The last of the sunset was vanishing, and a soca beat could be heard from the disco next door. "Maybe I will later. But the more people who know, the more likely it is that the whole scheme will fall apart. I'm sure I can count on your discretion."

"Of course," Andy said. "Always." Setting down the crab leg on which he'd been nibbling, he shook his head at the bizarre circumstances. "So… how many people *do* know?"

"Just the folks whose cooperation I can't do without if I'm going to keep pulling it off," Vic explained. "My ex-wife. My executor. They get cash to me bit by bit, siphoning it to me from my estate. And Fred, of course. I have to have somebody like him to look after the tape archive and make sure the music gets licensed in a way I can live with. I might not be Brad Taylor anymore, but I'll be damned if I'll let my work be turned into Pepsi jingles and background noise for used-car dealers' ads."

"Amen to that." Though Brad had essentially been a solo artist, writing all his own songs, Andy's bass guitar work was on the definitive recordings of seventy percent of those tunes, and he obviously didn't care to have his legacy diluted.

A bat sailed through the restaurant, over their table, scooped up a pair of fruit flies, and vanished in the direction of the beach. None of the staff or old-time island residents gave the flying mammal a second glance. These were the tropics.

Vic turned back to the table to find Andy frowning. "Aren't you lonely?" the bassist asked.

Vic coughed. "Yeah. That's why I had Fred arrange this meeting."

"In that case, how long you gonna keep this up?"

The "dead" man took a long, slow swallow of rum. "Don't know. Couple of years? Maybe by then, Lennon being gone won't sting like it does now. Doesn't it leave you feeling stung, Andy?"

"Stung by fire ants, my man. And it was even worse when I heard that *you* had died." He stared pointedly at his old boss.

Vic blinked, then cleared his throat. "Sorry," he muttered into his empty glass. "I just felt…mortal. I needed a break. Some time away, unhounded by fans, able to walk around without feeling like someone is looking at me every second. You know what I mean?"

Andy smiled wryly. "I quit being your backup man seven years ago next Tuesday, you know that? Even after all that time, even being off to the side like I was, it still takes hanging out in corners of the world like this to have any privacy at all."

"Well, there you go," Vic said. "Being dead is the most out-of-the-way corner I could find. I want to rest awhile before I go back to the rat race. Ask me again in a year. Maybe I'll feel differently then."

❄ ❄ ❄

A YEAR MIGHT HAVE been enough. Vic grew tired of never being able to call up old acquaintances. But 1982 contained the April from hell:

Bob Dylan was machine-gunned to death outside his front door in the presence of two of his children. Donovan Leitch was next, shot by a mental-hospital escapee who accused him of stealing the lyrics of "Sunshine Superman" and threatening to execute a host of other rock icons for similar "crimes."

McCartney was the last, but also the worst for Vic. It wasn't just that the bullet left him in a vegetative state, unable to die and unable to live. It was that Vic hadn't realized how much the other leader of the Beatles had meant to him until he was taken out. Vic had always been a Lennon fan, except to compare Yoko Ono's voice unfavorably with that of a macaw. Yet when he overheard a man joking that McCartney had always been a vegetable, he'd loosened the bastard's teeth for him and spent the next few hours at home playing "Yesterday" and "Got to Get You into My Life" and "The Long and Winding Road," forcing his bloodied, swollen knuckles to coax the tunes from his guitar or his piano.

Every megastar in the industry ducked into seclusion or hired the entire army of France to guard them. Caution reigned for a long time. Elton John gave up touring, releasing sporadic albums recorded at home behind barred gates. George Harrison vanished into his mansion for the next seven years.

Any thought Vic had of revealing himself disappeared. Brad Taylor remained victim number two on a list that had grown far too long. Vic Standish walked the planet in his place. He was rich. He lived a comfortable life. He wasn't going to fuck with that. His collaborators, who might have become careless and let something slip under other circumstances, understood the stakes, and kept their lips sealed.

In 1986 the detective on Grand Cayman confessed to his part. Annual, untraceable deliveries of cash, part of the original bribe, had not been enough; he thought he could get more money by selling his tale. The tactic did not harm Vic. For one thing, the detective did not know what name Brad Taylor had adopted, and second, the man was widely known as an unreliable witness. His testimony had been bought in more than one court case, which was a reason Vic had selected him. Fortunately, the coroner could offer no corroboration. He had already died, and better still, had passed away quietly of natural causes in a hospital, providing little fuel for conspiracy theorists. Only the *National Enquirer* and other tabloids paid any attention to the detective, and they only milked the story for two weeks. The reputable media shoved it in the same basket as Elvis sightings.

The likelihood of being exposed grew increasingly remote. With that sense of security, Vic ultimately could not resist the narcotic of having an audience. With a body gone overweight, minus the pretty-boy face of his younger days and with various cosmetic adjustments, he slid back into the music scene in 1989, given entrée by a few careful behind-the-scenes maneuvers by Fred.

Using Fred was a risk, because it linked him to his former identity. But Fred managed dozens of acts at any one time, and had hundreds in his résumé. Taking on another client set off no alarms. Without Fred, the goal would not have been approachable. Otherwise Vic used none of his old colleagues, and only two of the new crew—his sound man and his chief roadie—were added to the list of those who knew the real history behind Vic Standish, again because the scheme would fail without their assistance.

❊ ❊ ❊

AND HERE HE WAS. Victory's first album had gone nowhere, but the band had gained a touring reputation. The second album contained a hit single. Then the third went platinum, and now the fourth was into the stratosphere.

The success was the biggest surprise. All Vic had cared about was having the chance to get out there in front of a few thousand fans. If he had dreamed it would get this big—still not as big as his heyday as Brad Taylor, but huge by objective standards—he might have reconsidered the whole project, because it exposed him to the risk of discovery.

But the fact was, no crazed fan had gunned down a rock'n'roll star in over a decade. The fad, Lord be praised, seemed to have gone the way of all fads. Or maybe, thought Vic, shutting off the hotel-room TV and tucking the folded clipping into his valise, it was just his own paranoia that had gone away. Not that he didn't have his roadies observe heavy security precautions, but in hindsight his reaction to the events of December 8, 1980 seemed…excessive. Perhaps he'd been snorting too much coke.

He was clean now. He was clear-eyed. And he might not have enough excuses for denying the wish of a dying friend.

"God damn you, Andy," Vic muttered.

Finally his eyelids were getting heavy. He undressed, shut out the lights, and listened to the rain batter at the window. Tuesday was the gig in Amsterdam. Best not to think beyond that. One hurdle at a time.

❀ ❀ ❀

EMPTY SEATS DOTTED THE rear of the upper level. Judging by album sales, the Dutch fans were as loyal as those elsewhere, but it was a Tuesday night and sleet was falling. Vic breathed a small sigh of relief. As proven so recently, a capacity crowd generated a peculiar energy that was difficult to control. Here, the vacancies left echoes and reduced the hubbub from the drone of a hornet's nest to that of a few honey bees dancing between peach blossoms.

The concert hall was also smaller than the stadiums Victory played on its weekend stops. The venue reeked of hashish; the haze was so thick it dimmed the glow of the exit signs. The members of the band stepped gingerly across the darkened stage to claim their instruments. Dim blue, violet, and green spotlights roamed across the crowd, gradually shifting toward warmer colors of greater intensity as they prepared to converge where Vic waited on a dais in front of the huge array of drums.

Already the Amsterdam denizens were proving how little like the Berlin horde they were. Women stood and flashed their tits, knowing this was the one time when Vic could see clearly out into the galleries. Nearly half the attendees had long hair. Some wore tie-dyed shirts. He was sure he even saw one or two middle-aged types raising their fingers in the rabbit-ear symbol for peace: God, how long had it been since he'd seen *that*?

The beams struck him. The lead guitarist launched into the screaming opening chord of the title song from the group's third CD, and Vic raised the microphone to his lips.

His deep, potent voice matched the pulse-pounding music. Victory was a kick-ass band. For the ten-thousandth time, Vic made the mental adjustment needed to recognize that the lyrics bellowing from the speakers came from his mouth. It was *not* his true voice. He was a tenor, and there was no way he would have sounded like anyone other than Brad Taylor if his head tech hadn't modified the signal coming from the microphone. Though he was singing normally, what the audience heard was an entire register lower.

The crowd clapped and stomped their feet. First song down, the band lit into its second and third. By then, Vic was puzzled, though he tried not to let it show. These people were enjoying the performance, but they were doing it in a way no Victory fans had ever done. In simplest terms, they were *non-violent*.

The distinction was subtle. It was more a feeling than an observation, because the lights in his face kept him from picking up some of the visual details. But he'd been up there in front of so many people in so many cities that he could read an audience the way another man could read the emotions of a dear lifelong friend. When they screamed, they did not have their teeth bared and the neck muscles tensed; they were smiling. When they flailed their bodies to the drumbeat, they were not shoving the people beside them; they were swaying in unison. Far fewer asses than usual were encased in black leather; instead they were tucked into faded blue denim. And some of the women were still topless, without converting nearby males to testosterone hyperactivity.

It doesn't fit, Vic thought. The lyrics pouring out of his mouth weren't the paeans to love, the sly political commentaries, the personal transformation odes of Brad Taylor. They were supposed to be as far removed from Brad Taylor as possible. Nowadays he sang about fast chicks, hot motorcycles, or bitchin' scenery. When composing, he couldn't avoid inserting occasional clever turns of phrase, but such flourishes were buried within a cascade of primal drums and frenetic guitars, and no one had yet made the comparison between Vic Standish and any of the peace/love/dope generation of rock lyricists. Most of his fans didn't even know what the words to the songs were. They listened for more visceral reasons.

For the sixth number, Vic pulled out a harmonica, a rare departure, like his occasional use of a tambourine, from his role as vocalist. For five years he had avoided playing guitar or keyboards in public, because those were Brad Taylor's habits, but he was thankful for the feel of an instrument in his hands now. The concert was stirring old memories at a time when he was unusually vulnerable to their effect.

In a way, it all made sense. It jibed with what he had seen on the streets of the city the previous day and a half. Amsterdam was the last bastion of the Dream—the one that went "All You Need Is Love." Here the courts did not send recreational drug users to prison for decades. Prostitution remained legalized. The society tolerated alternate lifestyles, promoted the arts, provided sex education to minors. Yet Vic caught an undertone of desperation out in the seats. The Dutch were running scared, behaving with an exaggerated sense of abandon that recalled the stories he'd heard of the decadent moments in pre-Nazi Germany right before the iron fist squeezed shut. Individuals from many nations had thronged to the city of the famous painters, coming to the one place that was withstanding the tide of repression. In this milieu the free spirits of Europe could congregate in the open.

As Vic lowered the harmonica and bellowed out the first stanza, he faltered, almost forgetting the lines. He was only half in the moment. The rest of him was free-floating, touching upon events and conclusions of the past fifteen years.

America had once given him scenes like this. Then something had happened. The pendulum swung. Reagan came into office. The Republicans won a majority in Congress and never lost it. Now Bush was wrapping up a second term and the momentum was *still* gaining toward the right. The Pentagon's budget had increased every year. Social Security was being phased out. Carriers of HIV were required to wear ID bracelets to alert the general public to their malady—a public health issue, not a personal liberty concern, according to the new surgeon general. Abortion was illegal again in eighteen states.

Vic's stomach lurched. His knees went watery. What was it Andy had said about responsibility? Surely the period of hope between '65 and '80 was nothing over which he had control. People talked about the Beatles fueling societal change. They quoted lines from Brad Taylor and Bob Dylan. Sometimes they even threw into the mix the Doors and the Eagles, Jackson Browne and Crosby, Stills, & Nash. But that was all horseshit. No one had that kind of power.

Or did they? Vic Standish was worried. He looked back and saw a cusp point. The spirit of the sixties had faltered most visibly after its leading balladeers were cut down. Not until Lennon was taken out did the metamorphosis settle in, and then...

The heavy metal noise surrounding him turned sour to his ears. Not because it was bad music, or badly played—quite the contrary—but because it wasn't *him*. And because it symbolized a personal cowardice. He was envisioning a world in which he hadn't run for cover. What if he had contributed to the tide of events? What if his faked murder had set up the streak? With Lennon gone, then him, was that enough to establish the fad of offing rock stars? Was that what had given that series of deranged lunatics the confidence to go after Dylan, Donovan, and McCartney?

Absently he waved to the crowd. They cheered in spite of his wobbly performance of the last song. Did they see something in him that he didn't? Vic Standish was a fantasy, not a true identity at all. If they could cling to their faith in him in the face of a lie, who knew how much more could be birthed by the truth?

He fell back into his music, astir with a thousand thoughts. The songs were the same that Victory always played. He couldn't change that yet. But December the 8th was only three days away.

❊ ❊ ❊

LONDON. WEMBLEY WAS NEARLY sold out. Half an hour before the show, Vic peeked out as ticket-holders gravitated toward their assigned seats, many of them finding their places with a restrained, funereal pace. This wasn't Berlin, and it wasn't Amsterdam. These were the citizens of the country which had given life to John Lennon, and this was the anniversary of his death. Any rock event—heavy metal or not—that took place on December 8th carried a unique sort of emotional baggage.

Through binoculars, Vic saw fans running their fingers along their souvenir programs, noting the black trim. Only the very youngest attendees needed an explanation. All knew whose life and passing was being commemorated, though there was no indication that the accent had been added at Vic's instructions.

Vic was thankful only one death need be mourned. He was still worrying about Andy, no matter that the latter had assured him in a phone call that afternoon that he was doing well and yes, the odds of being able to host his New Year's party were still in his favor.

It was bad to be losing a friend, but it would be far worse if Vic lost this one before the month was out. The concert tonight was being recorded for a Christmas pay-for-view broadcast. This would be the one show of the tour that Vic's old bandmate might have a chance to attend, if only in the remote sense.

He counted down the minutes, conscious of each breath. Finally the moment came to step on stage.

The video cameras served as a wakeup call for musicians already riding a high. Victory pushed the envelope of its talent. Vic paced himself, maintaining the structure he wanted of the evening, openly asking the listeners to clap or sing along at precisely the places he wished them to. The crowd let themselves be wooed, all without losing their boisterousness. Vic was in sync with his listeners in a way he hadn't been since the last full-scale tour Brad Taylor had mounted in 1974, before Andy and a couple of his other longterm sidemen had gone their own way. Or maybe it was earlier still—perhaps since that fundraiser for peace in '72, the last time he had tried to make a concert more than just a musical event.

After nearly two hours, the lights went down. The roar from the seats was deafening even to ears shielded to protect them from the Pete Townshend syndrome. Vic and his mates walked off. Everyone knew they'd be back—Victory always did an encore of three songs.

"Still planning a surprise?" Lenny asked Vic in the tunnel backstage. In the stadium the cheers were turning into a chant: VICTORY! VICTORY!

"Yes," Vic said. "I'll give you the signal."

Even his colleagues didn't know what was coming down. Vic wasn't sure anything was. He was proceeding step by step. When the moment arrived, he might let it pass. Fighting the inertia of years was not a simple thing.

After the appropriate pause, before the fans became impatient, the band marched back onstage. The lights rose and Victory sailed into a high-energy rendition of their first hit, the song that had led the encore at every stop of the tour.

Anticipation rose. Sweat trickled down Vic's back. Hands reached for him, held back by the height of the stage and by the bouncers. Faces glowed. The third song, they all knew, was supposed to be Victory's new single. It had just gone to number one and was the most popular piece the band could offer at that particular time and place. They had not played it so far that night.

The second song ended. The sweat on Vic's body turned arctic. The plan now was *not* to follow with the expected song, but he saw that to deviate from expectations would be a mistake. Were he to defy the crowd that way, they would turn on him. He had to give them what they wanted, earn their gratitude.

He nodded to his bassist, and led off with the wild-man scream of the number one song. The crowd raved, able at last to reach the climax of their adoration. Vic shuddered, realizing how close he had come to fucking up. Now, more than ever, the Wembley faithful were with him.

The band stretched out the four-minute piece to six, repeating the chorus until the steel beams of the structure groaned from the decibel level.

The lights went down. The crowd cheered and held up cigarette lighters and burning matches, calling for another encore for the sake of form, even though they knew Victory didn't do second encores. A few practical souls made an early break for the exits.

A single, wide spotlight came back up. There was Vic, all alone on the stage. He held a guitar.

"Wait," he said softly, the amplified voice barely audible over the buzz.

The tumult gradually tapered off, if only because no one knew what to expect. Vic Standish didn't do solos. He didn't play guitar. And if he did, it wouldn't be an acoustic instrument with those strangely familiar gold frets and pearl white face, monogrammed with an elegant "B.T." One by one the people sat and waited, murmuring among themselves.

"I would like to share something with you," Vic said. Methodically, he lifted his wig from his head, put his contact lenses in their case, and placed a pair of granny glasses on his nose.

A handful of people among the crowd gasped as the gigantic viewscreen behind the stage lit up with a close-up of Vic's face, showing a heavyset, worn, balding version of a legend thought deceased. They paused, stunned, as Vic arranged microphones near his mouth and near his guitar strings—a different mike arrangement than he used as the front man of Victory.

The first soft notes flowed from his guitar. Utter silence fell over the crowd. They waited for the fourth measure when, if this were the song it sounded like, the vocal would begin. Exactly on cue, Vic opened his mouth.

He sang clearly, on-key, using the arrangement made famous in the original 1969 recording. His timbre had changed a little in twenty-six years, but there was no question whose voice it was.

The crowd began to stir as more and more people figured it out. The rumble was low and pregnant with meaning, as if everyone wanted to speak at once, but no one dared shout for fear of drowning out the anthem coming from the stage.

Vic reached the second chorus. A drum joined in, along with bass and rhythm guitars—gently, as befitted the tune. Startled, Vic glanced behind him and found his bandmates in their places. They had never rehearsed the song with him, and had no warning he would bring it out tonight, but no player of rock'n'roll, from the most acidic punkrocker to the schmaltziest Barry Manilow clone, hadn't learned the piece at one time or another in their garage band days. Vic grinned, and fell back into the song with renewed inspiration.

By the third and final chorus, the audience joined in. The voices, in a harmony rare for such a huge group of singers, mounted to a choir-like holiness, speaking of love and imagination and hope for the future. Vic—Brad—was thrust back to the era when he had composed the lyrics, back to a moment when he bled a drop of himself into every syllable.

The words were a kind of worship, but not the mundane sycophancy of fans toward a celebrity. Brad had never written them to make the world love him, but to show the world the beauty of itself. It was *his* worship of All That Out There.

The occupants of Wembley understood. They were on their feet, some hugging each other, some calling, "Brad! Brad!" Some praying, some shaking their heads—not in disbelief at what they were seeing down there on the stage now, or at what they were feeling in their hearts, but in wry self-reflection on what they had believed up to this point.

The euphoria spread. Brad could sense it washing out into London, over the island, skimming the English Channel and, in the other direction, gathering into a wave that would crash across the entire width of the Atlantic Ocean. It was not an illusion. It was a living force.

Out there, somewhere, a pendulum began to lag, no longer swinging unchecked. A tide was turning.

Brad caressed his guitar, letting the music flow from it, from him. He was no longer confused about his role or his identity. The choice was simple. The world needed a dreamer with a voice. He would serve as best he could.

❀ ❀ ❀ ❀ ❀

DAVE SMEDS IS THE author of novels, screenplays, comic book scripts, non-fiction articles, and more. His output extends across a range of genres including science fiction, sword-and-sorcery, superhero, alternate history, horror, erotica, contemporary fantasy, and young-adult. A major career focus is short fiction. His stories have appeared in such venues as the magazines *Asimov's Science Fiction*, *F&SF*, *Realms of Fantasy*, and *Dark Regions*, and anthologies such as *Full Spectrum 4*, *Peter S. Beagle's Immortal Unicorn*, *In the Field of Fire*, *The Shimmering Door*, *Return to Avalon*, *Lace and Blade*, and many volumes of the Sword and Sorceress series. He lives in Santa Rosa, CA with his wife and son.

Possibilities

Sarah Wells

Cindy's alarm pierces through the nostalgic dream she is having about her ex. She rolls over and hits the snooze button, trying to go back to sleep and continue the dream. God, she misses him. Sure, there had been issues, mainly the whole drug thing, but he really was a nice guy. Things were just easy with him. She could be totally herself and not have to worry if he was judging her. She should have insisted that he go to rehab with her and then they could still be together. This recovery thing is so hard without someone by your side. Maybe she will call him later today.

Shit, I'm running late. For the third day in a row, she misses her morning Serenity Prayer meditation meeting. Oh well, she'll just say it to herself on the way to her job interview. Cindy runs through her apartment frantically trying to get dressed and eat something. "Proper nutrition is very important to recovery," her therapist often lectures. *Screw that,* Cindy thinks, grabbing a pop tart. She never even looks at the post-it notes of affirmations on her mirrors, fridge and cabinets. In fact, she even takes one down from the medicine cabinet mirror and throws it on the floor in order to better examine a pimple she's getting. Must be all those damn chips and dip she'd been eating.

Cindy is late for the job interview. She comes in out of breath and sweaty. The man interviewing her seems somewhat creepy and has trouble keeping his eyes off of her chest. *He's just gross,* Cindy thinks. *There is no way in hell I'll work for him. Besides, this job seems stupid and boring. I'd have cravings all day and would probably relapse. It's probably healthier if I don't take this job. My parents will just have to deal.* She never mentions her drug issues or her time in rehab to the interviewer. *He doesn't deserve to know that about me.*

"What are your two biggest strengths and two biggest weaknesses?" Creepy Man asks.

Oh shit, I should have listened harder when they went over this question in rehab, she silently scolds herself. "I...I'm not sure. I guess I am a good worker and, well, I don't know. I just really need to make some money."

Cindy tells herself that it was a good decision to walk out of the interview saying she wasn't interested. It's important to be honest and to know your limits. She thinks her therapist will be proud of her. Before her meeting, she decides to get some coffee and call her ex. She hasn't talked to Billy in a couple months and wonders how he is. *Maybe if he sees how well I'm doing, it will inspire him*, she thinks. *I'm not really trying to fix him anymore.* Her therapist is always yelling at her about that.

She calls Billy and gets his voicemail. She leaves a message saying hi and that she'll try him later. Cindy realizes her meeting starts in a few minutes. The ninety meetings in ninety days are getting really old. She looks at her calendar with a bunch of X's marked off and counts how many meetings she has left: twenty-eight. Christ, she'll never make it. Everyone is so freaking whiny. She goes to the meeting, sits in the back playing Angry Birds on her phone, and gets her paper stamped saying that she attended. There, that should make her therapist happy.

She calls Billy again and this time he answers. He sounds high. She is supposed to go to her parents' house for dinner but damn, she is lonely. They say in meetings that you shouldn't let yourself get too lonely. What harm could it do? She misses feeling his arms around her and the smell of him. When he asks if she wants to come over, she only has to mull it over for three seconds. "Sure," she says. She calls her parents and tells them she doesn't feel well and she'll see them next week. "Oh, and please don't forget to send my monthly check. Money is tight."

Cindy goes over to Billy's. She lived there for two years so it's weird going back. It's his place now, not theirs. Billy looks the same: great smile, piercing blue eyes and that scruffy hair. The house is pretty much a wreck. His stuff lies strewn everywhere. *Why wouldn't it be?* She had done all the tidying and cleaning.

It's great and sad to see him again. They hug. Billy offers her something to drink and she accepts. The alcohol burns her throat and chest as it goes down. She coughs and Billy laughs.

"Out of practice?" he gently chides.

"I guess. All substances are frowned upon, supposedly." Cindy finishes her drink defiantly while never losing eye contact with Billy. They talk for a bit and it's nice. They end up making love in the living room and for a couple hours, Cindy isn't lonely anymore.

❊ ❊ ❊

CINDY'S ALARM PIERCES THROUGH the nightmare she is having about her ex. She jumps out of bed, trying frantically to shake the remnants of the dream off. *Jesus Christ, how am I supposed to do this recovery thing if I keep dreaming about drugs and Billy?* Billy and drugs, drugs and Billy. Which came first, the chicken or the egg? *He only got violent a couple times while high, so why do I have to keep dreaming about those things over and over?* She throws some cold water on her face, trying to clear her jumbled thoughts, then takes some deep breaths while sitting on the edge of the bathtub and says the Serenity Prayer. "Okay, I can do this," she says aloud.

She makes a point to go around the apartment and read each of the post-it notes. *I so don't believe any of this crap,* Cindy's inner demon taunts. Her therapist says she has to find a way to shut out that negative voice and strengthen the positive one. *What positive one?* It's there, the therapist insists. Positive affirmations are clearly not working today. Cindy mindfully sits down and has some fruit and yogurt for breakfast. She is doing her best to take care of herself in small ways. Her nerves are rattled for her upcoming job interview, though, so she can't eat a lot. She promises herself some chips and dip later as a reward. *Fatty!* says the demon voice. *Shut up,* says the other one.

Cindy arrives at the job interview and feels like she's going to throw up. She can feel the flop sweat dripping down her underarms and her back. *Don't fuck this up, don't fuck this up,* she repeats to herself. *You fuck everything up,* her monster-self mocks. *Just keep breathing, it's okay. If you need to leave, you can.*

The man interviewing her seems okay. However, Cindy is concentrating so hard on calming herself down that she's sure she's missed a lot of what he's saying. *Why is he looking at me funny? Can he tell I'm about to lose it? Why did he stop talking?*

"I'm sorry, could you repeat the question?" Cindy feels like she can't breathe.

"What would you say your two biggest strengths and two biggest weaknesses are?" he repeats.

"Um…I'm so sorry, but could I use the restroom?" Cindy is already out of her seat and bolting for the door. The man tries to give her directions but she is gone. She runs out of the building and down the block, hyperventilating the whole way. She is certain people are staring at her. *Told you you'd fuck it up. Shut up, just shut the fuck up.* Cindy stops at a bench in a little park and plops down. She starts crying while still breathing heavily. *Breathe…just breathe.*

Cindy tries to concentrate on the seemingly normal people in the park. She sees a couple on a blanket. *You'll never have that again.* She sees a father and son throwing a ball. People just living their lives and not freaking out every second of every day. Cindy sits and breathes.

She goes to her NA meeting. Getting there early calms her down, as she can be around other people who understand. She has only talked to a few people in passing, and doesn't have a sponsor yet, but she's getting there. There is a woman she feels a kinship with, but so far Cindy has been too chicken to ask about her being her sponsor. *Who would want to sponsor you? You're so pathetic. Go away; leave me in peace for the next hour, dammit.* The beast obliges, for now. Cindy sits at the end of a row, in case she needs to flee again. However, this has never happened in a meeting. She can usually get completely focused on the speakers and get out of her own head for the duration. But one must be prepared.

Dinner at her parents' is never a joyful affair. Her mother flits about as if all is always right with the world and her dad just throws back the whiskey. Her brother had the right idea to move to Costa Rica. Costa Ricans claim to be the happiest people in the world. *Maybe I should move there too. You'll never leave, you're too scared and needy.* The beast is back. *You couldn't even get through a job interview.*

"How was your day, dear?" her mom says cheerfully.

"Okay, I guess. My anxiety has been bad, though." Cindy is never sure whether or not to mention any of her problems. Her therapist says she should try and be more open with her mother but it has never gotten her anything but frustration.

"What in the world do you have to be anxious about? You don't have to work, you get to sleep in. Sounds like a good life to me. Pass the green beans, please."

Her father grunts and takes a large swig of his drink. "My parents would have disowned me if I didn't work. You don't know how good you have it, little lady."

And here comes the frustration. And anger. Cindy is so angry, but she pushes it down. She eats in silence while her mother goes on and on about happy current events; the neighbors adopting a puppy, a new Walmart going in down the road and the falling price of gas. Life is grand in her mother's eyes. Observing them, she thinks, *God help me, no wonder I'm so screwed up.* She silently looks forward to seeing her therapist tomorrow.

On the way home she stops at a convenience store and buys some chips and dip. Even though she ate until she was uncomfortably full at dinner, she really wants to reward herself for surviving this hellish day. *Fatty! Fatty! Shut up, leave me alone. Breathe.*

❀ ❀ ❀

CINDY'S ALARM PIERCES THROUGH the mediocre dream she was having about her ex. She rolls over and turns it off but lies there fuming. *Really? Wasn't it bad enough that our relationship was boring and mundane? I so don't need to be reminded of this while I sleep. Who actually dreams about eating and watching TV?*

Even the drug use got to be predictable. Billy would score some oxy's from his neighbor and they would take them, eat, have sex, watch TV, then go to sleep. Aren't most addicts' lives supposed to be full of drama and excitement? Guess not.

Cindy struggles into a sitting position and recites the Serenity Prayer out loud. Thank God she doesn't live with anyone, *they would be so annoyed by all this recovery stuff,* she chuckles to herself. As she moves through her apartment, getting ready to face the day, she glances at the post-it notes with positive affirmations on them scattered about: "Trust the Process," "One Day at a Time," "Let Go and Let God." Today would be a good day. She is allowing the positivity to permeate her being just like her therapist has taught her to do.

The job interview goes fairly well. It isn't Cindy's idea of a dream job, but she really needs the money. She can't keep relying on her parents: it isn't the healthiest of relationships. The man who interviews her seems straightforward enough and doesn't balk when Cindy tells him about her recent stint in rehab.

"What are your two biggest strengths and two biggest weaknesses?" he asks.

She is prepared for this question: it was one of the popular ones gone over in rehab. "I'm a very hard worker and I'm very loyal." *Even when it's detrimental to my health*, she thinks. "I guess my biggest weaknesses are that I can put too much of myself into my work and I can get too caught up on details." There, hopefully she has done that trick of making her weaknesses sound like strengths. This is all such a game. But she figures she can do data entry for a few months until something better comes along. It will keep her busy both physically and mentally and hopefully keep her cravings at bay.

Sometimes the cravings come on strong. She can feel them in every fiber and cell of her being. At times, they make her want to stop whatever she is doing, curl up in the fetal position and just rock herself until they pass. Of course, it isn't always possible to indulge this urge, so she just tries to breathe through them as she has learned. Other times, the cravings are just a thought. *Good God, I want to be high right now.* These are much easier to deal with and she can push them out of her head. She also has learned to focus on the reasons she went into rehab in the first place: she had lost control of her life, she yearned for more meaningful relationships and she really wants to go back to school to study horticulture.

Today's NA meeting is a speaker meeting. Cindy likes these; she can usually find something she can relate to with everyone who speaks. Martha is talking today about how she lost custody of her kids due to her drug use. Even though Cindy doesn't have kids, she relates to the feeling of loss that has been everpresent in her life.

Cindy has recently asked Anna to be her sponsor and Anna agreed. This is all so new to Cindy; she isn't sure how this works, but is willing to give it a try. It does feel good knowing that someone, well, if you count her therapist, two someones, have your back.

She is getting to know some of the regulars better and they often go out for coffee after the meeting. Cindy is proud of herself for getting through the job interview and is excited to share this news with her new friends.

But she's forgotten that she can't go out today as she has promised to go to her parents' for dinner. Damn, not her favorite thing to do, for sure, but she needs to keep relations civil, at least while she is still dependent on them. She'll have to chat after the meeting, then be on her way.

"I really think I nailed the interview today," she tells her small group of friends. *Friends,* she isn't used to having any, and it still feels weird to call them that. "I used the skills I learned in rehab and they worked!"

The women congratulate her and express disappointment that she can't join them this evening. They also wish her luck and strength regarding dinner at her parents'. Anna invites Cindy to call her after her dinner. Cindy feels a faint glimmer of hope as she leaves. *These people may genuinely care about my well-being.*

Every time she pulls up to her parents' house, she feels herself regressing. "Remember, you are an adult," she says out loud to herself. It doesn't help that the house looks the exact same, inside and out, since they moved there when she was five. Exact same drab furniture, dark curtains, the TV always on, and that smell. She would know that smell anywhere, though it's hard to describe. Smoke, alcohol, Italian seasonings and perhaps perfume? All she knows is that it disgusts her.

Dinner is the usual superficial event. Nobody in her family ever talks about feelings or the fact that Cindy almost died from a drug overdose or that Dad is an alcoholic. Mom just goes through life ensconced in her own little bubble which, oddly, seems to work for her. So far, at sixty-two years old, nothing has burst it. In a way, Cindy kind of admires this iron-clad shield of denial. But she also wonders, quite often, if Mom is really, genuinely happy. Her therapist thinks there is no way she is.

Cindy's dad never says much. Since retiring, he drinks steadily throughout the day but never seems to get drunk. Every now and then he grunts in response to a question but shows little to no interest in anyone or anything. Cindy has given up on trying to have any kind of meaningful relationship with him.

"How was your day, dear?" Mom asks cheerfully.

"Oh, the usual. Had a job interview and went to a meeting," she replies dutifully.

"Aren't you done with those meetings yet? I thought you were all better. Can you pass the green beans?

She thinks about trying yet again to educate her mother about the disease of addiction but she doesn't have the energy. She is working hard in therapy at accepting her family for who they are, limitations and all. She can't change them; they love her as much as they are able. She will have to get her emotional needs met from other, healthier people. Who these people are, Cindy isn't quite sure yet. But she is optimistic and believes she is off to a good start.

Cindy leaves right after dinner, using a headache as an excuse. She really just wants to be at home, snuggling with her cat. And she definitely will be calling her sponsor. Her family is exhausting. On the way home, she stops at a convenience store for some potato chips and dip. Apparently this is her new addiction; she finds them comforting. As long as she doesn't eat them every day, she figures it's okay. Besides, she deserves them after an evening with her family.

❋ ❋ ❋

It's a fall evening and Cindy is home alone. Her friends want her to go out to a bar and hear a band, but she has a headache. It was a difficult day at work and tomorrow is only going to be worse. Since moving into her first apartment, Cindy is trying to be very responsible so she doesn't need to rely on her parents at all. They have offered to help but there are always strings attached.

Cindy loves living on her own. Well, she does have a roommate, but it still counts. She had been eager to get out of her parents' house most of her life. Her father drinks too much and her mother is in denial. Classic alcoholic family. She is so happy to be away from all that. Now she can control when and if she sees them and she can leave when she wants. It feels like sweet freedom to her.

"Come on, Cindy," her friend Carrie pleads. "What are you, an old lady? A few drinks and you won't even feel your headache. Besides, I'm dying for you to meet my friend. You two would be perfect together."

"Let me take some Tylenol and lie down for a bit. I'll try to come later." Cindy hangs up and sighs. She appreciates her friends' efforts to fix her up, but so far, they've been way off the mark. There was Max, who lived over his mother's garage; she still did his laundry. Then there was Paul, who'd had something like fifteen jobs in the past two years. Oh, and we can't forget Artie. Poor, sweet Artie. He was "exploring" his sexuality with her and ultimately decided he was gay. Who would be next? An axe murderer? A drug addict?

Cindy's headache abates a little and she decides to meet up with her friends. *After all, I'm only having one drink and staying for an hour*, she tells herself firmly. She prides herself on her self-discipline. She arrives at the bar and her friends are thrilled to see her.

"Yay, she made it!" says Carrie. "Though I do have some bad news. My friend couldn't make it tonight. He got into some kind of trouble and is in jail or something."

"Really? What the hell kind of person were you going to set me up with? Like I haven't had enough bad experiences. Sounds like I dodged a bullet." She shakes her head in disbelief and goes to get a drink. "Never again," Cindy yells over her shoulder at her friend. But Carrie isn't listening.

Carrie turns to another of their friends and says, "Oh, Billy's not so bad. I'm still going to try and fix them up when he gets out of jail."

What kind of person does she think I am? I'm a responsible, employed, intelligent woman and she wants to set me up with someone who's been to jail? Maybe I need to get new friends. Cindy tries to calm herself by taking a few deep breaths while standing at the bar. She drinks her drink a bit faster than she realizes and is about to order another one, when she stops. She looks over at her friends. *Ugh, they are all drunk and making fools of themselves. I'm too old for this.* With this thought, Cindy sneaks out of the bar without saying good-bye. *New goal—get new friends!*

Cindy goes home to her apartment and changes into her pajamas. She makes herself some tea, turns off her phone and curls up with a good book. Eventually, she will set her alarm and go to sleep. A new day will bloom with endless possibilities.

SARAH WELLS IS A native of Pittsburgh, PA. She has been a mental health therapist for twenty-nine years and has dabbled in writing off and on for around twenty years. She co-authored two humor books in the late nineties: *Today I Will Nourish My Inner Martyr* and *Today I Will Indulge My Inner Glutton*. Sarah started taking Kung-Fu four years ago and is training for her black belt this year. This is her first published short story.

Another Catcher

Laurence Raphael Brothers

Winter of '46, all these fairyland people showed up in the world. Like they were waiting for the war to end or something. The crumby school I got sent to in Pennsylvania, the newcomers were satyrs. I didn't hate them at first. Why should I?

But in ninth grade I spent all year dreaming about a girl named Betty. I had these fantasies, like I'd protect her from some danger, and she'd be grateful and—well, you know.

Finally, I got to the point of asking her out. I was waiting for her one day after school when she went running right by me. She was eager to get where she was going, but I chased after her anyway, saying, "Hey Betty, wait up," but not so loud that she heard me.

I didn't have to follow her far because Georgi was waiting for her too. Georgi, from the other ninth grade class, stupidly handsome like they all are, naked from the waist up, just that kilt thing they wear around his waist, and furry goat legs below. Betty ran up to him and I could see she wanted to kiss him, but she didn't because there were people around, and so they just looked into each other's eyes. I'd never had anyone look at me that way, and I still haven't. It was a gut punch. So I gave up on Betty.

In tenth grade I tried out for the fencing team. Half the places were taken by satyrs, so I had to be an alternate for all the meets. Georgi was varsity in three weapons. Turns out satyrs are better athletes than humans. Better than me, anyway. By then he'd gone through Betty, Alma, and Rosamaria (I was keeping track), but they were pals afterward somehow, and I still didn't have a girlfriend.

Now I'm in twelfth grade, and my phony history teacher is going on about classical Greek and how we should find satyrs to teach us and all the girls have these sly smiles on their faces. Georgi is going to be valedictorian when we graduate, and my grades, well—they kinda suck. There's a big fencing meet in Manhattan coming up soon, and I'm not even going to be on the bus.

But I've finally had enough. I'm waiting for Georgi after school this time. The satyrs aren't all that big, I'm taller than him now, and heavier, too. There he is, laughing with yet another pretty girl.

I tap him on the shoulder.

"Hey, Holden." I'm surprised he even knows my name.

"Come on," I tell him.

"Where?"

"Just come on."

"But Jane—"

"Tell Jane another time."

He sees I'm serious, so he apologizes to the girl. I lead Georgi around back of the practice field.

"What's this about?"

"Come on," I tell him. "Let's do it."

"Holden," he says, "are you kidding or what? I was wondering…"

"What?" I'm confused.

"The way you're always looking at me," he says. "I thought you might… be interested, you know? But you humans can be touchy about that kind of thing, so I never asked."

I recoil. This isn't how it's supposed to go. I know I'm supposed to be disgusted but really I'm just ashamed. That's what makes me angry in the end, how much I hate myself for not even being able to pull this off like I planned.

"No," I say, "not that! I don't want—" I can't even finish what I was going to say.

Georgi looks puzzled. "Why did you bring me out here, then?"

I don't want to explain. I just want to hit him. That's what I'm telling myself when I raise my fists. When I sucker-punch him in the belly. It's like hitting a tree. He grunts a little, that's it.

"Holden? What are you doing?"

I try a roundhouse swing for his chin, but he dodges it.

"Fight me, damn you," I say, and—

I'm lying on the ground, and he's kneeling next to me, eyes wide.

"Are you okay?"

I sit up. My jaw aches, and so does the back of my head. As I try to stand, he has to hold me up until I get my strength back.

"Did you hit me?"

"I'm sorry. I shouldn't have. It's just—"

And suddenly, epiphany. I understand what I've been doing.

"It's just that I made you," I say. "Not your fault. It's mine. It's all my fault."

"What are you talking about?"

I tell him everything, starting with Betty.

"Oh, Holden," he says. "You're one mixed-up kid."

He's right. I just nod because I feel like if I answer maybe I'll start crying.

"Listen," says Georgi, "I'm sorry if it seemed like I was coming on to you."

"It's okay," I say, surprising myself. I'm realizing I'd been secretly worried I might be queer for him. I get it now, though; at long last, I get it. Georgi's not my type, but I know I have to change if I ever want to be *anyone's* type myself. I hold out my hand and we shake. Georgi grins, and just like that we're friends. He's so damn kind and good-natured, I want to call it phony, but I know it's not. He's just like that. And now that I think about it, I wonder why I'm not that way myself. People would sure as hell like me better.

I have a weird feeling now. Like I just headed off something really bad that would have happened to me, like I would have grown more and more bitter and fed up till at last— Yeah. I'm actually lucky I ran into Georgi, aren't I? And now I'm wondering if other satyrs, other fairy people, if they're making a difference to other people, too. Maybe they are. But all I know is I got another chance, and I'm not going to blow it this time.

❋ ❋ ❋ ❋ ❋

LAURENCE RAPHAEL BROTHERS IS a writer and a technologist with five patents and a background in AI and Internet R&D. His short stories have appeared in such magazines as *Nature*, PodCastle, the *New Haven Review*, and *Galaxy's Edge*. His romantic noir urban fantasy novella "The Demons of Wall Street" was recently published and its sequel "The Demons of the Square Mile" will be out soon. Follow him on twitter: @lbrothers or visit https://laurencebrothers.com/bibliography for more stories that can be read or listened to online. Pronouns: he/him.

Gateway

D. L. R. Frase

Holgersson glanced to the port. Although the shuttle cabin was designed to resemble an airliner, he knew the vacuum of *space* loomed beyond that thin barrier. Curiosity drew his attention, but his fragile composure dissolved when a slow roll brought Earth into view.

Earth should have been beautiful, would have, but for the fact that he was hundreds of kilometers *above* it. Flying had always been difficult for him, and this was far worse. Here he was: Flying for the holidays, not to be with friends and family but bound for a destination hundreds of thousands of kilometers from anything he knew. He clenched his eyes shut in an effort to stem the onslaught of vertigo and the nausea it brought.

Retching in spite of his empty stomach, Holgersson fought the unpleasant sensation. With altruism in mind, how could he let mere physical discomfort sway him so soon?

Earth was worn out; denying that was no longer possible. Although the past had always fascinated him, overlooking the present was becoming increasingly difficult. Holgersson had finally realized something must be done to ensure the future.

Little had he imagined his own role in that process, yet here he was. The forces had been set in motion, and now forces and motion were the problem: Holgersson's queasiness increased as he felt the shuttle turning toward the moon.

Instinct forced his eyes open. Even with a frantic search, he saw nothing stable to refute the conflicting information from his muscles. Sea-sickness, airsickness, space sickness—all the same; only stars were visible, aggravating the problem.

Earth and the Station slipped away and disappeared in seconds. The slight throb as the rocket motors sent the shuttle speeding toward its lunar destination would soon end, and the remainder of the trip would be freefall.

Spending a day on the Station with its rotational excuse for gravity had supposedly acclimated Holgersson for the lunar one-sixth G he would soon experience—his orientation had said so. Ha! Whose brilliant idea was *that*? Probably a physiologist who would never be anywhere near either the Station *or* the moon.

The engines shut down as he snorted a complementary derision toward all the other scientists in the world—in the entire *universe*—who look down their collective noses at archeologists. The past is no less important than whatever discipline *they* study; that old adage about repeating mistakes has been shown true time and time again. Possibly vindicating archeologists had been a factor in accepting this assignment.

Holgersson's tortured insides enjoyed weightlessness even less than the Station's "gravity." Perhaps knowing more about the negative aspects of the mission, many of which were still unknown, would have swayed his decision, but he smiled at the thought of an ancient proverb his mother had related many years ago. The modern translation would be something like this: Anything worth having is worth sacrifice.

Even if he wanted to quit, only physical or mental collapse could accomplish that now, options he refused to consider. He *must* become accustomed to the unpleasant sensations at any cost. Holgersson sighed. *Freefall,* he thought; *nothing is ever free.*

With no other scenery available, he swallowed a huge lump in his throat and glanced to the port again. The view lacked apparent motion, not much different from the starry nights he remembered as a boy, far from city lights and hazy air. He had braved the cold nights to search the sky for constellations in those days and tried to decide if they *really* looked anything like what the ancients had named them. Perhaps he should try to find some familiar stars now; he would make an effort to enjoy whatever part of the trip he could.

Aside from the crew, Holgersson was the only passenger on board, and that was fine with him. He preferred solitude to the obnoxious people invariably having the next seat when he was forced to fly. Since this was an unscheduled flight, only a load of cargo was sharing it.

Yawning as he stared into space, he was becoming almost comfortable with freefall. The cabin lights were low—no doubt a deliberate effort to induce sleep. He finally nodded off, succumbing to the combination of both boredom and sleep deprivation from the whirlwind preparations for the trip.

DISORIENTED, HOLGERSSON JERKED AWAKE; his body was straining against the straps. If they were braking to match velocities with the Lunar Orbiter, he was surprised to have slept through most of the journey, a feat difficult to imagine.

A burst from the maneuvering thrusters drew his attention to the port as the Orbiter came into view. Holgersson ticked off the facts he had learned during his orientation: The Orbiter is little more than an unmanned transfer point. Without special instructions otherwise, the shuttle crew would offload cargo and pick up whatever was awaiting transport. The Orbiter would then be abandoned until the next flight.

Gazing upward through the port, Holgersson was amazed to feel only limited discomfort. Rather than jeopardize the situation by analyzing it, he decided to accept his good fortune and take in the view: The shuttle was drifting toward the Orbiter's docking ring. A computer had controlled most of the flight, but now human skills would add the finishing touches.

Numerous tiny bursts from the maneuvering thrusters refined the approach until they seemed to hang in space mere centimeters from rendezvous. Holgersson released an expectant breath when the docking ring sealed into place. Was that a slight jolt, or had he only imagined it? *This guy's good,* he thought.

He waited. Preflight instructions had been quite clear: The crew would be occupied during and immediately after docking. Barring medical emergencies, passengers were low priority at that time—with no regard for how important they might believe themselves to be. He chuckled. *Someone* must think he was pretty important, or he wouldn't be out here on Christmas Eve with such short notice and no clear idea why.

The cabin door opened, and a crewmember entered: a woman Holgersson judged to be mid-twenties, as he noted her infectious smile and that she somehow made a pressure suit look attractive. The Orbiter's spin induced enough pseudo-gravity to make the floor somewhat useful, and she beamed brightly while making her way down the aisle toward his seat. "We're ready for you to disembark now, Dr. Holgersson."

Holgersson wondered if the pilot whose skills he had admired could be so young, but he regretted having equated "pilot" and "male," so he decided not to ask. Anxious to unfold himself from the confining seat, he shed his straps and retrieved the helmet tethered at his side. He mirrored her smile as he rose to tower over her, although the cabin wouldn't allow him to attain his full height of two meters plus change.

"My, my; you certainly *are* a big one. Let's get you out of here before that shock of red hair dents the ceiling. This way, please." She beckoned for him to follow while turning to lead the way toward the airlock.

She studied the display a moment and punched a button before turning his way. "We're securely docked, so you can carry your helmet. Maybe I'll see you again on your return trip. Have a nice stay until then." The smile was as bright as ever.

"Thanks." Holgersson focused on not launching himself upward in the low gravity as he mounted the rungs, but he couldn't help wondering if her behavior had been real or only a canned presentation for space-weary travelers.

When the inner door slid open, Holgersson pulled himself into the Orbiter. He stretched and released a heartfelt sigh while side-stepping away from the airlock door.

A sudden chuckle disturbed his moment of relief. "Don't get too fond of all that headroom; you'll hate the lander. I'm surprised they found a suit big enough for you. Spaceflight just wasn't made for someone your size."

Holgersson turned toward the source and began an almost clinical scrutiny. The man was shorter than the woman on the shuttle, no doubt older, and almost totally bald. He was well wider with a smile lacking her exuberance. The only thing he did for his pressure suit was make sure it was *full*.

The man thrust a hand toward Holgersson and continued, "Welcome aboard, Dr. Holgersson...uhh—Franz. This is our pilot, Kirk Mitchell, and I'm the site director, Nick Valentine. You can call me 'Stump' like everybody else does, for obvious reasons, without hurting my feelings. I learned to accept genetics a long time ago."

Holgersson accepted the handshake with a nodding smile before turning to offer his hand toward Mitchell.

Mitchell was a head taller than Valentine but still well shorter than Holgersson. He took the hand in both his own and pumped vigorously. "Stump's a 'Doc,' too, but I'm just the bus driver. Ain't no starships hereabouts, and I got no fancy sheepskin like y'all, but if it flies, rolls, or crawls, I'll make it jump through hoops. *Yee-ha!*"

Holgersson was at a loss after such a self-introduction, but Valentine cleared his throat and continued, "Even though Kirk may seem a little *wacky* at times, don't worry about it: He has the most capable hands in the universe. The shuttle crew gave us your gear, and it's already stowed aboard the lander, so let's go down and get you set up while they take care of the rest of the cargo." He motioned them ahead.

Holgersson retrieved his hand, gave Valentine a nod, and aimed a surreptitious glance toward Mitchell. "I'll keep that in mind."

Mitchell shrugged and took the lead. Holgersson followed, with the director close on his heels.

Using Mitchell's expertise as an example, Holgersson kicked off and was surprised as he learned the one-handed technique of gliding from handhold to handhold while carrying the helmet in his other hand. Gravity in the Orbiter core was almost nonexistent, and they crossed in short order to an identical airlock where he assumed the lander was docked.

Holgersson watched as Mitchell tucked his legs and spun to make a light landing on the wall opposite the one where they had started, and he drew a breath before making his best effort to match the maneuver. Not a bad attempt, but he had no time for self-satisfaction before the director arrived nearby and resumed talking.

"With the extra room, buttoning up here is easier than on board the lander. I assume you've been trained?"

Holgersson nodded before struggling to recall his crash course as all three locked their helmets in place and activated their environmental units. Mitchell verified Holgersson's job, then switched his radio on and selected the correct channel.

"Go any time you're ready, Kirk," Valentine went on. "We'll follow you through."

Mitchell disappeared into what seemed to be the floor while they waited for the lock to cycle and reopen. By the time they entered the lander, he had taken his place and was powering up. "Better shake a leg; we're coming up on two minutes."

Valentine ushered Holgersson to a seat. "Get strapped in, Franz; if Kirk casts off in time, we can drop straight to the base and save the fuel needed to maneuver toward it. That's important when fuel has to be ferried in." He slipped into another seat and busied himself with the harness.

Valentine looked up and continued his PR pitch. "With eight other bases scattered around the lunar surface, we all take advantage of the Orbiter's trajectory when scheduling flights. We could burn fuel indiscriminately, but somebody would be held accountable at the end of the month. This isn't exactly a tourist ranch; mining has to support the entire operation."

Holgersson could only admire Mitchell's skill as they spiraled down and settled onto the landing pad with almost no impact and only two short bursts for braking.

Mitchell powered down and cast his belts aside with a flourish. "That's all, folks. All ashore that's going ashore."

Valentine reached for his own belts. "Grab his bag and go ahead out, Kirk." He unstrapped while Mitchell retrieved the bag from a nearby storage locker and disappeared into the airlock.

Holgersson turned his attention to releasing the five-point harness as the airlock pumps whined. He had discovered how *tiny* the lander's airlock was when they entered; getting the three of them through simultaneously, even without his gear, would have been impossible. He rose and followed the director inside when the cycle completed. "I assume you have some kind of cargo bay for large equipment."

Valentine brushed off the question and resumed his textbook-sounding oration as the outer door opened. "That's right. You may be tempted to look at the sun, but *don't*. Your visor is filtered, but, with no atmosphere to block UV, the sun is pretty intense; don't push your luck. Keep your back to the sun whenever possible."

Holgersson was startled by the austere brilliance as he stepped out. "I thought this was the 'dark side' of the moon." He realized too late his com link was active.

Mitchell's partially-muffled guffaw was quicker, but Valentine continued in his best academic tones, "I'm not sure just when people started confusing 'back side' and 'dark side,' but the term stuck. The moon *is* in orbital lock, however, so everything here gets an equal dose of sunlight: days and nights are each two weeks long. Having one side always turned toward Earth merely confuses the issue."

Holgersson sounded, and felt, very much smaller than his actual size as he responded, "I never really thought about it before. You must think I'm pretty stupid."

"Nah. You're a geek maybe, but certainly not stupid. We have our share of geeks here." Valentine added a friendly punch to Holgersson's shoulder, and the lack of customary gravity sent him lurching off like a drunken kangaroo in an effort to catch his balance. Mitchell's laughter was no longer restrained.

Holgersson regained his footing but struggled with the puny gravity to stagger back toward the others. "You don't know how much better I feel knowing that."

"We're all one big happy family up here, Franz; you'll fit in just fine… geek or not." The director's tone conveyed a grin his visor hid. "Let's go meet some of that family. Uh—maybe you should keep carrying that bag, Kirk; I don't think he can quite 'walk the walk' just yet."

Holgersson split his attention between adjusting his gait to compensate for the low gravity and eyeing the base. He had envisioned domes scattered like soap bubbles on the lunar surface, but they were headed toward a formation of short rocky peaks. Except for the obvious airlock door, the structure looked like a full-sized mountain range seen from afar.

Again, Valentine broke into his thoughts. "I'd guess the place isn't what you expected. Plenty of potential nearby, so we figure on staying for a while. We carved our base from the rock and got some ore in the process. An airtight barrier with a layer of foam insulation is inside those rocks, and a second airtight barrier inside that. We've got all the comforts of home except windows, bugs, and excess room; you'll get used to it."

Mitchell had activated the airlock, and it opened as Valentine finished his spiel. They all fit inside with ease during the reverse cycle. Holgersson couldn't resist the urge to reply, "I'm hoping I won't have that much time here…"

When the inner door opened, Holgersson was quick to follow as the others doffed their helmets. He glanced around at the Christmas decorations draped from walls and ceiling.

Mitchell drew an exaggerated noisy breath and expelled a slow sigh. "Ahh...nothing like the smell of the freshly-recycled air of home after breathing *canned* recycled air."

Valentine shook his head and introduced the three crewmen on duty in the control room while explaining that a mining team was out and the rest were sleeping. He sent Mitchell to show Holgersson his quarters and stow his gear; they would be going out to the "dig" as soon as he had officially checked in and Holgersson was ready.

❋ ❋ ❋

HOLGERSSON HAD NO DESIRE to be treated like a tourist, but Valentine seemed to have only one mode of operation; he resumed his monologue when they left a short while later. "The rovers are battery-powered with solar charging panels; we only have to worry about conserving power at night. As a matter of fact, while you were stowing your gear, I arranged to have some of that cargo you shared your ride with picked up at the Orbiter by another crew and relayed here via rover. Doing each other favors like that is a way of life around here."

They had approached one of the rovers during this speech, and Holgersson gave it the once-over. He was forced to think of the device as a daddy longlegs with wheels; nothing else seemed reasonable.

"Betcha ten bucks you want to call that some kind of mechanical spider," Mitchell said. "I'd even give odds."

Holgersson shook his head before realizing the reflective coating on his faceplate hid the response. "No deal; what else could you call something like that?"

Valentine broke in. "The designers apparently decided this was best, and it works pretty well with the type of terrain we have and the loads we carry, so we're stuck with it. Mount up, at any rate."

He indicated which seat Holgersson should take and went on while they were settling in, "Watch your helmet when the canopy closes, Franz; I'm not sure if you'll be able to sit up in here. We could seal up and take our helmets off after the rover's pressurized, but a trip this short hardly makes going to that effort worthwhile. We just close the canopy to keep maintenance happy by not banging it around on bumps."

Holgersson scrunched down, an action long since perfected with compact cars, and watched the dome closing like a clamshell. *Wow! How can anybody talk so much?* he thought. *He must turn in some incredibly detailed reports.* When the canopy was fully closed and Mitchell pulled away, he discovered Valentine had placed him as close to the center as possible; he was able to sit up with only a minor slouch.

Valentine continued his relentless monologue: "We're surrounded by the broken rim of a wide but shallow crater. These miniature mountains are loaded with mining potential. That's our destination just ahead."

Holgersson savored the brief silence as they turned their attention toward the peaks Valentine had indicated and Mitchell skirted around to the other side. When they passed the formation and swung back toward it, what appeared to be the mouth of a tunnel was staring at them. Holgersson guessed it was about four meters tall and as close to a perfect circle as he was likely to come across; obviously artificial. "You cut that for a mine entrance?"

The silence stretched to uncharacteristic thinness before Valentine's terse reply: "No."

More silence. This didn't seem like Valentine at all. At last, Holgersson frowned. "Well?"

Valentine shrugged, a difficult enough maneuver while strapped in and seated inside the constraints of his pressure suit. "We were prospecting and stumbled across it."

Conversation came to a full halt while the trio waited for the canopy to pivot up before they could climb down.

As they approached, Holgersson gave the entrance a careful scrutiny. "You figure out how old this is?"

Valentine's speech seemed to have lost most of its previous gusto. "Five, maybe ten million years."

"Humph…interesting, possibly Pliocene, and hardly likely to produce an artifact here." Holgersson was almost musing out loud. He turned back toward Valentine. "You couldn't narrow it down closer than that?"

"That cave has some kind of *extreme* power source. It's shielded so we can't pick it up out here, but it screws up instruments inside. Dating removed samples was questionable."

"Oh? Exactly what does '*extreme*' mean?"

Valentine sighed. His uncharacteristic hesitancy was even more profound. "We'd measure something this potent in *megatons,* if we could find it, that is. Let's say: Big enough to split this rock in half and probably add some color to Saturn's rings in the process."

Holgersson wanted to scratch his head. The best he could do was spread his hands. "So, what am *I* supposed to do with something like that?"

"Well, we were hoping you could find it for us…"

Holgersson was becoming more confused by the second. "*Me?* I'm as far as you could get from being a nuclear physicist. It's amazing I decided to come up here at all with what I've been told so far, but they seemed to think getting me here was pretty important. So I'm here now; how's about a little more to go on?"

"Maybe you should just go see for yourself."

Mitchell had already entered the tunnel. By the time the others arrived, the portable lights were on, and he stepped aside.

Holgersson cared little that his gasp would be audible over his com link—or his quick comment: "Holy shit!"

Mitchell responded with a snicker, "Couldn't have put it better myself, Doc."

Holgersson drew a deep breath and released a heavy sigh. "What's that thing made of?"

Valentine slipped back into his lecturer role. "Platinum-iridium with some titanium and traces of a few other exotics; whoever made it intended for it to last a long time."

"The information I was given was sketchy, but now I can see why you asked for me."

"Yep, I was told you're the best there is."

Holgersson ignored the compliment as he approached the one-meter-square plaque and extended his hand toward it. He brushed his gloved fingers across the bright rune-covered surface, wishing he could actually touch the glyphs.

Valentine seemed to have a knack for destroying such moments. "I don't want to seem pushy, but we're under a lot of pressure from higher up, which is why your orientation was so abbreviated. Can you decipher that or not?"

Holgersson withdrew his hand with a sigh of resignation and stepped back. "These aren't Nordic runes, but they are quite similar. The plaque contains a veritable mountain of information, possibly enough to establish some rudimentary structure and get a pretty good idea, but I'll need time to wade through it all. How do I accomplish that?"

"We tried removing the plaque, but it seems to be an integral part of that wall—which is something artificial and we have no idea what it is. The hidden power source worried us when it comes to banging around in here, so we decided to leave it be. The radiation made it tough, but we figured out how to get pictures—*lots* of pictures. I guessed you'd want a first-hand look, but those pictures are the best we can do for extended study."

"Yes, that should work…but many thanks for the preview."

"Okay then; we may as well head home so you can get started."

Holgersson took a reluctant final look at a work of art that was an archeological enigma. He turned away as Mitchell switched off the lights and followed them out.

❉ ❉ ❉

TRAVELING SO FAR IN such a short time had destroyed his internal clock, so the endless hours Holgersson spent poring over photos and reference books while producing endless notes and sketches passed by almost unnoticed. They seemed of little consequence, but the strain was taking its toll. He refused to admit that days filled with caffeine and carbohydrates in lieu of rest and *real* food were pushing him to his limit.

Bleary-eyed, disheveled, and haggard, Holgersson stumbled into the mess with his stained cup clutched in his fingers. His timing was accidentally superb; a number of crewmembers, Mitchell and Valentine among them, were enjoying breakfast. He collapsed into a seat at their table. "I finally got it."

"That's great!" Valentine pried the cup loose and handed it to Mitchell. He went on as Mitchell scurried away, "With the hours you've been keeping, you no doubt haven't noticed our excellent dining facilities and superb chef, but now that you're here at the right time, I'll see that you do. First you'll have a nice big breakfast full of fat, protein, vitamins, and minerals just like Mama used to make—but no coffee. You'll hit the sack next, and everyone has orders to shoot on sight until I say otherwise. *Then* we'll go back out there."

Mitchell returned before Holgersson could respond and handed over a tray with a plate filled with scrambled eggs and sausage and a second plate loaded with biscuits and gravy. Barely enough room was left for the steaming mug of hot chocolate.

"You can tell us what you discovered while you're choking down every last bite on that tray, or I'll find *some other way* to get that stuff inside you. Etiquette be damned!"

After considering Valentine's expression in silence, Holgersson shrugged and sampled a bite. He raised an eyebrow while realizing he was famished. How long had it been since he'd had any decent food? What did it matter? Valentine had been correct: Their chef was indeed excellent, and this was a fine example of his craft.

Holgersson pointed to his watch. "I've lost track of time, but this tells me that it's New Year's Eve back home. I should be getting ready to have a nice dinner with friends and family. Although this isn't exactly traditional fare and not dinner, it will certainly suffice…if you'll permit me to count you among my friends. And so I bid you *Gott Nytt Ar.*"

Valentine smiled. "I told you we were all one big happy family up here; of course we're your friends. Enjoy your meal, but what did you just say?"

"Oh…I just wished you a Happy New Year." Holgersson turned his full attention to breakfast then, only pausing from time to time while relating his findings: "The tablet is loaded with information having no apparent purpose other than providing a basis to translate the actual text. Whoever wrote that knew exactly what it would take for someone to understand it. I could never have done it otherwise. As a matter of fact, I almost feel Nordic runes were *derived* from these, but that's neither here nor there. The tablet says, 'Here lies the way; follow when you are ready.' A number sequence describing the order to press certain runes is next, probably having something to do with that power source of yours."

Mitchell grinned and reached over to deliver a brotherly nudge to Holgersson's shoulder. "You did good, Doc—*real* good."

Valentine nodded. "That you did, Franz, but you've been driving yourself like a man possessed to accomplish it. That thing has been there for millions of years and won't be going anywhere in the next few hours; you've done a heck of a job and have no reason to cave in now." The authority in his voice had softened and was tempered by genuine concern. "Finish your breakfast and get some well-deserved rest; we'll go back later…"

        ❊ ❊ ❊

HOLGERSSON REACHED TOWARD THE plaque but hesitated. He glanced from it to Valentine. "What if this sequence sets off your *super-bomb*?"

Valentine shrugged. "Think about it: If you don't punch in the code, we'll never know. If you do, we'll follow them to oblivion—or wherever else they may have gone. If it's the former, *no one* will ever know. So you may as well go for it."

Holgersson shook his head. Valentine's logic was warped but irrefutable. Holgersson drew a deep breath and began pressing runes without hesitation.

Although he had finally developed his "moon legs," a wave of vertigo washed across him. He reached to the wall for support and realized a sizeable chunk had vanished.

Mitchell spoke up first. "What was that, a quake? Whoa! Check *that* out." He was pointing into a second tunnel.

Valentine released a huge sigh as if he had been holding his breath. "It isn't oblivion…at least, not yet. Well, Franz, you got what it takes to step in there?"

Mitchell intervened before Holgersson could reply. "Step aside, gents; *somebody* has to walk into the jaws of doom first." He disappeared into the opening.

"No! Wait!" Valentine was too late. Without even moving the lights to investigate, Mitchell was gone. "Oh well, I wouldn't be here if I weren't an explorer." He sighed and stepped through, leaving Holgersson little choice but to follow.

No words can fully describe how it feels to be *somewhere* one instant and *somewhere else* the next. How was it done? Disassemble the molecules and reassemble them elsewhere? Holgersson had no idea, but two facts remained: The increased gravity meant he was no longer on the moon, and he didn't care for the sensation of arriving wherever he now was.

Holgersson was shaken but decided he was still in one piece and functional before looking to his companions. Valentine was leaning forward with hands on knees as if he had just completed a 10K run; the transition apparently hadn't agreed with him, either. Mitchell was fiddling with an instrument he'd brought along.

"Damn!" Holgersson jumped as Mitchell's overloud expletive produced a burst of distortion in his headset. "Gotta get this helmet off!"

Valentine looked up. "No! Don't—"

He was too late again. Mitchell almost yanked the helmet away and drew a few rapid breaths before dropping to his knees and bending down to kiss the ground with elaborate, exaggerated ceremony. He sat back and concluded, "Whatever *that* was, I'm glad to be *anywhere* and still breathing after the trip."

Valentine sighed. "Yeah, I'm sure we all feel the same way about that, but you could have been a little more cautious about the air."

"See for yourself; it's fine." Mitchell rose and offered the device while drawing another deep breath. "The only problem is too much oxygen and no pollution; this is the sweetest-smelling air I've ever had the distinct pleasure to breathe."

Valentine checked the display and shrugged; Mitchell was still alive and breathing. He removed his own helmet, took a tentative breath, and signaled Holgersson to do likewise. "Well, Franz, where do you suppose we are?"

"Looks like a temple to me; if you mean 'where's the temple?' I haven't a clue, but I'd guess that's the way out." He gestured toward the apparent exit and started toward it.

The others fell in behind; *not* going wherever the doorway led was pointless, and any attempt at caution now seemed irrelevant.

Holgersson stepped into a lush garden bathed in warm early-afternoon sunlight. He turned back to view what could have been a perfectly preserved Roman Pantheon before refocusing his attention on the garden's centerpiece: a tall statue of polished white stone standing upon a stone dais. The figure was very much like an ancient Greek or Roman, but the features showed subtle differences; something seemed oddly familiar about it.

Mitchell had continued toward the statue and was rubbing his chin as he looked it over. "You know what, Doc? This thing kinda looks like you."

"What?" He took a closer look. Mitchell was right. The statue did have a distinct Nordic appearance. That's what seemed so familiar about it. Unable to resist, Holgersson approached with an outstretched hand.

The surge of power he felt through his glove took him by surprise. He snatched his hand away and stumbled back as the air began to shimmer. His vision blurred, and when the strange aura faded, the statue had been replaced by a living creature clad in flowing robes stirred by a gentle breeze not there a moment before.

The creature looked down at him and smiled. *After all these millennia, you come.* The strange voice wasn't a voice but a gentle intrusion into his mind: the sough of waves lapping a sun-drenched shore and the caress of butterfly wings rolled into one, yet the meaning was crystal clear. *We have remained here and held this place in stasis for ages in hopes of this day.*

Ages before, when we were young and brash but nevertheless powerful, we chanced upon your world in its embryonic stages. We committed a senseless fatal blunder and destroyed what would have been. Chagrined, we rebuilt what was possible and replaced what could not be rebuilt with traces of our own genetic material.

We prepared this place and left the path in hopes that you would one day follow. Eons ago, we matured enough to leave this plane of existence, but our penance was not yet complete. The potential fate of a damaged world can never be known for certain, yet it fills our hearts with joy and pride to see our progeny arrive here.

This world, fresh and unspoiled, filled with natural resources and teeming with ecological riches, is our gift to you. Use it well; we can offer no better.

As the flood of ideas ceased, the being stepped down to kneel with head bowed before Holgersson and continued, *We beg for absolution, Our Children. We have done whatever is in our power to emend this grave wrong. We can offer no more, and we deserve much less, but we seek redemption from those most wronged.*

Holgersson was stunned, deeply touched by such sincerity. He seemed to be watching someone else as he raised his hand and spread it across the being's pate. "You are forgiven—Our Fathers." He drew a deep breath and added as an afterthought, "Go…and sin no more." It somehow seemed appropriate.

He felt an incredible sense of peace flowing into his fingers as the being looked up with eyes glistening. *Thank you, Our Children. Heed the warning of our failure. With your pardon at last and hopeful that you will follow again one day, we go now to a better place.*

Holgersson withdrew his hand as the being rose, bowed, and stepped backward onto the dais. The shimmer returned as it dissolved into a swirling maelstrom of tiny bits of light, a churning firefly tornado that erupted upward to vanish. He'd heard no sound, but the resulting void *felt* like total silence.

Valentine approached the empty dais and looked up. "Did we just witness an entire *race* going to 'the promised land'?"

Holgersson looked up as well. "So, you 'heard' that, too. Yeah...I suppose you could put it that way."

"I doubt you have the authority to speak for *our* race, but I won't gainsay a pardon that moving; they seemed pretty darn sincere and deserving of forgiveness."

"Speaking of our race, what do you think about the logistics of getting everyone with enough pioneering spirit to take on a new world, through that portal?"

Valentine shrugged. "I'm not sure; knowing what we've done to one planet, do they really deserve a shot at another one?"

"Maybe *we've* learned from the past, too. A new year might be a good time to start a new life." Holgersson pointed upward. "We at least owe it to *them* to try, don't you think?"

Valentine's eyes followed the gesture before he looked back down and glanced around. He nodded. "You could be right. I'll start working on it."

❈ ❈ ❈ ❈ ❈

I'M EMPLOYED AS AN Electronic Technician by the US Air Force. Originally Buckeyes, my wife, Linda, and I moved to Georgia several years ago when the base where I was working was closed. Midnight, our black cat, grudgingly permits us to share her house. (No, she doesn't have a fiddle.) I've been in the Reverse Engineering Department at Robins AFB for the past fifteen years or so. We figure out how to maintain otherwise unsustainable avionics in order to do our part in keeping the fleet airborne. Although I enjoy my work and it is quite rewarding, I'm beginning to look ahead to a day when I might be able to devote more time to reading and writing fantasy and SF. (Of course, my fly rod is due for a dusting-off in the process.)

Esther

Fran Macilvey

"So, *my dear*, you want to stay, do you?" The unpleasant, oily tone said more than the words, and the sneer left no room for doubt. Esther Alambe was unwelcome.

"I have fled from my home because…"

Her words came slowly, one at a time. Not only was she unused to speaking the English she had learnt at school, but having a conversation, understanding what the man was saying, considering a reply, all took time. And there was the question of why. Why had she run away, concealing only her identity papers in her cleavage and disappearing into the night wearing her thin, evening clothes and light sandals?

"I was soon to be married and, well, in my culture, it is often that a woman is—" Unsure how to reveal what was so very private, she whispered to the woman sitting next to her, "Do I have to tell him, now?"

The quiet nod was enough, and Esther's hopes sank, just when she needed her courage most.

"In my village it is the custom to cut her before she is married!" She spoke more loudly than she intended, her cheeks flaring with embarrassment.

"All right, all right, no need to shout. Keep yer hair on. In your country…" There was a pause while the gentleman shuffled through a thin dossier that was at his right elbow. "In your country, it is illegal to cut a woman, according to your penal code. Is that not so?"

"I suppose it may be, but…"

"Well then, there was no reason to leave, was there?" The man shut the file and sat back, lacing his hands over his stomach.

"Yes, but you see, where I live, in my village, all the girls are cut before they marry. It is the custom and I cannot go against it. I am just a daughter. I saw what happened to my sisters. My two older sisters died soon after, from so much bleeding, there was so much blood on their clothes, on the bed. My uncle was negotiating for my marriage and the man who was to marry me was insisting that I should be cut, you see."

"You could just have refused, or run away to the city?"

It seemed obvious when he spoke like that, so that Esther was silenced. She could feel the woman beside her urging her to speak, because silence now might be taken for agreement, and that might signal capitulation. But Esther looked at the man before her and understood. He was pale, too broad around the stomach. His legs looked thin and his hair was thin too, from lack of exercise, from sitting at the desk all day, shuffling papers to one side and then the other. Bizarrely, she felt sorry for him and for his glib cruelty, his deliberate unkindness. He did not want to understand, and everything she managed to tell him would be twisted around the wrong way.

But why, she wondered, why the hostility? What had she done to deserve such stupidity? Was it because she was a woman, a black woman? A black woman from Africa who did not have any rights? *I do not fit here,* she thought.

"They would have found me and taken me home again. If I had run away to Accra they would have found me, reported me missing or— something like that. Afterwards they would always be looking for me. In our families everyone can find out. It is the way."

"Well, our way is a bit different, I think you will find."

Shifting uncomfortably in his seat, her questioner wanted Esther to leave. "Is there anything you would like to add to your statement before the end of our interview?"

"I miss my country and my family. I would not have fled at night unless I was very frightened. Cutting and bleeding and such pain would have brought only sorrow to me. But, in our culture, because I am a woman, whatever I could do would bring pain. It is the way."

He eyed her speculatively, as if wondering what to say next. "Well, you see my dear, your country's penal code makes it clear that cutting is illegal and anyone involved in it can expect to go to prison." He spoke the last words with deliberate slowness. "We accept that your government has a policy against it. So *officially,* there is little we can do, see? If the law was different, it would be easier…"

"But women live in the villages, with their fathers, husbands…even going to school is difficult. Unless our fathers protect us, we will be given in marriage…" *Like cattle,* she thought. "My father died."

Esther sat back, exhausted with emotion and memories. "Have you seen a woman being cut?" she asked, unexpectedly impatient. "They tie a little girl to a table, or they hold her down, two up top and two below, so that she does not move. They take an old knife, and they cut away all her private parts. Just like that. No stopping for the screams, or mercy. She is stitched up with a needle and thread and wrapped and left to heal all alone. That is what they call 'cutting'. Make it polite so that no one knows what happens." Esther's eyes sparkled defiance as she waited for him to close the file.

But he looked up, straight into her eyes, and she saw new respect. So, he was a bully, he liked women to talk back, eh? Esther was glad she had spoken out.

"I hope you wrote that down, what I said?" she asked, more politely.

The woman clutching a shorthand notebook beside her nodded sharply, her mouth set in a grim line.

"I'll defer a decision on your case. Meantime, see if you can rustle up some representation."

Esther nodded. She saved the small, grim smile until her back was turned. She had not been cut. She had escaped. Now, for now, there was a small window of light, a breath of air she might breathe. Someday, she might be safe. It was a hope she held close to her heart.

✼ ✼ ✼ ✼ ✼

FRAN IS AN AUTHOR and speaker based in Edinburgh, Scotland. The daughter of a Belgian diplomat, Fran was born in Congo in 1965 and spent eight years at boarding school, before qualifying and working as a lawyer for ten years. Her memoir, *Trapped: My Life with Cerebral Palsy* (Skyhorse, 2014, 2016) is an Amazon international bestseller for which

Fran has also written a radio play. Her second book, *Happiness Matters* and her third, *Making Miracles* explore how we can all find more fulfilment in life. Fran has also written three novels in a series about women in the law. When not writing, editing or blogging, she enjoys reading, horse-riding, singing, and dancing when no-one is watching. You can contact her at franmacilvey@fastmail.com or through her website at https://www.franmacilvey.com

Hope Jones

Susan Dutton

Once upon a time there was a young couple in southern California who were very much in love, but they were also very poor and had a difficult time making ends meet. However, they were so happy just being together that they decided they wanted a child to share this with, and lo and behold, a little girl was born to them one fine day.

They were so thankful and as a gesture, they decided to name her Hope. Her name would be Hope Jones. In those years, special names were not unusual; the world felt full of hope, particularly in southern California.

The little girl was very sweet and loved her parents dearly in her first years on this earth. With time, though, as she began to grow up, she began to not like her name. The other children at school laughed at her, saying that Hope was not a real name. She felt out of place; she wanted a new name, like Sharon or Patty or something normal. Patty Jones would be great, she thought, but she did not dare tell this to her loving parents; she kept it to herself, though this secret was difficult for her to manage.

Worse than the children's teasing, however, was the idea that somehow, hope in general was connected to her person. This caused her endless torment as to what her role in this life was to be.

Nevertheless, she continued to grow up. Other than the discomfort with her name, she followed the standard development of young girls in southern California.

At school she enjoyed learning other languages, most of all Spanish.

There were so many people who spoke it and she wanted to be able to understand them. Also, she loved Mexican food and art, with all the bright colors and festive atmosphere they followed. This also fit in with her desire to travel, and soon she also began to study German at her university, which she loved dearly. She was able to read great works of literature in the original language, finding that many words in German could not be precisely translated into English. She still was bothered by her name, but was so caught up in her studies that she didn't often dwell on it. But words were words and names were names; and this was the dilemma that followed her.

During her junior year she was able to travel to Germany with a scholarship. There she met and fell in love with a student from Iran. He did not make fun of her name, and this made her happy, to say the least. However, neither her loving parents, his loving parents, nor any of their friends approved of this relationship. They were told that it would never work out—they had different backgrounds, different religions; legal problems could come up; he was only wanting to go to California—so many objections. At the end of the year, she returned home alone.

It took her a long time to get over this situation. In fact, she did not ever fully recover from it. But since she was still young and resilient, in time things started to open up for her. She began to study Middle Eastern politics, a subject that she had grown interested in after meeting her Iranian boyfriend, fascinated by how complex the current situation there was. She was drawn to the ancient culture also. In her studies of the history of the Middle East in the contrast to the current situation, she was dumbfounded to discover that this part of the world had been virtually left outside in the cold for centuries. Hope was not able to accept this fact, so she started to think about what could be done to change this.

After completing her master's degree in political science with a thesis on the current Middle Eastern conflicts, she applied for a position in New York at the United Nations. To her delight, Hope was accepted and moved to the city. She was riding high in those days; the future seemed so positive and nearby, plus she was in the front line to do something useful and make her mark in life, even at her young age.

The UN helped her find a room to rent in Brooklyn in an apartment with two other girls who had also come to the city recently. They all shared many meals and stories about where they wanted to go and what they wanted to do in life. They also began to explore the city after work. One evening at a small jazz club, Hope met George B. Good, a musician who played the trumpet in a trio. Wham! She was enthralled. He came over to her table and said hello or something like that—she was so taken with him, she couldn't even focus on his words—and there she was, Ms. H. Jones, again smitten by the god Amore.

❀ ❀ ❀

Now, because the course of true love never is without complication, George—being a jazz musician—was African American. Hope had had very little social or professional contact with Black people. However, the thing that impressed her the most about him was his name. George B. Good sounded terrible to her—what a name, and he was not even bothered by it! In the face of this, she did not dare reveal her own problem with her name being Hope. His nonchalance about his name truly impressed her. In fact, he told her that he would have liked to be named *John* B. Good so he could be call himself Johnny Be Good, like the song by Little Richard. This was what enchanted her most of all about George.

Hope saw George fairly often, but they had little privacy in her room, and he lived with his grandmother in Queens. This, along with the fact that Hope's work was in the daytime and his was at night, meant that they did not get much time alone. In the big city, the prejudice against interracial couples wasn't as great as it was in smaller communities—at least to a degree. They were free and happy seeing one another; it felt like it was no big deal. But living together loomed over the horizon. Dating was one thing; cohabitating, much less marrying, would be quite another.

At the same time, her job was becoming more demanding. She was asked to travel with some of the delegates to conventions because of her specialization in Middle Eastern conflicts and culture, including abuse of human rights. This was a mission for her; she threw herself wholly into the task. For his part, George was very proud of her, but he began to feel left out of her mission, out of her life. They kept on postponing the question of moving in together. Inevitably, they began to drift apart, not being able to share much anymore like they had in the beginning of their relationship. His grandmother was kind, but she did not understand Hope and her ambitious career; she felt that George was being neglected.

Her parents in California had never even been able to meet him.

❀ ❀ ❀

AFTER THEIR BREAKUP, HOPE was on her own once more and open to
new horizons. She had learned so many things already during her studies,
travels, and relationships, and her world had grown substantially even
though she was still relatively young. "Now where can I go?" she wondered.

In her years at the UN, she became an important figure. However, one
day she realized that she needed to branch out and have more contact
with the real world; she needed to leave the city. She wanted to learn
about nature; she had become interested in conservation and pollution,
and for this, she needed contact with plants and the outdoors. She had
spent several vacations in the desert learning about the great outdoors,
camping in the parks and meeting nature activists at several conventions;
but now, in her desire for something different and challenging, she decided to quit her job and move to a rural town where she could see first-
hand what actually was going on for these people and the environment.
She would give lectures, write, organize conventions and projects—she
would manage to survive, somehow. Time was running out for our planet, she knew; and things needed to be changed.

After much deliberation, and to her own surprise, Hope decided to
move to Europe. The main reasons was that she thought it less materi-
alistic than the USA. Europe's socialism matched her way of thinking.
Besides, she thought it would be only for a short time; she could always
move back. She was still single and free as a bird—but where to go, how,
and when? She began to research possible choices and contacted some
of her favorite global organizations involved in conservation programs,
offering her collaboration.

Lo and behold, her choice fell upon Italy: Rome, specifically, the Food
and Agriculture Organization of the UN. But since she did not want a
desk job in the city, she joined projects in the field, bringing water to remote settlements and other initiatives like that. Best of all, no one found
her name silly here. She picked up Italian easily, learning another new
language in just a few months.

Hope had finally found her niche and was truly satisfied with her life.
Things weren't always easy, but she never gave up. Years went by, each

more interesting than the last, but one day she finally had to admit to herself that she was getting older, more fragile. Worse, this affected her work, which often was very physical. She tried to compensate, but in the end, the organization quietly but firmly suggested that she retire, so she did.

She considered returning to the States, but it was no longer home. Her parents had passed away; anyone she knew there, she had long since lost touch with. And it was expensive. So, she stayed on in Italy, moving to a small rural village in the Po Valley. She bought and fixed up a house with a big garden near a bird sanctuary, and slowly, inevitably, began withdrawing from the modern world—all its confusingly ever-changing technology; the absurd financial and political scenarios. Hope was happier keeping a very low profile, tending to her little home and garden, seeing her few friends.

HOPE HAD BEEN IN so many situations: education, human rights, interracial couples, Mexican immigrants, climate change, pollution, poverty, social unrest—yet for some reason, today she has fled to the sidelines, replaced with cynicism, greed, intolerance, and downright hate. It is still not too late to bring her back, but time is running out on many issues. Pandemic sweeps the globe; political upheavals bedevil communities the world round. Shall we not go looking for her today? There can be no future without Hope. Are we going to let this happen?

Is there room in this world for Hope?

SUSAN DUTTON IS A U.S.-born artist and writer living in Castelfranco d'Oglio, Italy. She is retired from a varied career including design and illustration consulting for music, history, and gardening publishers in New York, Italy, and Holland; cultural exchange program consultant; and sales manager for food packaging machinery with main markets in the Middle East. She speaks a half-dozen languages, has two sons, and enjoys good food and excellent wine. Find her at susandutton.com.

Puss and Jack Steal a Kingdom

Michael M. Jones

Once upon a time, there was a cat.

And that cat had a plan. A plan that would see it living in comfort for the rest of its life.

First things first, the plan called for an accomplice. A partner. (A catspaw, perhaps…)

To that end, the cat skulked around the local inns and taverns, begging for scraps from the kitchen—a humiliating practice, and one the cat planned to leave far behind someday soon—while waiting for just the right person to come along. Someone bold and brave, young and handsome, desperate and just gullible enough to take orders from a talking cat.

That's how, one fine day, the cat joined up with the penniless third son of a tailor, off to make his fortune in the world. "My name's Jack," said the son. "And if your plan to make us both rich is as good as you say, I'm all for it. I've tried it my way, and had a few setbacks as a result. So long as there aren't any giants, I'm happy."

"Congratulations. You're now the Marquis de Carabas," said the cat while grooming itself imperiously, "and within a month's time, you'll have a princess, a kingdom, and fabulous riches."

"What's the catch?" asked Jack, who was no fool.

"How do you feel about casual nudity?"

✵ ✵ ✵

ALL THE COURT WAS abuzz over the dashing young nobleman the king brought home after riding out in the countryside one day. "He was robbed by bandits! Stripped of his finery and riches, and left to die with nothing but his loyal cat for company! Why, who knows what would have happened if the king hadn't been there to save him?"

"I hear he's from the West, where his lands stretch from sunrise to sunset, and his fields grow the finest of crops!"

"He's single, too. Do you think he came to our land in search of a bride?"

"He's probably come to woo the princess."

"Good luck there. I don't think anyone's ever passed even the first of the three impossible trials she demands of her suitors. Though remember the knight who almost succeeded in scaling the glass mountain?"

"He just learned how to walk again…"

❋ ❋ ❋

WITH THE CAT'S DEXTERITY, Jack scaled the glass mountain like no one had before, and plucked the delicate white flower from its very peak, delivering it to the princess in a pot made of pure gold. (The cat did most of the work, of course, its claws finding purchase in the slick glass surface…)

With the cat's cunning, Jack successfully identified the princess out of thirteen spell-crafted duplicates. He claimed he recognized her eyes, into which he could gaze forever. (The cat was quite proud of that scripted bit of nonsense. No one needed to know that cats can see through illusions…)

With the cat's resourcefulness, Jack correctly solved a riddle whose answer was both ridiculously simple and pure nonsense. (The princess, who clearly never expected anyone to get that far, really shouldn't have written the answer down in her diary.)

With each completed task, the cat and Jack seemed that much closer to succeeding. The king had taken to calling Jack "My dear boy" as they drank and hunted and feasted together. Even the princess didn't seem quite so disgusted by the idea of marriage as before, gracing Jack with the occasional smile.

The cat kept its distance, to maintain its status as secret mastermind. There'd be plenty of time to assert its dominance once the plan had come to fruition and Jack was properly married off and had claimed his fortune.

❀ ❀ ❀

"Not the marrying type?" the cat asked Jack, aghast at this sudden deviation from the plan. "Since when?"

Jack shrugged. "Since forever. I'm too young to settle down, not with a big old world left to explore. I want adventure, not a wife."

"But our plan. The wedding. The kingdom. The princess." With each statement, the cat puffed up ever so much more, tail an indignant bottle-brush, eyes alight with angry fire.

Jack, unmoved by this display of temperament, smiled. "She doesn't want to get married either. The princess and me got it all worked out. The next time I go hunting with the king, I'll add a little something extra to his wine, which will put him into a deep, enchanted sleep. Out of respect and worry for her father, the princess will postpone the wedding. I get a nice payoff and hit the road, the princess gets to rule the land without a husband getting in the way, and we live happily ever after."

"And where do I fit in?" asked the cat.

"That's the problem, pussycat. I don't know if you've realized, but the princess is allergic to cats, so she's not going to want to keep you around." Jack shrugged. "And no offense, but I think I'm better off on my own after all."

"You ungrateful…what's to stop me from going to tell the king what you traitorous monkeys have planned for him?"

Jack gave the cat a crafty look. "You have to sleep sometime. It turns out that a lot of problems can be solved with a bag of rocks and some deep water."

The cat considered its options with varying levels of dismay and disgust. In all its careful planning, it had never planned for a partner's betrayal. It also knew when to cut its losses and move on.

The cat took its own sweet time in leaving the castle. Before it departed, it made sure to pee on all of Jack's belongings. It also shed copiously over the princess's chambers (including her bed), shredded valuable tapestries, chewed up essential documents, used the royal throne as a litterbox, and, for a final touch, knocked Jack's enchanted potion onto the floor, shattering the container and spilling the contents.

Never had one cat so thoroughly expressed so much disdain in so glorious a style.

✻ ✻ ✻

MANY DAYS LATER, IN an entirely different kingdom far down the road, the cat scoped out a different tavern, again looking for just the right partner. Someone bold and brave, young and handsome, desperate and just gullible enough to take orders from a talking cat. But maybe a little less intelligent, less ambitious, less likely to get ideas of their own.

And eventually, the cat found just what it needed, a miller's son cast forth into the world to prove his worth in some form or fashion. Though before making up its mind, the cat had one quick question.

"How do you feel about marriage?"

✻ ✻ ✻ ✻ ✻

MICHAEL M. JONES LIVES in southwest Virginia with too many books, just enough cats, and a wife who would totally help him steal a kingdom, if only they had somewhere to put it. His stories have appeared in venues such as *Unidentified Funny Objects 8*, *Mad Scientist Journal*, *Hexagon*, and *F is for Faerie*. He edited the *Scheherazade's Facade* anthology, and the forthcoming *Schoolbooks & Sorcery*. For more, visit him at www.michaelmjones.com.

The Garden

Scott Davenport

ONE

Martin Callahan sipped his coffee in silence as he stared out his back window and surveyed his wife's dead garden. It seemed appropriate the garden had died. After all, his wife, daughter, and his three-year-old grandson were all dead too.

It had only been nine months since that rainy night when the rest of the family had gone out to eat because he had to work late, only to never come home again. When the fire department arrived, the car was already fully engulfed in flames. And by the time the fire was extinguished, there wasn't enough left to even cremate. No graves. No park bench memorial. No drawer in some depressing mausoleum. There wasn't even enough left for some shitty, depressing vase on the mantel.

Weeds had invaded the garden almost immediately, and Marty was in no condition to tend to them. Truth be told, he never much cared for gardening. That was Celeste's true passion. She was always planting and tending, picking and pruning. Their nightly walk often stretched out for an extra half hour as she snipped clippings of the interesting-looking flora along their path. He often joked about how if he left a coffee cup unattended for more than ninety seconds he would come back and find a seedling planted in it.

It was annoying, really. It was one of the many ridiculous things about Celeste that used to annoy him constantly. And now, as he rattled about in the home they had shared for the last thirty years, he couldn't help but feel ashamed. He would have given anything to be annoyed just one more time.

As the sun started to peek through the window, Marty squinted and pulled on the cord to shut the blinds. He preferred the dark. The light was so jarring. So assaultive. As they slowly descended, Marty's eyes were drawn to a corner of the garden where Celeste's gardening gloves still sat. He couldn't bear to move them. Doing so would have been an admission that she was really gone. Now, it was as if Celeste had simply popped out for more tomato seeds and would be back soon. Something about seeing the gloves made him feel a little bit better.

A small plaque sat next to Celeste's gloves. Their daughter, Annette, had bought it for Celeste several years ago; it contained a quote attributed—perhaps incorrectly—to Audrey Hepburn: "To plant a garden is to believe in tomorrow."

Marty never really did understand the point of gardening. It was just another silly remnant of his wife's rural upbringing, people stashing tomatoes and jam in the garage like some inbred family from central Utah. So much work, when you could just pop down to the grocery store and pick up a jar of Newman's spaghetti sauce.

Marty smiled wistfully. Celeste's prized sauce, made from her own homegrown roma tomatoes, had always been part of their weekly ritual. Celeste always made a big family dinner after mass on Saturday night, and it always involved pasta. Marty had never really been one for church, but he found that if he went on Saturday nights, the music was better, the homilies were shorter, he got to watch football on Sundays, and he always got pasta on Saturday nights with the sauce his wife had put up the summer before.

He hadn't been back to mass since the funeral. It was just too damn hard. There were no assigned seats at St. Francis, but there might as well have been. When you turned to shake hands—or bump fists in a post-COVID world—it was always with the same familiar faces. How could he go back now and sit on the same bench by himself and have all those people stare at him with their big, stupid cow eyes? Not happening.

It really was funny how quickly all his plans had gone out the window. When their beloved daughter finally left home at the age of twenty-three, Marty and his wife had been excited about starting the next phase of their lives. They talked about selling the big house and buying a little condo on the water. They would try a new restaurant every night, drink wine in the middle of the week, and fly kites on the beach.

The dream was short-lived, however; Annette showed back up just eighteen months later, pregnant from someone whose name she did not know, needing a place to stay.

That was nearly five years ago. The condo-on-the-beach dream faded, and so did Marty's retirement plans. With two additional mouths to feed, he was going to have to keep working until he dropped dead. He was sick of being a damn ATM machine, constantly expected to spit out money.

He was convinced that his daughter named the baby Marty II (apparently Marty Junior was reserved for the child of another Marty, not a grandfather) in order to soften him up. After all, how could he say no to providing a home for "Little Marty"?

It had worked. And so, as he stood at the crossroads with more days behind him than ahead, he once again picked up the yoke and plowed forward. It was what he had always done. And in doing so, he watched his dreams of a future on the water and a happy retirement vanish before his eyes.

He had been angry, of course. Who wouldn't be? But he had suppressed those feelings, burying them deep inside. And every time he came home and had to park down the street because there were already two cars in the driveway or he stepped on a damn Lego with his bare feet, he grew more and more angry and distant.

Marty's stomach growled, bringing him back to the present. He instinctively reached down and pressed his hand on it like a pregnant mom trying to quiet a restless fetus as he got up and meandered slowly over to the Frigidaire. Inside was nothing but condiments and some leftover pizza.

There was a time after the services when his fridge had been stocked with all manner of casseroles brought over by well-meaning neighbors and friends from the parish, but those days were long behind him. Just as the phone calls withered from former friends who felt too awkward to keep calling, so too had the casseroles. People who had sworn that he could call him for "absolutely anything" now avoided his gaze when they passed him in the street. It wasn't just his entire family that had been taken away from him; it was his entire life.

Marty no longer lived. He merely existed on a day-to-day basis. Much like a recovering alcoholic, he did not look to the future. It was pure survival mode. Gone were the Costco runs. What was the point? In fact, gone was any form of long-term planning. A seventeen-year-old store clerk found that out all too quickly when she tried to upsell Marty an extended warranty.

"Do I look like I give a shit about what's going to happen in three years?" he'd said. "I am just trying to get through the fucking day with a universal remote that actually works."

His job had been understanding at first. What job wouldn't be? Diesel mechanics with a twenty-three-year track record were hard to come by. The guys at the shop couldn't help but imagine themselves in Marty's position and made a point of bending over backwards after the accident. But, as the months dragged on and Marty couldn't make it out of the house, they had to move on—even if he couldn't. And they replaced him.

They weren't completely heartless. They did give him a one-time bonus of three-months' salary, unheard of for a mechanic. But after funeral expenses and the bills were caught up, Marty had found himself with no stream of income and a mounting pile of debt.

He had considered calling up his boss and asking for his old job back, but he knew that was not an option. He also considered looking for some new challenge, but quickly realized that anyplace "new" would not give him the benefit of the doubt that he was going to need in order to keep going.

Marty might not have been a smart man, but he knew two things: he was running out of options, and he had already run out of money. Something had to change.

But he also knew that nothing would change. Nothing *could* change. His wife, daughter and namesake were gone. And there was not a damn thing he could do about it.

Marty rubbed the sleep from his eyes and realized that he was still looking into an empty box that used to hold food. He couldn't be sure how long he had been staring into the abyss, but it must have been for at least five minutes: the "open door" alarm was chirping. He pushed the door closed without getting anything out. It was a ritual that would be repeated several times today until he finally got hungry enough to either heat up the pizza or call Golden Chopsticks for a delivery. Assuming, of course, that he could get the credit card charge to clear.

He wandered back into the living room and flipped on the tube with his new, warranty-free remote. He was spending an ever-increasing amount of time watching old black and white films on Turner Classic Movies. There was something about watching actors who had all been dead for decades that was oddly comforting for him. It was as if by watching them perform on celluloid, he was actually keeping them alive.

Breakfast at Tiffany's was playing. Marty came in just as Holly Golightly was having a conversation with Mickey Rooney, who was giving one of the most racist yellow-face performances in the history of cinema. He flipped it off and chucked his new universal remote across the room—not because he was offended, but because that Audrey Hepburn was full of shit.

TWO

SOMETIME LATER—IT WAS HARD to tell *exactly* how much later—Marty was startled awake by his cell phone buzzing next to his ear. He was confused; he really didn't remember dozing off. What time was it anyway? Just how long *had* he been asleep? And what day was it?

"Williams & Riley" was on the Caller ID. The law firm where his wife had worked as a paralegal for the last ten years. Great. Just great.

Marty started to clear his thoughts—hoping he wouldn't sound as if he had been asleep—but then thought, *Who the hell am I trying to impress anyways?* He had always sensed that the lawyers at his wife's firm looked down their noses at him because he worked with his hands. "Hello?"

"Hello, Mr. Callahan. This is Kathy from Williams & Riley. I used to work with your wife before…" Her voice trailed off awkwardly. Apparently, this was an off-the-cuff call and Kathy had not practiced what she was going to say. Hell, she probably assumed he wouldn't answer.

Marty had no interest in making small talk, but he did manage to get out a "Mmm-hmm."

"Well, I am just calling because I need your help with something."

"I don't know what I could help you with. I really don't. But thanks for calling."

Marty started to hang up when Kathy started speaking quickly and loudly. "No, no, no, please, Mr. Callahan. Don't hang up. I have some paperwork here that I could use your help on."

Marty stopped. Paperwork? What kind of paperwork? Was there a possibility that this "paperwork" was additional benefits that they had dug up? Lord knew he could really use that about now.

"Who did you say this was again?"

"Kathy. I'm from Human Resources."

Bingo!

"Sure, Kathy. I would be happy to help. Anything you need." Even as he said the words, Marty couldn't help but be struck by the fact that it was the same thing funeral well-wishers had said to him. They must never have meant it either.

"Well, there is some stuff you need to sign. This week is busy, as we are gearing up for our big holiday party on Thursday. Hey, could you come in on Thursday morning? Maybe afterwards you could come to the party?"

"I really don't know about that..."

"Oh, please come down. It would be perfect. There are so many people who would be happy to see you. Everyone has been asking what they could do to help out."

Hmmm. Additional benefits *and* a potential fundraiser. Marty was suddenly glad he had picked up his phone rather than letting it go to voicemail. He really didn't have any interest in going down there, but if doing so would delay any possible decision on whether he needed to return to work, it certainly would be worth the trip.

"Okay, Kathy. Thursday it is. See you about eleven."

"Oh, this will be just great. Go ahead and park in the building. We will validate you."

You better, he thought. *Otherwise, I won't have enough money to get my car out of hock.*

❀ ❀ ❀

THE NEXT FEW DAYS passed in pretty much the same fashion as the 300 or so days before them. Marty got up. He meandered around the house. He ate a little bit during the day and drank himself to sleep every night. He was biding time, waiting for his Thursday meeting at Williams & Riley. It was not coming a day too soon. He had just received word that one of the automatic debits his wife had set up had come back "NSF"—

non-sufficient funds.

The morning came and after his usual coffee routine, Marty rubbed his hands over the stubble on his cheeks and tried to remember when he had last shaved. Was it three weeks, or was it four? And what caused him to do it then? He really didn't see much of a point to it anymore.

After cleaning up, he opened the sliders on his closet, this time to the right, where all his dress clothes were stored. Since this portion of his wardrobe consisted of two button-down shirts, a sports coat and a single pair of slacks, there was plenty of room for not only his winter gear but some of his wife's fancier dresses.

He stared at her wardrobe—her ridiculous wardrobe—wondering why the hell she had needed all this shit anyway. It was just one more thing he was going to have to deal with. But not today. Today he was going down to find out what sort of extra benefits this Kathy person had found.

Marty grabbed the slacks and slipped them on, marveling at how tight they had become. He thought about his recent eating habits and couldn't decide whether they resembled those of a grizzly bear rummaging through a garbage can or a twelve-year-old latchkey kid forced to fend for himself. If he felt like eating cold pizza for breakfast, he did it. If he wanted scrambled eggs at two a.m., so be it. One particularly rainy day he ate three packages of Rice-A-Roni in a single day: one for breakfast, one for lunch, and one for dinner. He couldn't remember the last time he had broken out their wooden teak bowls for a salad.

He struggled against the button on his slacks. The dress shirt was a little more forgiving, thank God, and the sports coat fit just fine—as long as he didn't try to button it. One last look in the mirror and he was off.

Marty drove to the office in silence, thinking about how many times he had been here over the last several decades. It usually was for something good: meeting his wife for an impromptu lunch, a celebration following a big trial win, or picking her up directly from work so that they could beat the traffic out of town for the weekend. He hoped that this trip for a holiday-party-slash-benefits-distribution meeting would be equally pleasant.

He wasn't sure whether he would recognize Kathy when he met her, but his apprehensions were quashed within three seconds of entering the lobby. She scuffled over to him, her Sketchers making an annoying squeaking sound on the granite floor of the two-story lobby. Marty wasn't sure what was more offensive: the stupid, slack-jawed "I'm so sorry your wife died" look on her face or the ridiculous snowman-riding-a-reindeer sweater she was wearing.

"Mr. Callahan. It is so nice to see you again. Thanks for coming."

"Marty. Please."

"Marty," she repeated, biting her lip, with the same stupid look on her face. No wonder she was friends with Celeste.

He stood in silence for a few seconds waiting for her to speak. Eventually, it became sort of a contest over who would speak first—the grieving widower or the HR gal with that ridiculous sweater.

Eventually Marty couldn't take it anymore. "So, I understand you have something for me."

Like a $100,000 life insurance policy?

"Oh, yeah, I do. We'll get to that. Why don't you come on up? There are a ton of people who would like to say 'Hi' to you."

Marty followed Kathy up in the elevator and through the maze of the fourteenth floor until he finally reached her small interior office. Unlike most offices, meant to maintain privacy, Kathy's had glass on every wall, making it a literal fishbowl so that everyone passing by could see what was going on inside.

It was important for HR to have witnesses. Lots and lots of witnesses.

Kathy wiggled through the stacks of boxes and squeezed into her seat, nodding at the empty chair on the other side of the desk. Marty slumped into it. Three or four inquisitive faces gawked in at him. How many other people had sat here just before being let go?

"So, I don't know if Celeste mentioned our involvement with the local youth center?"

"Not really. She didn't talk much about what went on at work."

"Really?"

"Yeah, it wasn't what you would call a 'career' for her. It was more like a job."

Kathy looked down at her desk. "Oh. I see."

"Not that she had a problem with anyone. It was just a way for us to pay the bills. You know what I mean."

"I guess I'm just a little surprised by that. She always seemed like she was such a big part of the family here."

"Yeah, well…" Marty trailed off.

Kathy's gaze grew distant. "She was my best friend here. She got me into gardening. You did know about the gardening hobby, didn't you?"

Marty ignored the snark. "It was kinda hard to miss."

"Anyway. For years, the firm has been involved with the youth center. Each December, the staff donates money to the kids. If you donate five dollars a day, you can have a casual day."

Marty nodded. "I remember something about the casual days."

Karen leaned over and whispered, as if she were sharing some forbidden secret. "It was purely voluntary, though. We said we checked, but we really didn't."

Marty nodded. "So, what's this have to do with Celeste?"

"Well, every year we have this big fundraiser...."

I am not donating her life insurance money to a bunch of fricking orphans!

"And..."

"And we would like to set up a fund in her name. 'The Celeste Callahan Teddy Bear Drive.'"

"What?"

"No, really. Everyone wants to."

"I really don't think so."

"It's just that she was such a big part of the Bear Drive."

"What's the Bear Drive?"

"What do you mean? She spearheaded it every year."

"What the hell are you talking about?"

"The Teddy Bear Drive. Where we donate teddy bears to children."

"Look, I don't know anything about my wife donating a couple of toys to kids, but I can assure you..."

"A couple of bears? Do you even know how big this thing has gotten?"

Marty stared at her blankly and shrugged.

"You don't know the story about this? Oh my God! You *don't* know! How can you not know this? It was such a defining part of who Celeste was. Are you sure?"

Marty slumped back in his chair. He had assumed that after all these years of marriage, he had known everything there was to know about Celeste. Was it possible there was something that he didn't know?

He turned his face away from Kathy. He just couldn't stand to look at that stupid sweater or her rapidly evolving judgmental face. But when he looked out the windows of the fishbowl, all he could see was paralegals gawking back in at him.

THREE

Marty leaned forward, placed his elbows on Kathy's desk, and buried his face into his palms. What kind of nightmare was this? What was this idiot in the perky sweater talking about? And where the hell was the extra life insurance policy that she found?

"I'm sorry, Kathy," he said, looking up. "But you said something about paperwork. I just assumed this was something about Celeste's benefits."

"Oh, no. Nothing like that. I'm sorry if I wasn't clear on the phone."

Marty started to stand up. "I'm sorry too. But I really need to be going."

"No, no, no. Please, Mr. Callahan. Just give me three minutes. It's important."

"Three minutes?"

"I promise."

"Okay, go ahead."

"All right. Where do I begin? Well, you already know about our casual December Days."

"I do now."

"Well, it used to be that we would give people the option of either donating five dollars or giving a small toy. The problem was that you really can't get a toy for five dollars. Not anymore."

"I wouldn't think so."

"We had a big box out there in the lobby next to where Martha answers the phones. People could drop off their toys in there. But, like I said, there never were that many toys. That is, until about six or seven years ago."

Kathy leaned forward again, as if whispering another juicy HR secret. "One Monday Martha walked in and there were about fifty teddy bears sitting all over the lobby. At first, she thought it was part of the holiday decorations, but it turned out that someone had bought them and come in over the weekend and placed them all over the office. They were all donated for the kids."

"That's all very interesting. Inspiring, even. But what does this have to do with Cel…"

"She bought them."

"She bought them?"

"All of them."

"All of them?"

"That's what I'm saying. She bought fifty teddy bears."

Marty rocked back in his chair, a wry smile crossing his face. "Just when you think you've heard every story about someone…"

"I'm not finished," Kathy said. "That was just the first year."

"She kept buying fifty teddy bears every year?"

"No, Mr. Callahan. Last year she personally raised $25,000 and bought 5,000 bears. They were delivered to children in thirteen different states."

"What the hell are you talking about?"

"She organized fundraisers throughout the year. She convinced some of the law partners to match other donations she had raised. Poor suckers had no idea what they had tapped into. She even contracted with a wholesale company to lower the per-item cost so that she could get more. It was like nothing I have ever seen."

Marty smiled. This, at least, was so much like his wife. That crazy, quirky soul who could have swapped snowman sweaters with Kathy.

"You know, for the first couple of years she did it, she didn't even tell anyone who it was. Boy, the rumors and speculation about who brought in all those toys were flying around like crazy. Everyone was sure it was one of the partners. Heck, one of them even attempted to steal credit for it. I mean, seriously! What kind of a narcissistic asshole does that? That's not even normal for a lawyer."

Marty smiled broadly. "My wife always was a bag of monkeys. Full of surprises. That must have made a lot of kids happy."

"Happy?" Kathy's voice rose, clearly agitated. "You're still not getting it, Mr. Callahan." She glanced down at her watch and scowled. "Come with me. You gotta see something."

Kathy was on her heels and out the door before Marty could offer a word of protest. She walked briskly through the halls like a woman possessed. It was all Marty could do to keep up with her.

Finally she stopped in front of a set of double doors, where she turned briskly and spoke in hushed tones. "This is the firm's multi-purpose room. We use it for client events, moot courts, mixers, continuing education and, once in a while, for firm-wide events. This is the holiday party. Come on in and follow me, but be quiet. The speeches have already started."

With that, Kathy threw open the double doors and marched through. Marty had already come this far, so he simply ducked his head and followed her inside.

As they worked their way to the back of the room, Marty could hear an older gentleman—he must have been the senior partner—droning on from the lectern with a big "W&R" logo on it.

"So, as you know, Williams & Riley have had a long-standing relationship with the Boys and Girls Clubs, and this year, we have made a record donation of 10,000 teddy bears which will be distributed not only across the nation, but also to thirteen different countries."

Marty exhaled abruptly as the room exploded into applause.

"But you don't want to hear from me. Let's hear from someone on the front line. Where the rubber meets the road. Bobby Santos: one of the graduates of the Boys and Girls Clubs."

The room obliged with polite applause as a young man—he couldn't have been more than nineteen or twenty—approached the lectern.

"Hi. My name is Bobby, and I am a graduate of the Boys and Girls Club of Los Angeles. I first became involved when I was ten years old. Our family had just come here from Mexico because my dad needed work. Although he was an architect in Mexico, he took work in the fields to pay the bills. Until one day an immigration raid swooped in and arrested him. He was taken into custody and deported. I never saw him again."

The room, which had previously been buzzing with idle side chatter, suddenly quieted down.

"My mom and I were alone in a strange place where we didn't speak the language. She had to get a job cleaning motel rooms even though she had been a middle school teacher. And I had nowhere to go during the day. No one cared about me. No one."

Bobby swallowed hard and continued. It was hard to believe this kid was only nineteen years old.

"I started hanging out at the Boys and Girls Club. There were a lot of kids like me. We had nowhere else to go."

Bobby took a deep breath and steadied himself.

"When Christmas rolled around that first year, I almost couldn't take it. I missed my dad. I missed my friends. I was so alone. And I just *knew* that I wasn't even going to get a single present."

A tear started to run down his face.

"And then, one day, a woman came driving up in a big SUV. The head of the club asked me to go out and help her unload a bunch of boxes. She had a ton of wrapped presents. More than enough for every kid at the place."

His voice was starting to get shaky.

"I brought that present back home, and it took everything in my power to wait three days to open it. When I finally did, I saw it was an *osito de peluche,* a stuffed bear."

Kathy grabbed Marty's hand. He glanced over at her; there were tears in her eyes.

"It's gonna sound stupid, but that little bear saved my life. It gave me hope. It meant that someone out there cared about me. Someone who had never met me before. I never even got her name. Just some old weird white lady in an ugly Christmas sweater."

Laughter scattered about the room. It was infectious.

"It really made me turn my life around. I was going in a bad direction. And now…" He paused. "I am attending college on a full scholarship, studying sociology. And I am working as the outreach coordinator for the very same Boys and Girls Club from ten years earlier."

The room erupted in applause. Kathy led Marty out the back door.

As she gingerly closed the door, Kathy leaned into Marty. "So, you see, Mr. Callahan. This is not just some silly bear drive. This makes a real difference in kids' lives. *Your wife* made a real difference in kids' lives! That is what I wanted you to see."

FOUR

MARTY DROVE HOME ON autopilot. By the time he pulled into the driveway, he had no memory of the route he had taken. He had simply driven on instinct.

He killed the motor and stared into space, shell-shocked. He felt blank, unfocused, emotionally detached from the realities of the conversation he had just had with Kathy.

He and Celeste had always been an odd couple. He had a solid and quiet strength, like a gunslinger in some crappy black-and-white Western on TCM. Celeste had always been the spice of the family. With the high-pitched diction of a kindergarten teacher and her silly hobbies, she had always seemed as if she had been born in the wrong era.

And now there was this silly bear business that he was trying to under-stand. But it wasn't just about the bears. At least it hadn't been for Bobby. And it wouldn't be for the lives of those that Bobby impacted. Each ted-dy bear was like one small ripple that kept expanding.

How was it that he had been married to this woman for thirty years and knew so little about her? Why didn't she share this part of herself with him? Was he really that much of a monster? Hadn't they been hap-py? And why all the secrecy? He would have understood if she had been humping the next-door neighbor or some slick lawyer from that law firm. At least that would have made sense. But to have this completely hidden side of her—one that demonstrated a humility and generosity of spirit that he had never seen? Hell, he would have loved to have been married to that girl.

That night, Marty had a terrible time trying to sleep. That Catho-lic guilt that had always hit both Celeste and Annette, but had always missed him, had finally found its mark. If you hung around long enough, it always did.

When he finally did wake up, he was even more tired than he usually was following a two-bottle night. He stumbled to the kitchen and got the coffee pot going.

As the pot was whistling and spurting, Marty's gaze was once again drawn to Celeste's garden, lying fallow just beyond the tilted blinds. And then his eyes fell on that stone—that annoyingly upbeat stone with the *alleged* Audrey Hepburn quote: "To plant a garden is to believe in to-morrow."

His eyes filled with tears. He really hadn't even considered that there could be a tomorrow. At least not since the accident.

Marty turned his attention to the pantry. No magic fairies had ap-peared during the night and suddenly filled it with staples. If it couldn't go in a microwave, it wasn't in there. But he was hungry and needed to eat.

After a cup of coffee, Marty got in his car and drove past Wally's, his home-away-from-home when he was in the mood for a Mexican omelet.

Instead, he drove to the grocery store and spent the better part of an hour picking out various meats, vegetables, juice, fruit, and even some herbs. Back home, Marty dined on his own homemade chorizo, mushroom, and avocado omelet, with a touch of cilantro, which was way better than anything Wally had served up over the last few months.

When he was done, he examined the mess that had once been the house he shared with Celeste. He exhaled sharply, surveying the damage and trying to come up with a game plan. It was as if the scales had fallen off his eyes and he could see how quickly his whole life had devolved around him.

Moments later, he was back in the car and off to the hardware store where he stocked up on cleaning supplies and garbage bags. Lots and lots of garbage bags. And as he was headed home, he swung by the gas station and paid the ten bucks to run his car through what would have been a free car wash had he merely filled up his tank.

As Marty cleared old pizza boxes and stacks of newspapers, the cute little Craftsman house started to re-emerge from the ashes. Marty cleared eight giant plastic bags of trash that had somehow accumulated *inside* his house since the last casserole-bearing guest had left. On his way back from dragging the bags outside, Marty couldn't help but glance over at that annoyingly upbeat Audrey Hepburn quote. But this time he noticed, for the first time ever, a small concrete statuette of a bear sitting next to it.

Exhausted from weeks of deferred maintenance, Marty collapsed on the couch and flipped on the TV. He started flipping through the channels. *My Fair Lady* was playing—his wife and daughter's *second* favorite movie. He shook his head at the gods that had chosen this particular piece of cinema to be played at this particular time and smiled.

He had never much cared for this movie, but this time there was something different. There was something to be said about Eliza who was able to pull herself up out of her situation—not to mention Eliza's drunken father. Especially her drunken father.

Maybe this movie was on to something. Maybe his wife and daughter had been on to something. *Maybe there was a reason to believe in tomorrow after all.* Maybe, just maybe, Celeste's death didn't have to mark the end of his own life. His problems didn't have to seem so tangled and out of control. And his life, much like Celeste's untended garden, didn't have to lie fallow.

The next day Marty got up early, opened the blinds all the way, went outside, and planted roma tomatoes.

SCOTT DAVENPORT GREW UP in a small Northern California farm town of 10,000 people—the kind of place where people stop for gas, go to the bathroom, and keep on driving. As soon as he was able, Scott escaped to Southern California where he met his future wife, El. It was to Scott's great benefit that El ignored his warnings to not get involved with him. They have been together thirty-five years and currently live in Sunset Beach, a tiny beach community forty-five minutes south of Los Angeles.

Scott became an appellate lawyer and won a case at the United States Supreme Court. He is also an avid hockey fan, and even played in an ice hockey beer league for the better part of a decade.

A firm believer that one should write what they know, Scott's first novel, *The Code*, is a suspense thriller which tracks the lives of two vastly different characters—a Southern California career prosecutor and a violent, minor league hockey enforcer—who are both mysteriously summoned to a small Northern California coastal town. For more information about this and other projects, visit www.ScottsFiction.com.

Blind Faith

Barbara Ware

The Kalalau lookout is a magical place on the island of Kauai. It's at 4,000 feet overlooking Kalalau Valley in all its splendor. Kalalau is the largest valley on the island, two miles wide, and beyond it stretches the blue Pacific. It is totally inaccessible by land except for by hiking an arduous eleven-mile trail: the terrain is so steep that it defies construction. The walls of the canyon are nearly vertical and look as if they are made from draped fabric more than stone. The ridges themselves are so narrow there is not room for a man to stand and so thin that in a few places a missing piece of wall lets you see light all the way through, like the eye of a needle. Kalalau was inhabited as recently as a hundred years ago and bears vestiges of its few inhabitants who farmed the land between its skyscraper walls. All the surfaces are a luminous velvet green of vegetation.

This is a place of deep nostalgia for me. I had made that arduous hike to Kalalau Valley in the summer of my twentieth year. I had just graduated from San Francisco State University, and my life lay in front of me like a blank slate to be filled with almost anything I could imagine. It was there I turned twenty-one, in July of 1970. I stayed for a full month with the food I carried in on my back and what I could gather from the leavings of the previous residents decades before and the gleanings nature provided: an orange tree deep in the valley, guavas growing wild on the hillsides, and taro was still growing here and there along the riverbank. I gathered limpets from the shoreline at low tide and freshwater shrimp from the creek. We made salads from the watercress that grew in the moist areas along the streambanks. Maybe ten of us populated that entire huge valley at that time.

To experience the many faces of the valley, I moved camp three times over my month there. My first camp was a cave on the beach. A week or so later, I moved to the bluffs overlooking the ocean at the mouth of the valley, and finally to a streamside spot deep in the jungle of the valley itself. There were no helicopters offering bird's eye views of the Na Pali coast, no boats landing with picnic fare for the so-called "adventurous" tourists. It truly was paradise found for a young woman like me exploring her identity and independence. It was my coming-of-age walkabout.

❀ ❀ ❀

SOME THIRTY YEARS LATER I was revisiting the island with my husband, Bob. No longer up for hiking eleven miles and camping, I was enjoying our condo and rented car. One of my goals, however, was to visually revisit this iconic valley from Kalalau Lookout and see from afar the place that had meant so much to me. Time was bearing down on the few days left of our vacation. As the days slipped by, each one became more and more precious. The greatest draw for us had been the beautiful beaches that offered incredible snorkeling opportunities. We loved seeing all the brightly colored fishes and the coral. We were especially delighted when we came upon a turtle grazing on the algae growing on the rocks or basking on the beach. My particular goal was to develop "octopus-eyes", to be able to see them even when they use their incredible ability to camouflage themselves against any background, even a checkerboard. I'd only seen them in the wild a handful of times and usually only when their movement gave them away. Of course, there was also the draw of the warm sun on the sand and just the thrill of playing in the waves and water while at our home in Potter Valley in Northern California, it rained, hailed and froze. There were beautiful botanical gardens to visit, and of course great restaurants to eat at and mai tais to drink. It was hard to pull away and make the long drive to the Kalalau Lookout.

With just a few days left, it was time to relegate one of the last ones to Kalalau Lookout. The road is long and winding, incredibly slow if you get behind a tour bus with nowhere to pass. It would take most of a full day and the view was never guaranteed, since it is right near Alakai

Swamp, one of the wettest places on earth. Clouds often filled the valley, blocking out everything beyond your hand in front of your face. We were warned to get there early since the clouds often blanketed the valley in the afternoon.

Nevertheless, we scheduled our second-to-last day for this escapade. My darling husband, who lacked the personal motivation to experience the nostalgia of this visit, kindly agreed to accompany me. We had trouble getting up as early as we'd hoped, but the day was beautiful, and the sky was blue. It was at least a half-hour drive to get to the foot of Kokee Road that snaked up the mountain, with a likely hour and a half of narrow windy road to get to the top. We passed by gorgeous vistas of Waimea Canyon and couldn't resist stopping for a photo op or two.

The road got worse and worse the farther we went, and we had to dodge potholes by the end. It was already well into the afternoon, but we were the closest we would ever be for years to come. As we pulled into the parking lot, it was obvious we were not going to have a clear view, but maybe the clouds were high enough that we could still look down into the valley and I could get a glimpse of that nostalgic place. We put on our coats, hats, and even a scarf. At the guardrail overlooking what was supposed to be a spectacular view, there was only a grey wall of fog/cloud obscuring everything. We joked that at least there weren't a lot of other people, though the disappointment of everyone was palpable.

My husband was not impressed. He was ready to leave, as were several other groups of tourists, but I begged for a little more time. Maybe we could look around for the rare I'iwi bird that feeds on the ohia lehua blossoms or the native nene goose. He is patient. He is kind. So, we stayed a while longer, but it was pretty cold. Just fifteen more minutes… PLEAAAASSSSE. We stayed.

Folks came and went, but finally weak rays of sun began to filter through. The gray turned from opaque to slightly more transparent whirling wisps. Ever so slowly, we watched as the wisps wafted upward and evaporated in the sun. Bits and pieces of the view emerged and then were swallowed up again, but finally the sun won the battle and we were looking at the full expanse of Kalalau Valley.

It was everything I'd hoped for. My eyes climbed along the trail that I had walked, searched the beach for familiar landmarks. It became an epiphany for me, not just because I persevered and got what I wanted.

What really became the teaching moment was that originally that grey wall had been truly all that I could see. I so wanted Bob to share the vision of the paradise I had found, but there was nothing to spark his imagination. The whole time that incredible view had been there, just out of sight.

The thing is that possibility can arise out of nowhere...barriers can literally evaporate. The world is so much more than form and function. It's magic and imagination as well. We can find strength by acknowledging our weakness; hope from embracing our despair. Now, if the future seems to hold no promise and the world seems bleak, I try to remember that moment overlooking Kalalau. With just a bit of time and faith, our whole perspective can be transformed to perceive what has been there all the time, so much beauty just momentarily veiled by clouds. Just because you can't see it, doesn't mean it isn't there.

Barbara Ware is the illustrious stepmother to the editor of this anthology. She is blessed with good fortune in the people she knows and the children she has raised. She has three now-grown, wonderful children, spent a life teaching English as a Second Language to a diverse assortment of non-English speakers, worked with mentally ill adults teaching arts and crafts, and enjoyed finding little audience as a watercolor artist. No other opportunity to publish her little- known and mostly unwritten works has surfaced, so she jumped on this possibility to soar from ignominy to public acclaim. We'll just see if this works. Thanks to Shannon.

Meditation on Persistence: 4am

Mark J. Ferrari

Discouragement is a wide, slow river
winding back across the plains
into the distant mountains of my youth.

Hope is a wisp of morning mist
that drifts across the water,
poised to shred and dissipate at sunrise.

Desire is a song bird that flies above the river,
landing now and then among the swaying reeds nearby,
then lifting off, and out of sight again before I've seen it clearly.

Oh, singing bird and morning mist,
how I often wish the still, dark river
were as tenuous as you are.

And yet, that mist keeps rising in the mornings,
and that bird, or others like it, keep appearing overhead.
And I have still not tired of watching for them.

MARK J. FERRARI HAS been a commercial genre illustrator since 1987. His fantasy novel, *The Book of Joby,* was published by Tor in 2007. He has recently launched an illustrated online fantasy serial called TWICE, which can be found at at www.twice-the-serial.com. More info on his art and writing can be found at www.markferrari.com.

Break the Mirrors

Jan Underwood

In a kingdom called Dill lived a queen who every morning stood in the single room of her unfurnished tower and addressed the mirror that hung on the wall, asking it—well, technically asking the royal adviser who lived trapped inside it—who was the fairest of them all.

It was a problematic question in at least two ways. First, this word "fair": it meant "beautiful," but of course it also meant "white." Dill was a kingdom in which whiteness was equated with beauty, and people whose skin was not fair were not considered beautiful. Also, why this obsession with appearances? The great majority of women in the Kingdom of Dill were serfs, who worked all day and did not have the leisure to gaze into mirrors nor even the means to buy them. But the Queen and a handful of other royals were born to be chess pieces in the shifting alliances between Dill and neighboring kingdoms. Their only role was to be rich and (according to the dictates of their culture) pretty, in order to secure marriages that would further empower the kingdom. Once married, they left off being chess pieces and devoted the rest of their lives to being ornaments.

The Queen of Dill spent nearly all her time in the tower. She was not locked in, but it was illegal for her to go most places and undertake most activities. (Many things were illegal in the Kingdom of Dill.) She spent her days admiring her ridiculous Queen shoes and her expensive silk stole (embroidered by serfs) and contemplating to what degree her face conformed to the standards of beauty set by her time and place. She did this in two ways: by staring at her own reflection, and by posing her problematic question to her royal adviser, who had been confined to the mirror by the King. The Queen sometimes consulted the adviser on matters of state. She liked to decide whom to knight and whom to behead. Mostly, though, she perseverated on the question of her face.

❋ ❋ ❋

As you might imagine, the Queen was very bored, and very boring. Her royal adviser was not pleased to live trapped in a mirror with only Her Highness to talk to. He had started out as the leader of the Wool Guild, deftly managing rifts between bellicose factions (spinners, weavers, dyers, and merchants) and between them and the shepherds. He had done such a good job with the Wool Guild that the King had poached him for a job in the Commerce Department, where he, the adviser, made trade agreements favorable to the kingdom regarding the exchange of spinning wheels and riding hoods. He also had a side hustle in public health; he had been able to reduce the number of fleas in the kingdom by having brewer's yeast sprinkled on compost piles and other things that black rats liked to get into. And he had started a campaign to vaccinate princes against frogism. One day, however, the adviser had been caught cavorting with a chamberlain. (Such cavorting was illegal in the Kingdom of Dill. Oh! So very many things were illegal in the Kingdom of Dill.) But the King needed the adviser. So instead of banishing him, or worse, the King had had him deposited into the mirror, and there he stayed—still of use, but out of sight to everyone except the bored and boring Queen.

Next door to the Kingdom of Dill was a small, hilly duchy called Agapanthus, inhabited by all sorts of women, none of whom were serfs. They were brown like leather and blue-black like the wings of the swallowtail butterfly (*Liminitis arthemis*) and milky-skinned with freckles and tan like a sandy beach. They had thin hair and thick hair and frizzy hair and lank hair. They had big bottoms like pin cushions and flat bottoms like trenchers; they had eyes with and without epicanthic folds. Some Agapanthans had a meniscus of flesh under their chins. Others were a bit gaunt. Some Agapanthans had gray streaks. Some had liver spots. Some had dimples. Some had big thighs like the trunks of strong trees. There were women who called themselves womyn and women who called themselves women and future women who were girls, and women with strong jaws and Adam's apples. There were boys and men, too; some anyway. And people who weren't women or men, and people who were both. And none of them was very interested in the degree to which they conformed to a culturally-determined standard of beauty which was, at any rate, very elastic in their particular culture. As a matter of fact, there were no mirrors in the Duchy of Agapanthus. Agapanthans served as one another's mirrors on those few occasions when they needed to look a certain way, asking one another, for example, "Is there broccoli between my teeth?"

In the Duchy of Agapanthus lived a woman named Star, whose skin was the color of cedar bark and whose hair, gray at the temples, formed a gigantic black nebula around her face like a towering storm cloud (though she had a sunny disposition), and whose body liked to be fed peanut butter to keep it nice and round and soft, and who had a Ph.D. in Fluvial Geomorphology. She was actually employed as a grocer, because she had been unable to find work as a fluvial geomorphologist in Agapanthus which, in spite of everything I've told you, was not quite a paradise. (The other nerve-wracking thing about Agapanthus was that it was just across the river from the Kingdom of Dill and was always being threatened by that kingdom in one way or another. We'll talk more about that in a minute.) So Star worked as a grocer and wore a white apron with big front pockets, and supplied the neighborhood with fresh produce, including a nice array of root vegetables that she grew herself. And like most people in Agapanthus, she kept a small dragon.

Now I'm sure you already know that most dragons are vain and greedy and shrewd and untamable. You may not be familiar with the rarer subspecies of dragon that lives in Agapanthus. These animals are smaller and more cooperative than common dragons, and they are not at all vain. I would not say they are terribly shrewd, but they're also not greedy (except for gummy bears. If you ever have a chance to ride one, you should be sure to have a supply of gummy bears on hand). Their scales are large and heavy but not as abrasive as other dragons' scales, and they range in color from rosy red to a pleasing apricot orange. Members of this dragon species are called dragonelles.

Well, Star kept a little dragonelle for transportation and company, and she fed it gummy bears and they got on well.

One day rumors were going around Star's grocery store that the Kingdom of Dill had plans to annex the river that divided its territory from the Duchy of Agapanthus. The River Agapanthus supplied most of the duchy's irrigation and drinking water, and was an important source of fish, as well as providing habitat to uncounted species of birds, amphibians and insects such as the swallowtail butterfly (*Liminitis arthemis*). Numerous treaties between Agapanthus and Dill specified that the river belonged to the duchy alone, and while the larger kingdom enjoyed a few recreational rights to the water, it had no business taking it over.

Star was unable to get much information about the annexation, so she decided to make a trip to Dill to find out for herself what she could. It was a good task for an aspiring fluvial geomorphologist. The next morning, she went to the barn with her apron pockets full of gummy bears. She spent half an hour going over the dragonelle's scales and pulling out all the loose ones. (It was molting season—a dragonelle molts two or three times a year—and it won't do, when a dragon takes flight, to have heavy scales falling onto pedestrians below.) Star took some gummy bears out of her pocket, picked the lint off them, and fed them to her dragon. Then together they flew over the green and hilly countryside of Agapanthus, crossing the disputed river and into the territory of Dill.

Star landed in a village there and hitched her dragonelle to a post outside a grocery store. She went inside and struck up a long, involved conversation with the Dillard grocer about root vegetables, and then she bought some, even though they were of inferior quality. Having won the grocer over, Star then turned the conversation to the question of the River Agapanthus. As she tucked inferior turnips into her large apron pockets, Star listened carefully to the grocer and some other customers telling her all about the kingdom's plans: they were going to build an enormous dam, which would supply power to the whole western third of the country. Of course, the river wasn't theirs to dam, but that was of little concern to these Dillards. They did not suspect Star of being Agapanthan; she lived so close to the border that they shared an accent and knowledge of local agriculture. And—since Star's skin was the color of cedar bark, and since her hair formed an enormous black nebula like a towering storm cloud (though she had a sunny disposition), and since it was graying at the temples, and since her body was well supplied with peanut butter so it could be nice and soft and round, and since she was a woman—they did not suspect her of being a fluvial geomorphologist. And they did not suspect her of undertaking an intelligence-gathering mission. They told her everything.

Star was troubled. She spent the flight back thinking over what she might do to protect her duchy and its river. Agapanthus had no standing army and not much of a diplomatic corps. If Dill wanted to flex its muscle, the duchy didn't have many ways to protect itself. Star had a cousin who had a position in the Dillard court. She might have a word with him, she thought, and see if he could dissuade the King and Queen of Dill from building this dam.

IT WAS NIGHTFALL WHEN Star got home. She tossed the inferior root vegetables into her compost pile, except for a couple small turnips that had lodged in the corner of one pocket. Then she unsaddled her dragon and gave her a handful of gummy bears. The dragonelle made irritated smacking noises. "Oh," said Star. "Sorry about the lint." Threads from her apron and root vegetable roots and other bits were forever sticking to the gummy bears. Star's pockets were always full of stuff.

Meanwhile, the Queen of Dill, in her tower, stood before her mirror and intoned the old familiar poem.

The royal adviser was getting annoyed. He had been in the mirror for more than two months now and was finding the Queen's company very trying. "I have a name, you know," he said. "My name isn't 'Mirror.'"

"Andrew, Andrew, on the wall," said the Queen, in a rare moment of good-naturedness.

Andrew the adviser would not be humored. When Her Highness repeated her rhyming inquiry, he said, "Define 'fair.'"

"You know perfectly well what I mean."

"If you mean 'pale,' well, yes, you are the palest of them all," the adviser said truthfully. The Queen's face was as white as a hibiscus flower. In fact Andrew suspected the Queen of being iron-deficient.

The Queen glowered.

"But if you mean 'beautiful,' I have to tell you, beauty is a cultural construct, derived from whatever is most difficult to attain in a given societal context. In Herrenfolk democracies it is often limited to phenotypical characteristics of the ruling ethnic group—"

"Shut up," said the Queen, and she threw her expensive silk stole (embroidered by serfs) over the mirror.

❁ ❁ ❁

A WEEK OR SO later, Star took another trip to the neighboring kingdom. After making inquiries, she learned that her cousin had become adviser to the Queen. Star and her dragonelle flew to the Queen's tower, a tall stone structure at the edge of a wood near the famous river. The tower had just one room, on the top floor, and a single window.

Star wanted to have a private word with her cousin, out of earshot of the Dillard Queen, so she and the dragonelle hid in the wood until they saw the Queen exit through the heavy door at the base of the tower. (Her Highness took a walk once a day). When the Queen had disappeared in the distance, the dragonelle glided, swift and silent, to the tower. Star scrambled out of her saddle and wriggled through the lone window. The room was empty.

"Darn it," she said aloud.

"Star?"

Star looked around but saw no one.

"Over here. In the mirror."

Star crossed the room and spotted Andrew standing in the mirror next to her own reflection.

"Been a while," her cousin said. "But I'm sure you're not here on a social visit."

Star got right to it: the river, the annexation, the dam. Said dam would not be the blessing to Dill that the kingdom might imagine, she explained. Dams blocked fish migrations, which could cause food shortages for the people of Dill. They trapped sediments needed by the fertile floodplains downstream, on which Dillard agriculture also depended. They caused significant erosion, and often lowered the water table. All these effects would have a negative impact on the kingdom's food supply. Star did not mention the numerous treaties between Dill and Agapanthus, nor the rights of Agapanthans to their water, nor the habitat of uncounted species of birds, amphibians and insects such as the swallowtail butterfly (*Liminitis arthemis*), which would also be threatened by the dam. Her cousin was fond of her, but Star knew he had his career to think about. Andrew listened without comment, arms folded.

"I understand you have some influence with the Queen," Star said.

"I do," Andrew conceded. "But she is not going to be pleased to hear this analysis."

Star nodded. These revelations might cost the royal adviser.

"So," said Andrew. "What's in it for me?"

Star's heart sank. She had nothing to offer him, except a nice array of root vegetables, superior to those grown in Dill. The royal adviser declined them.

Then they heard the heavy door of the tower opening, and the footfall of the Queen in her ridiculous Queen shoes on the stone steps below.

"I'll be back tomorrow," Star said, "with a better offer."

Her dragonelle was waiting at the window. Star scrambled out and they flew away just as the Queen entered her room.

The trip home was slow. A dragonelle can fly backwards and forwards, but hovering like a helicopter, the way she'd done outside the tower window, is fatiguing. The little dragon had to stop and catch her breath several times on the way back to Agapanthus. But by the following day she had recovered, and she was always eager to please her human friend. She and Star set out once again for the Kingdom of Dill. As they were gliding low over the hilly green country they called home, one of the dragonelle's scales sloughed off. As it started to tumble, Star caught it. It was the size and heft of a ceramic roof tile. You wouldn't want it dropping from the sky on people below. Star slipped it into one of the pockets of her apron.

In a couple hours they arrived at the tall stone tower, just after the Queen had left for her daily walk. The dragonelle zipped to the lone window and Star scrambled from her back and into the Queen's room. As before, she crossed to the mirror and greeted her cousin. "I can tell you what's in it for you," she said without preamble.

In exchange for advising the Queen against the dam, said Star, she would break her cousin out of the mirror. He looked surprised, and Star could tell he liked the idea, even though he kept his arms folded. "And if the Queen doesn't follow my advice?" he said.

"That wouldn't be your fault," Star said. "I won't hold it against you. We have to try, don't we?"

Andrew pursed his lips, considering.

"What would you do with freedom, Cuz?"

Andrew was thoughtful. "Honestly," he said, "I think I'd like to live in Agapanthus."

So he agreed to the arrangement, and they were beginning to work out the details when the Queen stepped into the unfurnished room. She must have seen the dragonelle hovering at the window and known someone was here, and she'd crept up the stone stairs without a sound. She had probably overheard their whole conversation.

Star and Andrew looked at one another in horror. Star bolted to the window, but her dragonelle wasn't there. The creature had tired from hovering and was waiting for Star at the foot of the tower.

The Queen began to stomp toward Star. She was a tall woman, long-legged, and daunting in her fury. Star thrust her hand into her apron pocket to see if she had anything she could use to defend herself. She found only a turnip. She grabbed it and threw it at the mirror. Star had good aim, but the inferior turnip was soft and only bounced off the glassy surface. The long shadow of the Queen fell over Star's face. Desperate, Star stuck her hand into her other pocket and seized the dragonelle's scale.

The sound of shattering glass caused the Queen to turn in dismay. When the mirror broke, Andrew was released. He jumped out of the frame and in three long steps had reached the women. Between the two of them, Star and Andrew overpowered the Queen. They tied her hands behind her back with the expensive silk stole (embroidered by serfs) and took her with them.

The way home was halting. The dragonelle was able to carry Star with no difficulty, but the combined weight of Star, the tall Queen and a grown man was a heavy burden for the little dragon. She flew slowly, sometimes only gliding, so that they came uncomfortably close to grazing the treetops. Normally it was a two-hour flight to Star's house, but now they were proceeding so slowly that Star was afraid they would not make it home before nightfall. She was relieved when they crossed the familiar river, but within minutes, they began to lose altitude.

"Come on, baby," Star whispered in her dragon's ear. "You can do it." She reached into her apron pocket, but she had no gummy bears to offer as encouragement.

The dragonelle struggled to flap her wings. They continued to descend until it was clear she needed to stop and rest. She alighted on a grassy knoll.

The westering sun had just slid below the horizon. Star didn't say anything, trying to think of a way to account for their stop without appearing vulnerable in the Queen's eyes. But before she could turn and address the other passengers, the Queen slipped from the dragon's back and took off running. She was remarkably swift, even with her iron deficiency and her ridiculous Queen shoes, and even with her hands tied behind her back. Her long-legged Highness covered a lot of ground with each stride, heading toward a copse. Star was afraid if the Queen went in among the trees, they wouldn't be able to find her.

With a holler, she too sprang from her dragonelle's back and began to run after the Queen, Andrew close behind her. They ran down the grassy knoll and into a meadow, through drifts of wildflowers and sweet vernal grass. The footing was uneven, and they were unable to gain on the Queen. Star squeezed her eyes shut and willed her legs to carry her faster. The sky was going dark. After a short time, the royal reached the edge of the copse and disappeared.

Star and Andrew stopped, gasping for breath. The wood ahead was an undifferentiated tangle of trees, shrubs and underbrush, all dark now in the gloaming.

"There," whispered Andrew.

Star narrowed her eyes at the woods before them, but she could make out nothing.

Andrew tugged on Star's sleeve and they crouched in the sweet vernal grass so the Queen could not spot them spotting her. Andrew pointed. Star followed his gaze and saw, among the dark brambles, a single smudge as white as a hibiscus.

They crept closer, staying low to the ground and keeping the smudge in their sight. The Queen must have decided not to go very far into the copse, perhaps for fear of getting lost herself. They could see her hibiscus-white face moving parallel to the edge of the wood, traveling away from the grassy knoll where they had landed, but not moving deeper among the trees and brush. It was very nearly dark now. Bent double, Star and Andrew made their way diagonally across the meadow to intercept the Queen. When they were half a furlong from the trees' edge, Star checked her apron once more. The second inferior turnip was still lodged in the corner of one pocket. She stood suddenly and lobbed it at the pale target of the Queen's face. It landed on the Queen's noggin with a satisfying thud, knocking her out cold.

❊ ❊ ❊

THE FOLLOWING WEEK THE Duchy of Agapanthus sent a message to the Kingdom of Dill, demanding that the kingdom relinquish all plans to annex the river and build a dam, in exchange for the return of its Queen unharmed. A day or two later the Agapanthans received a reply. "We want our adviser as well," the Dillards wrote. "Send him home with the Queen."

But Star had another idea. The Kingdom of Dill had shown its willingness to break agreements, after all. She suggested that they keep Andrew there in Agapanthus, to guarantee the kingdom would abide by its word. If the King of Dill wished, he could continue to employ his worthy adviser. Andrew could telecommute via dragonelle. The Kingdom of Dill would continue to avail itself of his services; Andrew would live freely in the community of his choice; and his value to the King would secure the King's promise to leave the River Agapanthus in peace.

The Duchy of Agapanthus rewarded Star's heroism with a job offer, which she accepted: she would become an official State Fluvial Geomorphologist. She would also be honored in a ceremony, for which she would have to ask her friends if she had broccoli in her teeth.

Andrew bought a house in the traditional Agapanthan architectural style, without mirrors and without towers, but with a garden and a spacious barn for dragonelles. He lived right down the road from Star and the grocery store.

As for the Queen—she was returned to Dill unharmed, but not unaltered. Not much would change in the Kingdom of Dill after her adventure. A great many endeavors continued to be illegal there. But without her mirror, the Queen had to find new ways to spend her time. She started extending her daily walks until eventually she was spending most of the day out walking. (She had to swap her ridiculous Queen shoes for hiking boots.) The more she walked and looked about, the less she thought about her face, and the less she thought about her face, the more beauty she saw in the people and things around her. She found beauty in the woods and along the river, in meadows of hibiscus and sweet vernal grass, among the uncounted species of birds, amphibians and insects such as the swallowtail butterfly (*Liminitis arthemis*). She saw beauty in the people of Dill, too: the wool spinners, the weavers, the dyers, the merchants; the shepherds; the princes, vaccinated and unvaccinated; the cavorting chamberlains; the serfs. She saw beauty in advisers with their arms folded, and in heads of Commerce and heads of Public Health, in fluvial geomorphologists and in knights; in skin like leather and in skin like milk and in skin with liver spots; in green hills and knolls and copses; in fertile floodplains and villages with grocery stores and compost piles; in fields of inferior turnips; and in dragonelles rosy-red and pleasing apricot orange and in frogs and even among black rats. She found beauty everywhere and in everyone. It was as though, when her mirror broke, a spell was broken too.

JAN UNDERWOOD IS THE author of a magic realist academic satire, *Utterly Heartless*, as well as two collections of short stories, *The Bell Lap* (a work of cli-fi—climate change science fiction) and *Day Shift Werewolf* (about monsters with hangups). She lives in Portland, Oregon, whose endless rains and offbeat culture have inspired the kooky cities and whimsical characters in her work. Find her at funnylittlenovels.com.

Times Fifty

Brenda W. Clough

Danielle was fifteen and a half, her sweet tooth still untamed. When she heaped three spoonfuls of sugar into her pepper-mint tea, Wendy rolled her eyes: "That's *her*, you know."

The teaspoon clattered to the table. "Aah! Don't say that! I'm switching to honey, as of right now."

Sitting across from her in the harsh light of the hall was a girl with the name tag 'Amanda.' "You know we're allergic to honey. And cilantro tastes soapy," she said darkly. "They're both genetically linked traits."

Danielle set her mug down hard. She surveyed the drinks table, where cans of soda were nestled in a plastic tub of ice. The crowd had cut into the supply of orange sodas and colas while a dozen cans of lemon-lime lay untouched. She snatched a lemon-lime up and opened it, took too big a gulp, and almost choked. It tasted dreadful. She glowered at the fifty girls milling sullenly around the hall. Every one of them was also fifteen and a half years old, brown-eyed and lean and well-muscled, five-foot-five or -six, brimming with good health and sporting a stick-on name tag. But at least none of them was drinking a lemon-lime. Danielle took another defiant swig.

And at least none of them had the same hair. All of them were dark and curly, but their hair was styled with wild variation in the teenage spirit of continual experimentation. Danielle could pretend she was looking at a hairstyle Pinterest page, or one of those customized beauty programs. She saw her own hair short and velvety, or in a huge cloud of ringlets, or tied back in a sheaf of sleek braids. The neat topknot over there on Lora looked the best—she'd have to try that when she got home. But every nose around her was narrow and aquiline, every mouth under the different lip glosses or glazes firm and dimpled. Mortification crept down her spine.

"I hate you all," she announced.

Nods of agreement. "You'd feel better if you drank cola instead of that disgusting lemon-lime," Olga remarked. She looked around, nerving herself to mention the taboo subject. "Do any of you do—*sports*?"

"Soccer." "Soccer." "Soccer."

"Softball!" Danielle announced. The other girls glared at her with undisguised envy, each scowl an exact replica of the other.

"But you're good," Tia predicted in flat tones.

Danielle's well-toned shoulders slumped. "I'm only a sophomore, and I'm already on the varsity team. It wasn't like Mom and Dad pushed me into it, or anything. It just happened."

"Doesn't any one of us do anything of our own?" Bev asked. "Does anyone do drama, or cooking, or build miniature railroads?"

Danielle couldn't bear to drink any more lemon-lime. Meeting for the first time like this made her queasy, the eerie revulsion in the unnatural act of meeting yourself forty-nine times over. Mom had tried to help, comparing her with Sleeping Beauty—the beloved daughter, highly prized and sought after for her natural endowments, farmed out to nice folks who would raise her as their own until she was old enough to meet her destiny. Until, Danielle said to herself, the wicked witch came knocking at the door. That day had come. Only times fifty.

No one replied to Bev's question because the hall's tall door swung open. One man held the door while another pushed the wheelchair through, and a third—tall and imposing in his navy blue suit—followed behind. They pushed the woman in the wheelchair up the ramp leading to the little stage so everyone could see her.

Danielle had been told that Tanya Haynes was only forty-five. How many other girls get to see what they'll look like in thirty years? A frizz of gray on the temples, those deep curving lines around the mouth—the wicked witch, Danielle thought. She studied the wrinkles around the older woman's eyes and resolved to start moisturizing and using sunblock daily.

The formidable executive beamed down at them, his giant hands clasped across his stomach. "Now don't they look great, Tan? We got here the makings of three or four of the most dynamite soccer teams in history. You ever see such a beautiful crop of girlhood in your entire life? Girls, you are bee-you-tee-ful."

A hostile silence, broken by Tanya saying, "Thank you, Earl... I've been trying to think what to call you, dears. You're not my daughters. You have parents, all your wonderful adoptive parents around the country. Not my sisters. My twins? Not exactly."

Earl grinned. "They're your clones, hon."

"I won't call you that," she said to the girls. "Let's just say I'm your aunt, your Aunt Tanya. And when a niece comes to visit, auntie has a present for you. Earl, take your boys and go up to my room. Get those big bags down."

"Bill and Ricky can handle it," Earl said, dismissing the flunkies with a wave of his hand.

"No, you go too, Earl. There's three bags, heavy ones. I'll be fine right here."

Muttering under his breath, Earl took his boys and went. Tanya waited until the door shut behind them and then rolled her wheelchair to the edge of the little stage. "You, dear," she said, pointing. Danielle was nearest. "Come a little closer, would you please? My eyes aren't good enough to read name tags anymore."

Back in South Carolina her parents had raised her to be polite to her elders. Danielle hopped up onto the stage. Close to, she could see the metal braces on the older woman's knees. A car crash when Tanya Haynes was twenty-nine—Danielle's parents had shown her all the newspaper files and sports videos last month, when they broke the news to her about the cloning. The great athlete, the most stupendous female soccer star ever, had never been able to walk again.

"Danielle," Tanya said, reading the name tag. "I can't hold fifty hands, so I'm going to hold yours, all right? As a representative. The rest of you, listen to me, please."

The hands clutching Danielle's were lighter than hers, and the skin was looser and rougher. But the fingernails were exactly the same, the distance between the joints, even the little bump on the outside of the wrist bone. She had no words for how strange it was, looking down at two pairs of identical hands of different ages. Silently Danielle measured her palm and fingers against them. Exactly the same length.

Tanya's voice was harsh. "My dears, this wasn't my idea. I would never have consented, if I had known what it meant. Earl thought that—he just couldn't stand the idea of the U.S. women's soccer team without me. And the soccer federation had their hearts set on another Olympic gold. They filled up my head with all this stuff about the legacy of the sport and the future generations of soccer players, and then when Earl offered to pay all the medical bills if I'd contribute the tissue cultures…" For a moment she faltered. Then she said, simply, "I'm sorry, girls."

We're slaves, Danielle thought. *Not even that, we're photocopies of an original.* Danielle's entire future was laid out for her in sports, and there was nothing she could do about it, in this chain gang with her fifty sister-selves. She wanted to cry. Instead she said, "Do we apologize for being alive, then?" Then she wanted to stuff the angry words back into her mouth. But several of her—sisters? twins?—nodded their approval, with sullen, hard faces.

"Don't you *ever* do that." Tanya's older mouth pursed instead of dimpling when she set her teeth, but otherwise the expression was one that Danielle had seen in her own mirror. "They cloned me to make all fifty of you. The plan is for you to dominate sports for the rest of the century. But you are your own women. Do you hear me? They wanted to give you my legs, my lungs, my muscles. But I'm giving you my heart. Don't you let these sports moguls run you. They made you in petri dishes and paid for your births, but they don't own you. Seize your lives, and make them yours. You can do it, because you are champions, girls. It takes one to know one."

The strength that had won Tanya Haynes the gold medal in 2022 seemed to radiate out of her as she leaned forward in the wheelchair, not the long-gone strength of the broken body, but deeper, hotter—the strength of her spirit. Danielle could feel the heat of it in the bony hand clasping her own. It was like touching a burning match to an unlit new one. Tanya—Aunt Tanya—wasn't the wicked witch. She was the Sleeping Beauty, trapped in a tower shaped like a wheelchair and guarded by creepy fat cats, and she was never going to escape now. But she had given them, her twinned progeny, the key.

The will and power flared up in Danielle's middle. She was a champion too—of her life. She could be whatever she wanted to be. They could make her, but they could not mold her. "And don't forget," she said, "we're teenage girls. Rebellious by nature."

Tanya grinned at them all, a dangerous grin. "You go right ahead and rebel, dears. Explore the world. Find your place."

Then the door opened again and it was like a curtain falling over Tanya's countenance. Earl staggered in hauling a large canvas duffel bag, the other two following behind with more. Tanya smiled up him as he dragged the bag up the ramp. "Now aren't you sweet. You know I can't do very much these days, girls, but I've taken up lace knitting. And luckily I didn't have to worry about the colors that would suit you. Danielle dear, try this one."

She took a vivid blue scarf from the bag, neatly folded and tied with a ribbon. Danielle carefully slipped off the ribbon and shook the scarf out. It was beautiful. The blue triangle pattern was perfect for her, alone. Danielle tied it around her neck. The scarf felt light and warm as a hug. She met Tanya's eyes, exactly the brown of her own. The older woman winked at her.

Beside her Amanda held up a green scarf, awed. "Look at that," she said. "Mine has hearts."

"They're different." Bev's smile was wicked. "Every one is different."

Danielle grinned back. All fifty of them looked just as dangerous and beautiful.

❋ ❋ ❋ ❋ ❋

Brenda W. Clough is the first female Asian-American SF writer, first appearing in print in 1984. She has been a finalist for both the Hugo and the Nebula awards. Her latest time travel trilogy is *Edge to Center*, available at Book View Café. *Marian Halcombe*, a series of eleven neo-Victorian thrillers, appeared in 2021. Her complete bibliography is up on her web page, brendaclough.net

My Man Left Me, My Dog Hates Me, And There Goes My Truck

Joyce Reynolds-Ward

Whirr!

Was that Dumbass starting up? Shouldn't be. Maybe Laura was hearing things. Her head was still throbbing thanks to the half case of generic beer she'd chugged last night after Jeremy announced he'd had enough of isolated ranch life and was leaving for town, thank you very much.

She finished tightening the middle fence wire, just as the truck's electronic parking brake released with a *clunk!*

"What the…?" She straightened up in time to see the white pickup execute a sharp three-point turn on the rocky slope and slowly start grinding its way up the dirt track. "Aw, shit!" Laura dropped her tools and ran after her truck.

"Cody!" she bellowed, hoping the truck hadn't run her dog over. "Aw, *shit*," she panted as the border collie's head popped up in the driver's seat, black ears perked, muzzle open and tongue lolling in a big doggie sneer. "You didn't…"

The dealer had *sworn* that starting Dumbass took her fingerprints. Laura had paid extra for that feature to make it harder for Jeremy to leave her with his impractical little two-seater just when she needed to haul hay or go hunting. But she wouldn't put it past Cody to have figured out a way to bypass that lock. Damn dog had been in a sulk ever since

203

Jeremy left, staring at the gun cabinet and whimpering. If the mutt had the strength and dexterity to unlock the case and handle a weapon, she'd be really worried.

Laura gritted her teeth and sprinted. She *might* be able to beat Dumbass to the flat. Once the truck got there, it could speed up enough to outrun her. Then she'd be afoot.

At least I could hobble and tie a damn horse. That is, if it wasn't Tricky, who could untie any knot with lips and teeth and run almost as fast with hobbles as he could without. That was about the only skill the bay gelding possessed—he'd turn tail and run from a cow that looked cross-eyed at him, and he stumbled all over the trails. But Laura kept him anyway because Tricky made her laugh. And he was company. She'd wanted Dumbass for the work company since Jeremy wouldn't join her in the woods. Even though she'd spent good money on a hotspot as part of Dumbass's configuration.

Laura put on an extra burst of speed and reached Dumbass, hoping Cody hadn't figured out how to lock the doors.

No. One thing in her favor. The dog growled as the latch moved under Laura's hand and she swung the door open.

"Get over there," Laura snapped as she levered himself into the seat using the locked steering wheel and the doorframe. "Dumbass, what's going on?"

"My name is not Dumbass," the tinny monotone voice programmed into the truck responded. "Jeremy called me. He needs me to move his things."

"You aren't Jeremy's truck." There was a way to shut down independent mode in this rig. Now what was it? "We're not done fixing fence."

"Jeremy needs me," the truck repeated. Laura fumbled with the lock override. Now, how did this work? She'd looked forward to the self-driving parts of this damn truck. It made life easy. Just tell Dumbass the coordinates and sit back.

Except Dumbass never seemed to get it quite right on the ranch. Off the ranch, no problems. But here? It never went where Laura wanted, and sometimes if she didn't watch out it would take her into a ditch or through the river. Dumbass was a good drive…as long as it wasn't on the ranch.

Ah. There. She found the buttons and tapped in the code to unlock the wheel. Was it her imagination that the truck fought her as she wrenched the wheel around to head it back toward the fence?

"What are you doing, Laura?" Distress shaded the truck's monotone.

"Gotta job to finish."

Pixels flared on the truck's camera screen. Jeremy's image appeared. Right away she noticed he'd done something to his hair, silver tips on neatly styled short black. *Mmm.* Damn, that looked good.

"What are you doing with the truck, Laura?" His voice twigged something pleasurable deep inside of her, despite its angry tone. Cody yelped happily.

"Work to do."

"I need the truck."

"Whatever for?"

Exasperation twisted his face. "To move my things, of course!"

"Can't we talk it out tonight?"

"No. Donnie, override."

"Who's Donnie?"

"Me," Dumbass answered.

The wheel locked under her hands. "What the hell—Jeremy, what's going on? Dumbass, you're mine, not *his*."

"My name's not Dumbass," the truck responded.

"You're sure acting like one."

Before she could say more, Jeremy sighed. "Laura. I programmed Donnie remotely this morning. My choices were either him or the ranch. Since you were so stupid as to drop money on the truck instead of my server farm, I decided I'd much rather have Donnie. I don't need a ranch."

I would have to marry a remote IT specialist, she thought. "Look, honey, I'm sorry. I didn't realize that latest high-speed satellite uplink was so important. Two months ago you'd said what we had would be fine."

"That was two months ago. Things change in tech."

"We can make it work out."

"With what?" he snapped. "My lawyer audited your accounts this morning. Everything's tied up in land, cows, and that damn truck—sorry, Donnie. I'm frustrated right now."

"That's all right, Jeremy," the truck said. "I understand."

"We can sell cows to get your satellite uplinks," Laura said.

Jeremy snorted. "You said yourself that the market's down and the sale

herd needs to get bigger for the best prices. I can't wait. I'm losing con-
tract possibilities while we argue. You had your chance, Laura. Now I'm
taking Donnie and going."

"No. Honey, please."

"Donnie, override her and return to the ranch. Lockdown."

Straps she didn't even know were there snaked out from the ceiling
and door and restrained her arms and legs. She had to do something.
Wait. Did Jeremy really want Dumbass or did he want the money the
truck represented? What was it the salesperson had said? *These trucks don't
like changing hands because they have to be reprogrammed. Sometimes that
means losing their personality. So you need to commit to owning this rig until
it drops.*

Shoot, she'd been all right with that notion. Tricky and Cody were still
on the ranch, when a harder-hearted person would have dumped both
of them. She just had to figure out ways to work with them. So maybe
she needed to use that argument with Dumbass—*no, call him Donnie.
He likes that name.*

"Look. Donnie. You realize that Jeremy doesn't really care for you,
right? He just wants you to move his gear and then he'll dump you like
he's doing to me."

"Don't listen to her," Jeremy said.

"How do you think he's going to finance his satellite link, Donnie?"
Laura pressed. "He's right about the accounts. If he's taking you then
you're his only source of cash."

"Donnie, she doesn't like you. She cusses you out."

"Yeah, but I do the same with Tricky and Cody." The dog whimpered at
the mention of his name. "Other ranchers would have gotten rid of them
by now. I want to work things out, Donnie. I *like* having a self-driving
truck. You and me just need to have more fun together. Jeremy doesn't
need you except to move his stuff. He doesn't care about you like I do.
Have I been stupid with you? Probably. But I *need* you. I want your
company."

The truck stuttered. "Are you sure?"

"Why would Jeremy want a truck like you once he's moved? He'll sell
you. Probably lobotomize you first so you don't rebel. You won't gain
anything by locking me out." How on earth had Jeremy gained control
of Donnie in the first place?

Oh. He *was* on the title. That gave him programming rights. She'd thought it was a good idea at the time. In-house programmer and all. Saved her the price of upgrade and maintenance contracts.

"She's just saying that," Jeremy said.

"Think about it, Donnie. He needs funds. What better way to get cash than to sell you? I need *you* and what you do to help me here on the ranch. He won't need you when he's moved out. You're just a source of funds." *Like he thought I was.*

"Would you sell me, Jeremy?" Somehow Donnie's monotone sounded sad.

"Donnie—there are realities."

"So you *will* sell me." The sad monotone changed to anger. "Laura, are *you* going to sell me?"

"Not if you let me loose and take me back to the fence," Laura said. "Look, Donnie. I need your help. *Really* need your help on a daily basis. More than that, we can have fun together. Cruise the woods. You like that, don't you?"

"Well…yes. I'm still learning about things. You get mad at me about things I don't know."

"Donnie, you need to tell me when you don't understand. I thought you came with the backwoods package."

"It's a learning program. I'm still figuring out the algorithm."

"Wasn't Jeremy supposed to help you learn the details about backwoods?"

"Why would I do that?" Jeremy interjected. "It's not important to me."

"The map data is all wrong," Donnie said. "That's why I took you into the river that time. I'm sorry. Jeremy told me not to ask you questions. It didn't feel right, but he told me the map data was okay."

"Damn it, Jeremy, you were supposed to help, not sabotage me."

"And you were supposed to help *me*," he retorted.

"I told you it was going to take time! I can't control all the markets!"

"I don't have time if I'm going to be the best IT specialist ever. Not if I'm going to take advantage of the latest updates. I'm losing money right now. It's time for me to get out of this backwoods. All you do is live and breathe cows, land, and hunting."

"Getting into the woods *is* fun," Donnie ventured. "You should try it, Jeremy."

"And why would I do that?" Jeremy sneered. He shuddered. "It's dirty out there! And I have to drive too far to find a good stylist!"

"But getting dirty is fun, right Donnie? You *like* mudding. Remember? We can figure out more fun things to do as we train your backwoods program."

"That sounds even better! Sorry, Jeremy." The straps undid themselves and retreated to wherever they'd been. She could turn the wheel again.

"Lock him out," Laura ordered. Cody whimpered from the other seat. She'd have to do something with him. Maybe she should send Cody to Jeremy since the dog didn't like ranch life either. She'd bet Jeremy wouldn't have the guts to dump Cody like he would the truck. He genuinely liked Cody.

"With pleasure," Donnie purred. "Do you want to send him a message?"

"Yeah. We're shipping Cody to him. Tell him that." Laura slapped the dashboard. "It's you and me, darlin'. You're the only man I need in my life!"

"You and me," the truck hummed.

At least she had her truck if not her dog. She wondered what Donnie would think about herding cows. Couldn't be worse than the inept mess Tricky made of it.

"Think you can herd cows?"

An eager shudder rippled through the truck. "Like a dog or horse?"

"Yep."

"I can try."

"There you go." Laura grinned. "Can you lock Cody down? Don't want him running off."

"With pleasure." The straps snaked out again and restrained the dog, who shrank down in the seat. Donnie stopped where he had been parked before.

"You wait for me," Laura said, patting Donnie's dash again. "Can you give me some music to work by? We'll take a fun route home and you can learn more about the backwoods."

"What would you like?"

Laura considered. "Willie Nelson."

She had a bounce in her step as she returned to stretching fence wire and the strains of "Time of the Preacher" wailed from Donnie's speaker.

Just about everything a cowgirl could want. A faithful truck, good music, and a job to do, she thought. *Who needs the man and the dog?*

JOYCE REYNOLDS-WARD HAS BEEN called "the best writer I've never heard of" by one reviewer. Her work includes themes of high-stakes family and political conflict, physical and digital sentience, personal agency and control, realistic strong women, and (whenever possible) horses. She is the author of *The Netwalk Sequence* series, the *Goddess's Honor* series, and the recently released *The Martiniere Legacy* series as well as standalones *Klone's Stronghold* and *Alien Savvy*. Her latest work, *The Heritage of Michael Martiniere*, will be released in late February. Samples of her other fiction can be found at Curious Fictions, and her nonfiction on Substack at either Speculations from the Wide Open Spaces (writing) or Speculations on Politics and Political History (politics). Joyce is a Self-Published Fantasy Blog Off Semifinalist, a Writers of the Future SemiFinalist, and an Anthology Builder Finalist. She is the Secretary of the Northwest Independent Writers Association and a member of Soroptimists International. Find out more about Joyce at her website, http://www.joycereynoldsward.com. Joyce is @JoyceReynoldsW1 on Twitter.

The Waiting Room

Judith Newcomb

I am early. This is a skill I've developed to get myself here. I don't know what's going to happen today. I feel new each time. I chant my usual phrase on my way up the steep staircase: "You promised yourself that you would commit to these sessions." My brain feels shaken and empty.

But the waiting room invites me to take off my coat and toss it on a chair as I kick off my winter boots and leave them near the door. I am at home, a stubborn child dumping her personal belongings.

This room does feel like mine. I often experience it with all my senses. It really has no smell of its own. When I am the occupant, it smells like me, burnt coffee and nervous sweat that layers of deodorant and baby powder can't hide. It looks like me, clothing and accessories put together for their functionality and most from second-hand sources.

When I arrive early, I can make a cup of chai tea that I drink quickly, scalding my mouth, as though I don't want to get caught in the act when the long hand reaches the hour. I save the tepid travel-mug coffee for his room across the hall. I guess it's to match his taste and scent and to have something to sip, quelling the anxious thirst as we talk.

I settle in after grabbing *Letting Go of Fear*, an "inspirational" book from the shelves. I might have scoffed a bit out loud at this title, but I need something besides the promise, and him, to keep me from running. I look around for what feels like the thousandth time as I flip through pages of the book. This room is visually inviting—someone knows that second-hand home furnishings are appealing, and that they can combat all the whiteness of the walls, ceiling and floor with IKEA sheer but floral-patterned blue curtains that cover the large window and cast their hue into what would be a dreary place without them. The rest of the furnishings consist of dark and scarred wood and a seen-better-days, shiny green floral area rug. Although ugly and worn, they are comforting in their familiarity.

The only sound in this space is the plug-in kettle boiling. If the heavy window is allowed to be cracked open, the faraway sound of cars parking and students walking to class can be heard. The solidness of the building, with its heavy, thick walls and doors, is a comfort to someone like me. It feels like it will keep all my secrets safe, those spoken and unspoken secrets, that visit here.

I'm often surprised that the tea bags don't scent the room, even in a small way. The lack of an engaging scent which might evoke another era allows me to take my mind off myself, leaving me to imagine what it smelled like when it was being used for its original purpose. I think of all those smelly bodies arriving home after ROTC drills across the huge campus, the same odor that wafts from their sports equipment and gym clothes that they have inadvertently taken back to the dorm instead of leaving at the gym to be cleaned, while they change to rush off to class. It is a pungent aroma that permeates the building every year those men worked through school on the G.I. Bill. This barracks building makes me wonder if the U.S. university system, prepping itself for the returning soldiers, built the dorm buildings in this fashion to welcome home the veterans. Or was it just the most simple, quickest and cheapest solution?

The real beauty of this room is the rare human occupant. Every so often I will not be alone. Unlike in other waiting rooms, they make eye contact and speak up. Like me, of course they are here for all types of issues. I've never seen more than one at a time. I'm very private and maybe these other clients are too, but surprisingly, in this room, people are willing to tell all—as though to "warm-up" for their therapy.

Some are so bold as to ask me why I'm here. Most of the time I sit alone reading my book, and this fact is not lost on the therapist. He knows I come here even when I don't have a session. He doesn't know that I've bookmarked and selfishly hidden my book to ensure it will be here every time.

❋ ❋ ❋ ❋ ❋

JUDI IS A MOM, a foster mom and a grandmother to little Daisy. She has taken writing workshops and creative writing courses in NYC, and is a retired kindergarten teacher, living in Western Massachusetts with her husband, Bob, and daughter, Olivia. Her eldest, Madeline, lives in Oregon with her husband, Andy, and their daughter. Judi is inspired by real-life grittiness and stories of resilience.

The Boggart of Campsite C47

Holly Schofield

Boggarts don't generally pick up rubbish but Moulde has no choice today. Loosening tent pegs, pouring water on sleeping bags, opening cooler lids—nothing discourages this year's campers. Like wild boars across Yorkshire moors, the bloody pillocks just keep marauding through the campgrounds of Alberta Western Provincial Park. What Moulde wouldn't give to be back in the Old Country, back in the olden times when humans weren't such arseholes.

Beyond, down at the slough, the current occupants of campsite C47 are faffing around, throwing rocks at sandpipers and such. Moulde pulls a reeking, empty milk jug out from under a scraggly cedar, a plastic marshmallow bag off struggling bunchberry, and a beer can crushing some long-suffering moss. She fills her cracked leather rucksack with the trash, the one she's been using since 1504. It's got a few centuries left in it, too, because it was crafted with respectful hands, from leather and hemp and magic. Not like today's offensive plastic shite.

When she gets to the campsite, she tips the rubbish out. It makes a right fine pile on the scuffed ground between the campers' shiny minivan and purple nylon tent.

Voices grow louder. With luck, the campers will react to the heap with dismay, and then realize how they're part of the problem. A thick pine next to the picnic table makes a good boggart-sized hiding spot to watch the fun. Moulde crouches on a lower branch, ignoring her rumbling belly. The foothills are scant on edible forage, other than parasite-filled pike or cattail bulbs tasting of sewage. And the campers always bring wrongly-colored food, like hard tiny circles of cereal or that shoe leather they call pizza. What she wouldn't give for a raisin bap or a simple baked potato.

"Holy crap, look! All the crap that we threw away is back here! Gross!" The campers' vocabulary doesn't seem to be any larger than their understanding of how to live a harmonious life. Moulde wants to leap forward and screech, "Ah'll tear ye limb from focking limb, ye dozy bleeders!" but the other boggarts have threatened to cut out her tongue if she does that again. She makes do with a low, disgusted "Pshhh".

The smallest camper, a wee bairn with a fringe of black bangs, stares curiously right at Moulde's pine.

Moulde scuttles away, out the pine's backside and through tall grasses, then past the raspberry hedge she's planted at the bottom of the scree. She scrambles up the rocky slope on all fours to her cave near the top of the ridge and heads right to the back corner. She huddles there, hands trembling on knobby knees. The world is going to eat itself alive, with all this waste and ruin. Humans have lost their way, lost their very nature, more so than any time she can remember—all of 'em, every last one.

Finally, as dusk threatens, she flicks a finger at the empty oyster shell sitting on the ledge and whispers a few words. The memory of seal oil grows fainter every year but still there's enough magic left to create a faint greenish comforting glow for the next century or two.

A crunch of gravel outside, then: "Found you!" The black-haired girl stares in from the cave entrance. "Hide and seek is my favorite game!"

Moulde screeches and jumps to her feet. "Bloody 'ell! Off wi' ye!"

"You talk funny!"

Moulde studies the girl's bramble-scratched arms, grubby face, and dirty pink overalls. Only one other camper has ever made it this high, a loud posh berk with synthetic clothing. Moulde arranged a "climbing accident" for that one. The campground closed down for a whole peaceful week. Eyes on the girl, she creeps an arm toward the cudgel leaning on the wall.

The girl holds out a fist with something in it. "Wanna share my toast?" Crumbs fall onto the cave floor.

Moulde darts forward, snatches the whole slice, and crams it in her mouth.

"Wow! You must be hungry."

"That I am." Moulde swallows the last bit and clears her throat. "... And I thank ye."

"Karina next door back home says that we are all on one small planet and we have to be nice to each other. So I am!"

Moulde licks butter off her lips. "Does she now?"

"And she says that we are part of the forest and the prairie and the ocean."

"Aye?" Moulde rubs a hairy ear. Was it possible? Could there be a few less daft humans about these days? Her heart feels a warm tinge of long-forgotten pleasure.

"And that we should practice self-care. To the planet, I mean. Because we're part of it."

Moulde sets the cudgel back down. This Karina-next-door-back-home that the bairn is rattling on about sounds like they might have a proper head on their shoulders. And so does the bairn. Such things should be encouraged. Never let it be said that auld Moulde doesn't do her part. She pulls the oyster shell off the shelf and blows out the flame. Shared magic led to increased magic, and that could help the world, p'raps. "Take this home wi' ye, there's a lass."

"Thank you. Um..." The girl turns it over. "Is it special?"

"Aye. It's got a sense o' the world, it does. A memory, like." Its influence on the bairn would be small and the nights ahead for Moulde blacker than treacle, but it's all she has to give. She makes the flame again and douses it, then has the girl practice until she can do it too. The bairn's enough in harmony with nature that she learns quickly.

"Cool! I gotta go. Mom'll be worried."

"Off wi' ye, then. And, lass—" Moulde gives her the look that makes brownies keel over in a faint. "This chat we've had—it's secret, mind!"

"Okay! I like secrets almost as much as forests!"

"Remember today when tha grows auld. Magic be real if ye live in harmony." She squints up at her. "And teach the others? To stop wrecking the forest and the oceans? Will ye?"

"You betcha!" The girl beams and puts the shell in her overall bib pocket. She disappears down the slope in a clatter of pebbles.

Moulde curls up in the dark on her damp cattail mat. Tomorrow, if the next batch of campers have as much in their noggins as this bairn, she'll go easy on them. Just a few wee spiders in their coffee mugs, p'raps—not a whole nest.

HOLLY SCHOFIELD TRAVELS THROUGH time at the rate of one second per second, oscillating between the alternate realities of city and country life. The author of over eighty short stories, her works are used in university curricula and have been translated into multiple languages. Holly's stories have appeared in *Analog, Lightspeed, Escape Pod,* and many other publications throughout the world. She hopes to save the world through science fiction and homegrown heritage tomatoes. Find her at hollyschofield.wordpress.com.

Coffee Break

Gregg Chamberlain

There is nothing like that first coffee of the morning, or, in my case, the first mocha of a winter afternoon.

Seated at a window table in the Sparks Street Tim Horton's, I cupped my hands around a large mocha, the heat seeping through the cardboard cup, warming fingers still numb from the January cold outside. All too soon, I would be heading back out there to join my fellow members of the Ottawa Press Gallery for the daily session of *théâtre bizarre* known as Question Period with the Prime Minister.

Then the alien entered the restaurant.

Right on time, I thought. The Korubian—that's which type of alien he was—had become a regular part of the clientele at the Sparks Street Tim Horton's.

I knew the Korubian was a high-ranking male by the caste gender mark between his large, faceted eyes. Part of his people's trade mission, I suspected, though I could not swear to remembering seeing him specifically during any of the past couple months of "official" meetings between the Korubian delegation and External Affairs officials that were open for media coverage.

I saw him and other Korubians, though—along with other aliens— often enough on the Hill. The office building that served as a joint consulate for many of the various ET trade missions, cultural exchanges and other post-Contact purposes was a couple blocks over on Wellington Street, right across from the Parliament buildings. There was even an

annex under construction now behind the West Block that would feature special consulting rooms designed to accommodate introductory
or negotiation meetings for both aliens with special habitat needs, like
methane breathers, and human government officials. All in the spirit of
reducing the risk of potential conflict-provoking situations.

I sat, sipping my mocha, and watched as the Korubian made a slow
shuffle away from the coffee shop entrance to the nearest empty table.
Most of the folks in here today paid him little mind. Both the staff and
other regulars, like myself, were used to seeing the Korubian here. Familiarity breeds content and all that.

Though, truth to tell, I never understood why the Korubian came in
here. It wasn't like I ever saw him do so much as eat a timbit. Well, it
takes all kinds to make all the worlds these days. Maybe he was under
orders from his embassy to study Canadian coffee break behaviour for
unknown diplomatic reasons. Who knows? It could happen.

As the Korubian carefully settled himself down on the chair at his chosen table, I went back to skimming some of the bookmarked news sites
on my tablet. What Korubians do during their downtime might be an
interesting little feature piece, but my focus was on preparing to deal
with the local politicians, not their galactic cousins.

After a moment, hearing footsteps, I looked up to see Zena, one of the
staff, come around the counter carrying a regular-size china mug of coffee in one hand, and a plate with what looked like a honey cruller on it
in the other. She set both on the table in front of the Korubian, smiled at
the alien, then went back behind the counter. I glanced down at my tablet, then looked up again in time to watch the alien's coffee break ritual.

The Korubian sat and regarded the cup of coffee. Finally he lifted an
arm and wrapped the wriggling mass of slim tendrils at its end around
the cup. Which must have been hotter than he expected. The Korubian's
"hand" jerked loose. The cup spun around but didn't tip over. A good
portion of its contents did slop over the rim and onto the table.

Quick as a cat on cream, Zena was at the table with a cloth and a
bunch of napkins. She mopped up the spilled coffee with the cloth, lifted up the cup and wiped it down with the napkins, then finished up by
wiping the entire table top dry before setting the cup back down.

"There you are, I'm sorry about that," Zena murmured. "Would you
like another cup?"

The Korubian's faceted eyes looked up at Zena. "No. Thank you," whispered out of the voder around his neck.

Zena shrugged, smiled, and went back behind the counter. The Korubian regarded the half-empty mug. Then he looked over at me. I lifted my mocha in salute. After a moment, the Korubian did the same with his cup. I went back to scanning headlines and he resumed contemplating his coffee. I glanced up again to see him holding the cruller up close to his eyes, as though examining every crystallized bit of honey in the glaze.

To dunk or not to dunk? I thought, with a smile. *Will this cruller go the way of all doughnuts? Who was it, that first man, to have dunked a doughnut? Like the nameless caveman who watched a stone roll downhill and thought "Uhg! Wheel!", who was that anonymous java drinker, sitting with cup and sinker in hand who said to himself, "Hey, I wonder what this would taste like if I dunked it in my coffee?"*

Was this Korubian the first alien to ever dunk a doughnut? If so, has he passed on this human cultural oddity to his fellow Korubians? Would dunking doughnuts—or other alien snack foods—become a new interstellar First Contact tradition? Or the first case of interstellar conflict through cultural contamination from our own world courtesy of a Canadian culinary icon?

I smiled again to myself, as I imagined alien "doughnut wars" inspired by disputes over what is and is not worth dunking. Would alien politicians and religious leaders, inspired by the conspiracy fringe paranoids of their own worlds, preach against dunking as a plot to weaken the moral fabric of the galaxy?

The mind—well, mine at least—boggles at the possibilities. In the end, I suppose, we all have our coffee rituals. Or at least something similar. I shrugged and went back again to my tablet.

After a while I felt the cold air draft hit me. I looked up to see the door slowly swing shut. Through the display window, I observed the Korubian pass by on the sidewalk, cross the intersection with the light, and shuffle on up towards Wellington.

I watched him until he disappeared behind the buildings. Looking over at his now-empty table, I saw Zena already collecting the cup and plate. The honey cruller was all crumbled up and I could see at least half a piece sticking out of the cup where the Korubian had dunked it. As usual.

"Does he ever drink any of his coffee?" I asked. "Or eat anything?"

Zena shook her head. "Never. Coffee, tea, or juice, makes no difference. Never seen him drink any of it any time I've been on shift." She set down cup and plate for a moment to collect some coins off the table, then gave the surface another wipe. "Just dunks everything. Even timbits." She thought a moment. "Maybe he saw someone dunking doughnuts once and figured that was the thing to do."

"Then why," I wondered, "does he even bother coming in?"

Zena shrugged. "Beats me, and I really don't care. I could wish more like him came here. He's quiet, polite, never makes a fuss or ever bothers anyone."

She held out her hand to show me the three five-dollar Maples the Korubian had left behind.

"And besides," Zena said, grinning, "he's a good tipper."

I smiled in response. She headed back behind the counter, leaving me to finish my mocha. Before I left to head on up the Hill for the media session, I made sure to leave a toonie on the table.

I was just a poor working reporter but I had at least one thing in common with the Korubian. We both appreciated and rewarded good service.

It's only the proper thing, after all, for any civilized being. Besides dunking doughnuts.

❀ ❀ ❀ ❀ ❀

GREGG CHAMBERLAIN IS A community newspaper reporter, living in rural Ontario, Canada, with his missus, Anne, and their cats, who let the humans think that they are in charge. He writes speculative fiction for fun and has several dozen published examples of the fun he has in venues that include: *Daily Science Fiction*, *Ares*, *Mythic*, *Polar Borealis*, and *Weirdbook* magazines, and various anthologies.

Tea with Superman

Liam Hogan

I scooted over to the front door and swung it open. Superman stood there looking down at the concrete ramp and then at my wheelchair. But he didn't say anything and for that I was glad.

"I've been expecting you," I said, spinning around to start my trundle back down the tiled hallway. "But I doubt the neighbours have. You'd best come in."

He glanced over my shoulder into the empty corridor and shrugged, pulling the door shut behind him. We sat in the kitchen where two mugs sat either side of the freshly filled teapot. I'd offered to pour for him but he'd declined, as I thought he might. The pot was only half-full on that account.

"You know," he said, glancing around, taking in the specially lowered worksurfaces, "I kind of expected something more impressive."

I took a moment to look at him, perched there all ready to spring into action. You don't often think of Superman seated and I suspect he'd have been happier if we'd both been able to stand. As would I. I took in his brightly coloured outfit, the vaguely ridiculous red cape (I imagined it getting snarled in my wheels and almost laughed), his chiselled jaw and sculpted muscles, the brightness of his all-seeing eyes, the perfection of his limbs… All that, *and* white, *and* male. It was difficult to imagine someone more privileged, even if he was an orphan and technically an immigrant, whatever his passport said. I contemplated a very rude retort in a dozen languages including at least one I suspected he didn't know, but contemplating it was enough. For now.

"You think I do what I do for my own benefit?" I asked. "Because of a desire to get rich? I can show you my tax returns if you like. They're scrupulously honest, every penny in and every penny out accounted for. I live comfortably enough and more possessions…would just get in my way." It was my turn to shrug.

He nodded. You never really saw Superman at red carpet events either, and a one-bed apartment in an unfashionable quarter of Metropolis was a pretty humble abode for the Man of Steel.

"And what is it *exactly* that you do, Ms. Okafor?"

"Please, call me Khadijah. Or K-O, if you prefer. And I figure you know what I do. Otherwise you wouldn't be here?"

He waved a hand, a hand that was as perfect as the rest. No callouses for him from pushing around a wheelchair, even one as well engineered as this one. "Snippets, Ms. Okafor. Rumours. Conjecture. Enough to suspect that you're behind more than a dozen hacker aliases, all with Interpol warrants for their immediate arrest. Aliases associated with crashing banking systems, with meddling in elections and bringing down foreign governments, with destroying any number of companies by zeroing their share prices."

I took a sip of my tea. Too hot to gulp, but that first sip was always blissful, always calming. Even when faced with the ultimate do-gooder. "You could have sent the police?"

"I could have," he conceded. "But they didn't catch you in Mumbai, so I wasn't convinced they would catch you here."

I shrugged again, adjusted my wheelchair infinitesimally closer to the table. "I was never in Mumbai. Most of what I do is done remotely. I work from home."

His lingering glance suggested he'd probably just X-ray visioned the layout of my downstairs, two-bed maisonette. The office, with its three separate high-speed broadband connections and the panoply of computers and monitors; the bedroom, with bars mounted on the wall to help me in and out of bed; the extension roll-in wet room and shower. There's also a lounge with a couple of sofas and a TV that I use when I'm entertaining, which is rare enough it always feels like I've discovered a space I didn't know I had when I do happen to enter it. I prefer the kitchen; it's more homey. More at my level.

All of it paid for by my day job, as a freelance problem solver and bug finder for the video games industry. Like a script doctor for films and television, I get called in when something goes fundamentally and drastically wrong in a game in the final stages of development, usually when there's a tight release deadline.

It's a job that doesn't care that I'm in a wheelchair, that I'm mixed race, that I'm female. Or even that I'm in a different time-zone than most of the people I work for. It's almost funny, on the occasions when I have to present my findings over a webcam, when the people I've been working with realise who it is they've been working with. Watching them adjust their assumptions, lower their expectations... Not that it's something I hide, even if I routinely sign-off emails with my gamer-tag initials, but nor is it something I advertise. Life seems simpler that way for a geeky girl from Harrow. I'm niche, and I'm expensive and, once I've waded my way through gigabytes of code to fix their obscure bugs, they know to come back to me the *next* time they have an impossible problem to solve.

Other than legitimising my overpowered computer setup and keeping the tax man happy, I do the day (or more often evening) job because it's a genuine intellectual challenge, which is rare in today's workplace. And it's *fun,* which is even rarer. The fantasy world of computer games is a welcome escape from the actual dystopia we seem to be living through. But I'd be lying if I said it was a full-time occupation. I always invoice for the task, not the hours spent. And, because I'm very good at it, it really doesn't take me long to make a respectable living.

Freeing me up for my hobby, my passion, my true calling. And the reason for Superman's Tuesday afternoon visit.

On which note, it's a good thing his X-ray vision can't read what's stored on USB drives, particularly encrypted ones.

"Hacking computer systems? And you do that because?" His eyes didn't dip to my useless legs, but they may as well have. The assumption that I was somehow broken, and therefore compensating... I felt the warm, familiar flush of anger and was glad my dark skin would hide the blush. Though perhaps not from the man who sat across the table from me.

"I am not my *disabilities,* Superman. Any more than you are your superpowers."

He frowned. "I didn't say—"

"—It is a peculiar imbalance, is it not? Superheroes get to be insanely strong, impervious to bullets, able to fly. Whereas your average super-villain has exactly none of those advantages. Your average supervillain is merely super-clever, and willing to use it. Almost as if intelligence and knowledge is being demonised, hmm?"

He drummed fingers lightly on the pine table. Not for the first time I wondered at Superman's remarkable self-control. When you can pul-verise steel with your bare hands, it can't be easy to pluck a flower, or to hold an egg, or a baby. Was there a barn in Smallville filled with the things an infant Superman had once trashed?

I glanced, embarrassed, towards my fridge. To the grooves and dents along the white metal at the exact height of the top of my wheels. Sure, I could easily afford a new fridge. But I'd only end up scoring the front of that, over time. And not just the fridge; I kept pots of paint to fix up the door frames. Even though they were wider than usual, there was always a chance I'd clip them as I passed through, especially when I was in a hurry.

"Super intelligence can be put to great good," Superman observed.

"And super strength could be put to great evil. We are not what we *can* do. We are what we *do* do." And we're not what we can't do, either, I didn't bother to add.

"So what have you done with this intelligence of yours?"

From anyone else I could imagine this being said with condescension. With air quotes around the 'intelligence', despite my half-dozen degrees, despite the job few if any others could do—the one on my business card, as well as the one that wasn't. But Superman was *also* super-smart, with a natural knack at picking up languages, as well as other things. With a few possible exceptions, he was probably the biggest brain on the planet. That he didn't make a big thing of it always seemed somewhat wasteful, to me. But I had to remind myself: Superman's biggest superpower was the way people looked up to him, how they *respected* him. Today's de-monisation of experts, of knowledge, even of truth, could just as easily be levelled at him, if he weren't super-careful with his talents.

"Well, for starters," I said, "I'm the one who left a digital trail of crumbs for you to follow."

His pleasant demeanour flickered. For a moment, and only the briefest of moments, he looked wary. I took that as a compliment, of sorts.

"Why? Is this a trap, Ms. Okafor?"

I laughed. "Of course not. You're *Superman*. I can't stop you doing whatever you want, whatever you feel is right. What this is, is an invitation."

"Explain, please. An invitation to what?"

I savoured the last of my tea. We were into prepared speech mode. I didn't want to interrupt the flow and I didn't want to waste my hot drink.

"Saving people from burning buildings is all very *nice*, but that building shouldn't have been burning in the first place, should it? A dozen building regulation violations, all to scrounge a few pennies for the stockholders. Stopping a jewel thief is also well and good, but what about when the jewel in question was stolen a hundred-odd years earlier? Who is righting *that* historic crime? And stopping a mugging without stopping to think why that mugger was driven to such a desperate act, and doing something about it, is just a band-aid at best, isn't it? We live in a time of fear and inequality, all of it deliberate. Our true enemies don't stroke cats or have underground lairs. They have penthouse suites and privately owned golf courses."

None of which was news, to either of us. But Superman was curiously constrained, for all his powers. In not wanting to do any harm even when he was doing good, he was relatively impotent against anyone who was bad in any kind of morally grey way. It was like playing chess (another black and white analogy for you) but not being willing to sacrifice a single pawn, not even to win the game.

And it was those bad guys (and yes, they're almost entirely guys), the ones no court was going to touch, who were the *real* supervillains. Who were cunning enough to exploit Superman's weaknesses, his good versus evil dichotomy.

But it's hard to be critical of a guy who was just trying to do his best. And I was on a strict timetable, here. "Have you never wondered who is drip feeding your enemies to you?"

Because of *course* they were. A steady diet of bad people, *genuinely* bad, psychotically bad, for Superman to mop up, to keep him busy, lest he dare set his sights somewhere higher.

Those bad people were mostly stupid. Disposable. Inexhaustible. And of absolutely no interest to me.

The world was waking up, I hoped, to the fact that we needed a different approach. To the fact that the status quo wasn't worth preserving, except for a small number of very rich people busy getting even richer.

Superman didn't have a Twitter or Instagram account, so it was tricky to know exactly what causes he believed in. But he hadn't been seen leading the front line in the Black Lives Matter protest. And that was kind of worrying. People were beginning to jump to the wrong conclusion. People were beginning to *talk*.

The little-known fact he'd marched as Clark Kent wasn't going to shut them up.

In this modern era of CCTV and a high quality video camera in every pocket or handbag, Superman had delineated his personas with surgical precision. Clark Kent never used his powers, in *any* circumstances, because sure as eggs is eggs he'd be captured doing so.

Superman sat, watching me. Waiting. I suspected he didn't much like being told he wasn't *actually* helping much.

"The really bad people sit back and push the buttons, yours included. As, I admit, do I. Which means there's not much to show you but…call me old fashioned, if you like. Here. I keep a scrapbook."

Superman flicked through it, reading at a pace far quicker than a normal person. That scrapbook alone would have seen me extradited and wearing an unflattering orange jumpsuit, never to be seen or heard from again. It contained details of the bank accounts I—*we*—had frozen, just before they would have been emptied by embezzlers. The top secret government reports into human rights abuses, that suddenly became less secret and toppled a dictator. The pharmaceutical company faking its medical trials so its directors could unload their stock options. That their little deception resulted in a dozen dead patients seemed to have meant little to the board. It meant a lot to me. And that was just a few of the highlights. We had been busy.

Towards the back of the thick book, about the time I began to leave clues of my cyber existence, the accounts are less showy, the dealings equally sordid, but without the clean resolution, without the happy ending. Because just releasing information doesn't help when the miscreants control the narrative, and when a company isn't publicly traded, the share price isn't that important. There were plenty of targets we couldn't touch, couldn't stop. Could only watch, and, perhaps, pass on the details to someone who might do something.

Like the latest find: a junta general in Latin America, ordering supplies of chemicals, and the recipe for the nerve gas they will produce. A satellite map, showing the exact location of the laboratory. Nothing short of an air strike could stop the death and misery to thousands that that general was planning.

An air strike, or a superhero.

Actions that would make a lot more difference than rescuing a cat that I was ninety-five percent certain could rescue itself, and probably would just as soon as you turned your back on it.

Superman closed the scrapbook and pushed it thoughtfully back.

"It's dangerous, to do this sort of thing alone," he commented. "You need someone to keep your moral compass where it should be."

"I'm not alone," I replied, truthfully. The hacker community is a peculiar animal and not all of those dozen aliases were mine. Over the years, I'd found a network of others similarly minded. Me and my merry band, the Robin H∞d hackers. "But *you* are."

His eyes widened at that. What must it be like, to be Superman? To be as much a symbol as a reality? One that, perhaps, lost its edge with every appearance. One that people ignored, whenever it suited their purposes. Was he still the people's hero? Did the owner of the supertanker bound for Metropolis take extra precautions, because he knew it was the home of Superman? Or did he cut corners, save money by skimping on safety, secure in the knowledge that if things *did* go wrong, Superman would be there to save the day?

But if someone were to hack into that shipping company, those penny-pinching safety breaches would be laid clear. And, if that hacker, or community of hackers, couldn't stop that tanker before it left the refinery by corrupting a few crucial documents, then it would be *really* handy to have Superman's mobile phone number.

There was a ping from the oven. Superman sniffed the air. "Raisin and oatmeal cookies?"

"Your favourite, I believe. With a pinch of cinnamon and ginger, the way you like it."

He quirked a perfect eyebrow. "You *have* been doing your research."

I wheeled myself over to the oven. "They'll take a couple of minutes to cool. Shall I put the kettle on again while we wait?"

He smiled and actually relaxed in his seat. "I'd like that very much, Khadijah."

❀ ❀ ❀ ❀ ❀

LIAM HOGAN IS AN award winning short story writer, with stories in *Best of British Science Fiction 2016* & *2019*, and *Best of British Fantasy 2018* (NewCon Press). He's been published by *Analog*, *Daily Science Fiction*, and Flame Tree Press, among others. He helps host Liars' League London, volunteers at the creative writing charity Ministry of Stories, and lives and avoids work in London. More details at http://happyending-notguaranteed.blogspot.co.uk

A Very Old Story(teller)

Bob Page

Okay. Full disclosure: I know the boss. You know, that person who is putting this anthology thing together—Shannon. She's my daughter. I have an inside connection. Unfortunately, she knows me very well and can be very persuasive. "Come on, Dad, write me a story. You're a natural! You're a great writer!" But I can see through her guileless flattery.

That said, she does know I have a problem. I have an itch that I've been trying to scratch for exactly forty-nine years and it won't go away. The last time I wrote a story was in 1962 in my favorite high school class— Creative Writing. I loved writing short stories, a chance to let thoughts flow without all the hard work—like research and all that unrewarding refining bother. My most favorite teacher, Mrs. Lee, would sit us down and say, "You have thirty minutes to write a story involving 'fear'" (or happiness, solitude, etc.) We would grab our writing pads and begin free-forming beginnings to what we (in our youthful naïveté) felt could someday be on somebody's best seller list.

I loved the freedom to let my imagination go wild, and on occasion, I actually had a few good ideas. In that class, I produced three stories that were selected to appear in our annual literary magazine, *Satori* [see p. 235]. One was even honored as the "Best Prose" submission. Now, let's put this in perspective—we're talking Tustin Union High School—300 students in our graduating class. A very small fish pond. And then, life kind of got in the way of my written words—for about fifty years.

So with such an "illustrious" writing history, I was blindsided by Shannon when she began tickling that sleeping itch. Thank you, Covid-19! I'm stuck at home every day with all my self-imposed writing roadblocks unavailable to automatically say, "I'm too busy!" Where to even begin? A story involving "hope," with forty-nine years of possible storylines—funny moments, serious moments, magical moments, crossroads, roads taken, roads not taken—or none of the above and just a clever piece of fiction.

Well, I'm overwhelmed. Every possibility is a book of its own. For example, how about leaving my good-paying job just out of college, Shannon five years old and her brother, Erik, one; selling all our furniture and appliances and buying seventy-two acres of raw land on the Eel River in Potter Valley, Mendocino County—"going to the country, build us a home"—thank you, John Prine! We welcomed any "like-minded" visionaries to help us fulfill our dream. After four very memorable, and mostly painful years, we realized we had the wrong mix of "family members," little or no knowledge of "living off the land," and no sustainable direction. My high school sweetheart falls in love with a long-haired sixteen-year-old guitar player and I head back to Los Angeles to rearrange my mind—leaving my family (Donna, Shannon and Erik) literally "in the dust." Okay, so for this writing exercise—I don't think so. But maybe someday.

Possibility number two: I head back to visit my kids at "The Land," and visit a previous acquaintance from my commune days who had been partnered when I knew her. A beautiful woman to whom I had always been attracted. So what magical moment caused me to make the right turn toward her house instead of the left to see my kids? Fate? Divine intervention? She and Bruce had split up! Sparks ignited, and I felt like I had won the lottery! We never looked back! Barbara is my soulmate, wife of forty years, mother to my third child, Toby—her first. What a wealth of adventures and stories we have created and shared. Years of trips to Mexico, camping on beaches, hammocks between perfectly spaced palms, windsurfing whenever possible and creating a relationship base so strong it solidified the majority of our adult lives. A love story with the natural bumps in the road, but a road taken that I'll never regret. This most assuredly was the best decision I have ever made. Definitely a topic worthy of sharing, but by no means a "short story." But please, don't get me started pondering this amazing experience. Life's too good right now in this territory and I don't want to look forward.

Final contender: the health clubs. After moving back to Mendocino County to live with Barbara, a close friend, Jack, and I got a wild hair to try something that we had absolutely no understanding of or experience in: opening the second health club in the county. It's 1979, and a health club was definitely not a business even on the map nor an industry that had blown up to the amazing magnitude of today. Thank goodness we never knew how little we really didn't know. Miles of setbacks, unbelievable roadblocks, not close to enough money, but we somehow blindly succeeded and started Ukiah's first ever health club.

After a few years, Jack moved on. I led the Redwood Health Club for twenty years, survived and flowed with the growth of this burgeoning industry, added a local country club, and even was convinced to open a third club in Santa Rosa (the Airport Health Club)—a managing partner in three facilities who was in way over his (my) head. So the wisest decision—abandon ship! Sell the country club, then sell the Redwood Health Club and concentrate on the Airport Health Club—the largest, most successful of the three and so well placed in an exploding population area that success was almost guaranteed. A good choice. We'd found a blueprint that really worked. The "bigger mousetrap" that accommodated all ages—kids, seniors, and everyone in between. We seemed to have done everything right. Voted the Best Health Club in Sonoma County for nine years running! Seven thousand members! A slam dunk...

Until Covid-19 and now, are we being challenged! Another topic in and of itself. But forty years in the health club business has left me with a cornucopia of fascinating stories. For example: a confused little senior woman hits the accelerator when parking instead of the brake and plows through our fence and into our swimming pool—just missing swimmers and a woman and her child on the deck. A man sneaks into the women's shower area and as a member screams from her shower, her husband (a cop) hears her from the men's showers, confronts the intruder, and knocks him to the ground and pins him there until the sheriff arrives (while the policeman is still naked). The stories are unlimited and great material for a complete novel (or better yet, a miniseries), but alas, this is not the moment or place.

So what now, Shannon? The floodgate has been opened and maybe, someday the flow might start, or maybe not. For now, I'd like to conclude with a few thoughts that are a little more appropriate to the nature of the assignment. I expect this perspective might even have already entered your anthology. Four years ago, almost to the moment, a dark, evil, sinister cloud engulfed the skies of our country. It further polluted our atmosphere, added new and permanent scars to our landscape and endangered many more already fragile species towards extinction. This cloud swept across our nation, oppressing those who couldn't easily stand up for themselves, and rewarding those who were "entitled." We closed our doors to the rest of the world and divided our nation in ways one would never have conceived—neighbors against neighbors, families against families, races against races, and we all know the rest. Throw in the totally unexpected viral scourge that swept over our nation almost completely ignored by a leader more interested in personal aggrandizement and his golf game. Hundreds of thousands of lives could have been saved.

But...I believe I am seeing a small beam of light breaking through the oppressive shadow over us. Real compassionate people are actually being recognized, placed in positions of influence, with actual expertise in their new important responsibilities. People who love humanity, the earth, and all living things. I am so hopeful that a "new day is dawning." May wisdom and compassion bolster what I would love for us all to truly achieve—hope for a better world.

❊ ❊ ❊ ❊ ❊

BOB PAGE IS A fastidious and committed writer. This story is the result of fifty years of preparation. One story every fifty years—a good plan! When not contemplating his next literary project, he runs a health club he started in Santa Rosa thirty years ago—currently operating all services outdoors, in swimming pools and under tents. At seventy-six, Bob is often asked when is he going to retire. He sometimes responds with a favorite pilfered comment from an eighty-year-old pathologist friend of his who was still working and was constantly asked, "Hey Hershel, when are you going to retire?" Hershel's reply (and Bob's on occasion): "Not today!" And the date of Bob's next story release? "Not today!"

GRAVE WITHOUT A HEADSTONE

By: Bob Page

Empty words. Drawn out negotiations. But then there's man's basic wisdom. His instinct of self-preservation. Surely these will win out over narrow self-interest. These thoughts echoed back and forth through the mind of Glen Powers as his speedy jet rushed him home from another futile peace conference. His mind wandered as he viewed the beautiful scenery of the African land below. The bright sun beat down on the plushy green trees as they slowly waved back and forth in a gentle breeze. The plane was flying along a large blue river where dark vegetation grew to the river's edge. A family of zebras that had been drinking from the river ran into the dense brush as the noisy bird thundered over them.

What have we done to this world, Glen thought. There are so few places left as beautiful as this. He leaned back, and a pleasant feeling of sleepiness took hold. Just as he dozed off, he felt a mighty lurch, and then darkness came.

Out of the blackness of unconsciousness Glen awoke to the blueness of night. He had a terrible pain in his side and a lump on his head, but he could move, although slowly and painfully. He checked the shambles that were once the inside of the plane, hoping desperately to find another survivor, but everything was dead and still. Oh, God, he mumbled. He climbed out of the plane to escape the scene of death and destruction. He had to think. Was it a miracle, a relaxed body, or a chance in a million that let me come through this?

In the morning Glen set out in the direction in which he thought the large river might be, feeling it would be his best bet for survival. After an hour's painful fight through swamp-like jungle, Glen came to a clearing. Giand branches and vines still blocked out the much needed light, but the ground had been cleared away. At the far end of the darkened clearing was a large formation with many cave openingd. From

end of the darkened clearing was a large rock formation with many cave openings. From one cave which seemed to be the main one, Glen heard voices. He was startled by the voices, for he had feared he would find no one in this wilderness. He walked to the mouth of the cave, peered in, and listened. He heard footsteps and then saw a small group of men coming to the entrance. Though they were bearded, their garb was civilized.

"Any of you speak English?" asked Glen hopefully. One of the men nodded. Glen couldn't believe his luck. Not only did he find someone living in this uncivilized part of Africa, but also at least one of them spoke English. Glen held back his overjoyed emotions and told of his disaster.

"I was on a commercial airline. It crashed yesterday, and I'm the only survivor. I sure am lucky I found you."

"Yes, we heard the crash yesterday," one man said. "We kept pretty close under cover, because we thought it might have been a bomb or something." As the man continued, more people came out of the cave: men, women, and children. "I'm Johnson," he said, "and I'm from the States. We're from countries all over the world. We're as far away from nuclear bombs as we can get. There's no target near here for a bomb, and these caves go deep enough to protect us from fall-out. We figure it's just a matter of time before Hell breaks loose. We figure we'll pull through and start civilization again. Your plane crash was just about the luckiest thing that ever happened to you, mister.

You can stay with us, and your life will be safe."

Glen was shocked. "Who do you people think you are? Don't you realize that by running away from a problem you don't solve it? You people are wrong! You've got to realize we have to clear up the issue that brings the threat of a bomb; otherwise, survival is of no value. You can't just give up and crawl into a hole. There's not much I can do about you, but as far as I'm concerned, you can count me out, because I think there's still hope." He turned his back on the group of people and headed into the jungle. He would rather brave the wilds than stay with these people. A feeling of disgust weighed heavily within him. A number of men ran after him and grabbed his arms.

Johnson said, "Sorry, mister, we may not like you any more than you like us, but we're stuck with each other. No one leaves here to spread the word. We're too crowded as it is, and the less the world knows about us the better, because we don't want any more people. Believe it or not, you're lucky. You'll thank us soon for saving your skin.

BULLETIN   September 17, 2203

A United Nations raw materials expedition radio-phoned a most unusual find. Probing one of the few remaining unexplored areas of Africa, it came upon a primitive society of humans. Almost naked and huddled around fires in a large cave were some hundred men, women and children. The near-blind people made a strange noises, and it is questionable whether they could actually communicate with each other. Where they came from and how they got there are still unknown. The expedition said it would radio any further findings.

About the Editor

SHANNON PAGE WAS BORN on Halloween night and spent her early years on a back-to-the-land commune in northern California. A childhood without television gave her a great love of the written word. Edited books include anthologies *Witches, Stitches & Bitches*, the *Book View Café 2020 Holiday Anthology*, *Black-Eyed Peas on New Year's Day*, a forthcoming anthology of ghost stories (with Marissa Doyle), and the essay collection *The Usual Path to Publication*, as well as novels for Per Aspera Press, Ragnarok, and Outland Entertainment. She has also authored a number of books under several different names—including her own—along with dozens of short stories.

Shannon is a longtime yoga practitioner, has no tattoos (but she did recently get a television), and lives on lovely, remote Orcas Island, Washington, with her husband, author and illustrator Mark J. Ferrari. Visit her at www.shannonpage.net.

Copyrights & Credits

Black-Eyed Peas on New Year's Day: An Anthology of Hope
Edited by Shannon Page

Individual Story Credits:
"At the Night Bazaar" by Sherri Cook Woosley, copyright © 2021 by Sherri Cook Woosley, original to this volume.
"The Last Date" by Sarina Dorie, copyright © 2021 by Sarina Dorie, original to this volume.
"The Family Business" by Melissa Mead, copyright © 2021 by Melissa Mead, original to this volume.
"Thank God for the Road" by Nancy Jane Moore, copyright © 2010 by Nancy Jane Moore. First published in *The WisCon Chronicles*, vol. 4, edited by Sylvia Kelso, 2010.
"Changing of the Guard" by Mindy Klasky, copyright © 2021 by Mindy Klasky, original to this volume.
"In Case of Emergency" by Karen G. Berry, copyright © 2021 by Karen G. Berry, original to this volume.
"Circus" by Paul McMahon, copyright © 2021 by Paul McMahon, original to this volume.
"Fire Cat" by M. J. Holt, copyright © 2021 by Marilyn Holt, original to this volume.
"Letters Submitted in Place of a Thesis to the Department of Chronology" by Stewart C Baker, copyright © 2021 by Stewart C Baker, original to this volume.
"The Eighth of December" by Dave Smeds, copyright © 1995 by Dave Smeds. First published in *David Copperfield's Tales of the Impossible*, edited by David Copperfield & Janet Berliner, HarperPrism, 1995.
"Possibilities" by Sarah Wells, copyright © 2021 by Sarah Wells, original to this volume.
"Another Catcher" by Laurence Raphael Brothers, copyright © 2021 by Laurence Raphael Brothers, original to this volume.
"Gateway" by D. L. R. Frase, copyright © 2021 by David L. Frase, original to this volume.
"Esther" by Fran Macilvey, copyright © 2021 by Fran Macilvey, original to this volume.
"Hope Jones" by Susan Dutton, copyright © 2021 by Susan Dutton, original to this volume.
"Puss and Jack Steal a Kingdom" by Michael M. Jones, copyright © 2021 by Michael M. Jones, original to this volume.
"The Garden" by Scott Davenport, copyright © 2021 by Scott Davenport, original to this volume.
"Blind Faith" by Barbara Ware, copyright © 2021 by Barbara Ware, original to this volume.
"Meditation on Persistence: 4AM" by Mark J. Ferrari, copyright © 2021 by Mark J. Ferrari, original to this volume.
"Break the Mirrors" by Jan Underwood, copyright © 2021 by Jan Underwood, original to this volume.
"Times Fifty" by Brenda Clough, copyright © 2015 by Brenda Clough. First published in *Christianity Today*, 2015.
"My Man Left Me, My Dog Hates Me, and There Goes My Truck" by Joyce Reynolds-Ward, copyright © 2021 by Joyce Reynolds-Ward, original to this volume.
"The Waiting Room" by Judith Newcomb, copyright © 2021 by Judith Newcomb, original to this volume.

Book View Café 2021
ISBN: 978-1-63632-006-9
Copyright © 2021 Book View Café Publishing Cooperative

Production Team:
Cover Art: Susan Dutton
Cover Design: Mark J. Ferrari
Proofreader: Shannon Page
Copyeditor: Paul S. Piper
Ebook Formatter: Jennifer Stevenson
Print Formatter: Shannon Page

www.bookviewcafe.com
Book View Café Publishing Cooperative
304 S. Jones Blvd. Suite #2906, Las Vegas, NV 89107

About Book View Café

Book View Café is a professional authors' publishing cooperative offering DRM-free ebooks in multiple formats to readers around the world. With authors in a variety of genres including mystery, romance, fantasy, and science fiction, Book View Café has something for everyone.

Book View Café is good for readers because you can enjoy high-quality DRM-free ebooks from your favorite authors at a reasonable price.

Book View Café is good for writers because 90% of the profit goes directly to the book's author.

Book View Café authors include *New York Times* and *USA Today* bestsellers, Nebula, Hugo, Lambda, Chanticleer, National Readers' Choice, and Philip K. Dick Award winners, World Fantasy, Kirkus, and Rita Award nominees, and winners and nominees of many other publishing awards.

www.bookviewcafe.com

Made in the USA
Columbia, SC
07 April 2021